THE SEVEN DEATHS OF QUINCEY RADLETT

C.J. EMERSON

Someword Publishing

For Kirby, my amazing wife

FRASERWOOD

The girl still isn't used to the cold even after twelve white winters here, thousands of miles and an ocean away from home, surrounded by brittle firs on the foothills of the Canadian Rockies. She coughs, drops the cigarette butt and grinds it into the snow under her cheap sneakers. They pinch her toes – too big when she was fourteen, too small now she's fifteen. And her feet are frozen, but she barely notices any more. '*Don't fight what you can't change,*' that's her mother's motto, and for now it will have to do. Just for now.

A wind is rolling down from the higher peaks, sharp with frost and fragments of ice and snow whipped up from the ground. She was promised a coat this year, but promises are no different from fairy tales and it's been a long time since anyone read her one of those. She hugs herself to keep the cold at bay and scrapes towards the door of the trailer. She needs to keep off the path, of course. Under the fresh coating of snow it will be a river of ice, and the soles of her sneakers are as smooth as glass.

A dog patters across the snow towards her, looking for

company. It had arrived in the trailer park one day, ribs like a concertina, grinning the way dogs do when they want something. But scavenging in winter is hard and it's limping, one eye weeping.

Her kick lands on the side of its muzzle and it whimpers in pain, backing away but still hopeful. 'Fuck off, you bag of shit.' She kicks out again, and the dog limps off towards the trees.

The bucket by the steps is upside down, the agreed sign to stay outside; her mother is entertaining again. At least these days she doesn't pretend they are uncles. The girl hesitates, then decides to go in anyway. If she's belted by her mother or whatever man is with her, so be it – at least she'll be warm. Warmer. She opens the door softly, listening for voices, hoping to judge the mood, but there's no sound. Crashed out of it on ice, then, the other kind. She sniffs the air, sampling and confirming; the faintest hint of cheap plastic curtain, always a giveaway if you know what to expect, and she's had years of experience.

The girl makes her way into what passes as a bedroom and stands looking at the two bodies passed out on the bed. She hasn't seen this guy before; she prefers the regulars, at least she knows what to expect. The one-offs, they have nothing to lose. And this one is no different; blood has barely congealed on her mother's cut lip and a bruise is already spreading under her left eye. The guy hasn't even untied her hands. Sex games; where's the play? How can any woman want a man when they act like this? How can anyone be so stupid? And as her mother tells her, stupid people get what they deserve.

Despite the sounds of her movements, the bodies on the bed haven't shifted. The girl walks softly across to the man; she notices fragments of something in his beard, crumbs of pizza, and a scattering of empty beer cans on the floor next to a fogged glass crack pipe.

Something's wrong.

She watches as his chest rises and falls and his breaths bubble through lips rimed with dried mucus. Her mother, though, is still and pale. Too pale, even for her. The girl moves around to the other side of the bed and reaches out softly, a feather landing on skin, but the cheek she touches is cold.

She studies her mother's body as if it is a waxwork; hair a matted motley of reds and greys, scabs and scars along her arms, the cheap green skirt rucked around her thighs. When your mother dies you are meant to mourn but when she examines her feelings, testing for tears, there is nothing. Love has never been part of the bargain, never asked for, never given. Better that way.

At night, in her own bed, she has often planned what she will do when the chance arises and she finds her Get-Out-of-Jail-Free card, her passport to freedom. And, unlooked for, today is the day. It will be a shame, in a way, but needs must when the devil drives. *You ruined my life,* the refrain of her childhood. Well, no longer.

First things first. She finds her mother's purse and takes out the only note, five dollars, and a few coins. Not a lot to show for a life. And an old-school photo, creased and faded. Her mother and a man with their arms around each other and the sea behind them. She turns it over: *Hugh and me, 1983.* Her mother looks young and happy. Almost unrecognisable. The girl lets it fall to the ground, then picks it up again. You never know.

The man's leather jacket has been thrown carelessly over a chair and she makes a better haul there; over two hundred bucks. The driver's licence will be no use to her but she studies the photo; so gross to think that her mother would let that thing touch her. Earl Lekker, even the name creeps her out. The cellphone is tempting, a new Motorola StarTAC, and she stuffs it into the back pocket of her jeans. Then into her bed area to look around; nothing worth taking except for the backpack she uses for school, when she bothers to go. Anything valuable that she owns, she's wearing.

Now into the kitchen area to take a knife from the drawer, the one with the long blade and the pointed end. Her favourite. It will be a sacrifice and sacrifices are sacred, aren't they? So it won't be all bad.

The man hasn't moved. She hefts the knife, considering. He's heavy. Under the skin will be layers of fat and gristle, and she has no illusions about her own strength. She allows the fantasy to roll through her mind for a few more moments; the point of the knife held against his throat, her weight pushing down, blood and air foaming and bubbling out as he realises too late what is happening.

But what if the point strays, if she scratches rather than stabs, if he wakes before she's done? Too risky, and perhaps there's a better way, something more fitting, more ceremonial.

The girl goes to the door and looks outside but no-one is around, even the dog has disappeared. She turns back into the trailer, closing the door behind her, and twists the gas taps on the ancient hob. The hiss is gentle, almost a lullaby. Very fitting. She sits and listens for a moment or two, making sure that the flow doesn't cut out, and then collects the pizza box and whatever paper and cardboard she can find, the makings of a small bonfire laid next to her mattress. She takes the lighter from her pocket, one of her mother's that she'd pilfered along with a couple of darts a week or so ago, and watches the flames grow more quickly than she'd imagined. So much smoke; it catches in her throat as it roils around the small space. The cellphone is bulky in her pocket; probably best not to have that just in case she's picked up by the cops or the social, so she drops it to the floor.

She moves back to the outside door and listens, but there are no sounds from inside the trailer, nothing except the duet of gas and flame. Probably best to leave before the finale. She closes the door behind her and walks quickly through the gathering dusk towards the road. Where to go? Away from here, that will be a good start, and the road has to lead somewhere better than this. She starts walking, turns back for a last look at the sign – 'Fraserwood Trailer Park' – and barely travels another hundred metres before she smiles for the first time that day as she hears the explosion.

N o mobile signal this lunchtime; the wind was in the wrong direction again. Not for the first time he wondered why they didn't allow landlines in beach huts. Surely it was easy enough to lay cables under sand, not that there was much up at this end of the beach, more a combination of mud and pebbles. The sea, fed by the estuary on this edge of England, was no more than a glimmer on the horizon now that the tide was out, a line of light strobing intermittently whenever the sun appeared through a rip in the clouds – and there were always clouds.

He would have to re-frame his Practising Certificate; it was hanging at a slight angle, as usual, and he leaned across to straighten it. Under a crack in the glass, the blurred black dots of mildew were advancing on the beginning of his name: Quincey Radlett, solicitor. He was never sure whether the name gave him an imposing air or simply made him seem like a knob. He knew what his wife would say, always assuming she was talking to him again.

The thought of Cath made his back twinge, just above the left kidney. When does a play-punch cross the line into assault? An interesting question, if a little academic in the circumstances, and the truckle bed hadn't helped. Perhaps he should have left it in the basement study at the house instead of bringing it here for those times when home was less than welcoming.

The kettle had boiled at last. Old Fencible, his physics master, had taught that sea level was the same everywhere. The kettle, on the other hand, seemed to believe it was being used in an Everest base camp rather than a Kilvercombe beach hut. Or had he got that wrong? Air pressure and boiling points; physics had never been a strong suit. He took the mug of coffee – black, three sugars – out onto the small area of decking where his two spare shirts were drying over the rail, along with the maroon Speedos that served as emergency underpants and the socks with holes on each big toe. Perhaps he should learn to darn, but who mended clothes these days? There were more at the house, along with his second-best suit.

Quincey tried to remember if this was one of Cath's court days. He hoped so: that would mean less chance of her coming back to find him furtling around in the house, and appearances in court always put her in a good mood. He often wondered how such a beautiful woman could have so much testosterone oozing from her glands. And who would have thought it; married to a silk, him, a provincial solicitor with ginger hair and asymmetrical testicles. He'd managed to go through life quite contentedly, not being a self-studier, until she pointed out the discrepancy to him one night as she cupped his balls in one hand like a couple of Chinese gooseberries. Her image, not his. She could be quite earthy sometimes, just when he was least expecting it.

Rain was approaching; he sensed a rawness in the air,

and that would mean working inside the hut rather than on the decking outside. It wasn't his preference; now he'd have to keep the door open or risk asphyxiation from the smell. He'd thought it was a leaking gas canister but when he'd persuaded a plumber to have a look last week, the man – a mournful wretch with a dignified attitude to his craft – had said there was nothing wrong so perhaps it was all in the imagination. As if. He couldn't turn the gas on and off every time he needed a caffeine fix; the tap was so tight that his palm was still lacerated from the last attempt, and he had always healed slowly. *Weak blood,* Ma used to say, j*ust like your father.* Hers oozed like treacle and set like concrete, so perhaps she had a point.

He still couldn't decide whether to go home to get changed. He considered clambering up onto the roof of the hut where a mobile signal was more likely so that he could message his wife and find out if she was likely to be around. On balance, though, that was probably a bad idea. The last time he tried, he'd slithered off the slick coating of slime and guano and twisted his ankle.

At some point he would have to get a new briefcase; the tattered bag-for-life lying on the floor by his feet wasn't quite the image he needed to portray, but it had been all he could find earlier and God help him if he were to drop the green ring binder and lose any of the papers. *Dr Joanna Dust vs. Uskmouth University*, an employment tribunal case. Why had he agreed to take it on? The woman had been in touch a couple of days ago and at first he thought it was Cath; the same sharpness, the same faint air of condescension, the same voice that made his bowels seem hollow.

Dr Dust had talked at him for over an hour; at one point he realised she was quoting arguments from previous cases that he'd never even read. At the end, when she asked his opinion, he had used his usual fall-back; give me some time to think about it, send me everything you have. *That will not be possible,* she'd said, as if he'd asked her to amend the second law of thermodynamics, *I'll send you a synopsis.* Synopsis? And here it was, God knows how many pages of printed e-mails, letters, handwritten diary notes. And today of all days, the dyslexia had really kicked in and the whole lot could have been written in cuneiform for all the sense it made. He sometimes wondered whether a different profession might not have been a good idea.

A tennis ball landed on the binder with a soft explosion of grey sand, bounced up onto his nose and then dropped to the decking.

'Damn this contraption!' The woman's voice sounded slightly military, with overtones of boiled cabbage. 'Charlie. *Charlie!*' She waved a giant plastic ladle in the general direction of a small terrier further down the beach. It trotted towards her with what looked suspiciously like a half-eaten hotdog in its mouth. 'Charlie! Drop that, dirty boy.'

She waddled across the pebbles towards Quincey, her brown tweed skirt skimming a pair of ancient green wellingtons. 'Quincey, isn't it? One of the Radlett brood? Thought you'd moved to London; someone said you'd snagged a high flyer. Who would have guessed.' It took a few seconds before she registered in his memory; Mrs Brown, his form teacher in Year Six at Kilvercombe Primary. The same grey hair and rimless specs; she'd seemed ancient then. Surely she should be dead by now.

She glanced at the clothes drying on the rail. 'Not still wetting yourself, are you? Maroon, poor choice. People think dark colours don't show the stains but they're wrong. It didn't matter how many spare pairs your mother sent you to school with, you'd go through them all. She was a saint, your Ma, especially after what happened with your father. I remember her saying, there is no justice. After parents' evenings, we'd always wonder what she'd done to deserve you. No offence.'

She and the terrier, minus its wilting snack, stood side-by-side on the damp sand, looking at him. 'If you'd be so kind, Charlie would rather like his toy back.'

Quincey reached down, picked up the ball and threw it as hard as he could down the beach, realising only as his body jerked forward that he'd gone commando that morning, the Speedos still being damp, and forgotten to fasten his fly.

As he stuffed the file and papers back into the plastic carrier, a 'missed delivery' card fell onto the slatted floor of the decking. UPS, parcel left with neighbour. He must have missed this when he picked up his post - it had to be the new bike. A man needs a hobby, he'd told himself, and he quite fancied leading a peloton through the streets of Kilvercombe, up around the cliffs, past the pier and back through the cheering crowds.

He'd ordered the machine a week ago after spending days of research online; 27 speed Shimano shifters, Reynolds frame, Schwalbe tyres. Metallic porn, with a little gel and rubber thrown in. And completely under his control.

He checked the card again, dated three days ago. So which neighbour had the delivery, and why hadn't they said anything? Surely the bike hadn't been stolen already, before he'd even put a photo or two on Instagram - five followers, all strangers, but it was a start. Maybe Cath had intercepted the delivery and sent it back out of spite. Or perhaps it was already in the shed at the end of the side entrance. Marcia at number 37 was like that. She might have popped it in there for him and forgotten to say, not that he'd been around much.

What to do? There was no point in continuing to stare at the indecipherable files, and in any event he couldn't face working inside the beach hut. He could go home, but what if Cath were still there? He wasn't sure he could face her at the moment; he ached for someone to make him feel that he deserved a place among normal people, rather than be forced to suffer the condescending company of his wife.

The wind must have changed. His phone pinged with a text from Cath; *Staying over in London*, it said, with no kiss at the end. It had been a long time since they had shared any kisses, real or virtual, and he liked kisses. Quincey had to work hard to remember how she smelled, the intimacy of a lover's body. The scent of her skin used to be so important to him; for some reason, it always reminded him of tangerines. Sweet and ripe, warmed in the sun. Not the texture, though; her skin was the colour of a banana smoothie and as soft as velvet. He'd said that once, in the days when he was still allowed close enough to tell, and she'd boxed his ears, the way his father used to. He'd never quite seen where the box came into it.

He made a decision. Screw work; he would drive over the bridge to Uskmouth and drop in on Esther. It was only two days since the last time, on her birthday, but they hadn't spoken since. She hadn't even replied to his texts, which was unusual, so the personal touch seemed in order. With Cath away, there wouldn't even be any explaining to do. Men have needs, he reminded himself, and he'd long since suspected that Cath's nights away from home weren't spent streaming 'Friends' in lonely hotel rooms.

He hadn't made up his mind about Uskmouth. Despite the new restaurants around the Bay it still carried an air of loss, a decline from grandeur, as if pretending to be something it wasn't. His most recent therapist would have called that projection, but what did she know? He'd only gone to her - six months of almost silent staring - because Cath had insisted. No, not insisted; threatened would be better. A battle of humiliations.

He pulled into the next petrol station and chose a bunch of carnations from the bucket outside the sliding doors, got as far as the cash desk, then changed his mind, went back outside and swapped them for roses, just in case. His lover's sense of smell was rather overdeveloped, and carnations might have tipped the balance the wrong way. He never could tell which Esther he'd encounter; like most women, she moved in mysterious ways. Or was that God? Sunday school had never been a strong point.

The next question was, would she be in? Probably. Very diligent, Esther, an over-achiever. She'd be there, working on a dissertation, reading and scribbling. She'd shown him one of her essays once, on what was thankfully a good day for dyslexia even if she wrote all her first drafts longhand in purple ink. Most of the words made sense, even if the concepts didn't. He seemed to remember a discussion on the Philosophy of Law, a subject that had eluded him throughout the eighteen months spent studying for his Graduate Diploma; what on earth was wrong with the real world of employment tribunals?

He thought of texting to say he was coming, but perhaps surprise would be better, and he'd never mastered the art of one-handed typing on the move. As he swung onto the A48 towards Uskmouth city centre, he pictured her face when she opened the door; a smile, surely, that special nervous twitch of the left eye showing, as no words could, her pleasure that he was back again. Would she expect sex? He tested his state of potential arousal, but he wasn't in the mood. A shared supper would go down well, though. He'd missed lunch and a shish from Kev's Kebab on Cathedral Street would hit the spot.

At first he thought Esther must be out, but then he saw her car parked a hundred metres or so down the street, a Vauxhall Astra so old that the red had faded to pink, with a dent the shape of Australia on the driver's door. The houses were late Victorian, three stories high, with yellow brick picking out detail against the dark background of old soot. At this end of the street, they were semi-detached with narrow side entrances. Esther's flat was on the ground floor, back, and he'd gone into the garden once from the French windows in her living room. Near the middle of the lawn an apple tree had toppled, its trunk split as if by lightning, and what had once been flower borders had turned into thickets of barbs and thorns. Something had shifted in the long grass, slithering unseen away from him, and he'd moved back quickly inside. Wild crepuscular landscapes had never been his strong point.

He wondered if he should knock or use his key. The bell had been broken since he'd known her; he'd promised to fix it in a fit of misplaced helpfulness and was glad when she had said that she preferred it broken. Analogue announcements are so much nicer, she had said, but he hadn't known what she'd meant.

He drove around the corner and found a place to park. She didn't like his car in sight of the house, for reasons which had never become clear. Another one of her obsessions, one of the rules to keep anxiety at bay. Funny how some people wanted him to change his behaviour because of their problems.

He felt mildly foolish, walking along with the thin bouquet of roses held as if he'd merely borrowed it. Someone was making curry, and the pungency of cumin and turmeric filled his mouth with saliva. So many fluids in his body, all out of control. There was music too, a scattergun of words to a violent beat. He was glad it was still daylight.

A gaggle of dustbins partially blocked the side entrance that led to her front door on the side of the building. Her bin was there, its lid cracked but perched at a jaunty angle with '5b' painted on the top in white. It was unimaginable enough that they could carve five apartments out of one house, let alone split them down further with As and Bs. What sort of person would live in a 5b?

Of course, there was always the possibility that she wouldn't let him back in after what happened the last time they met. Women crying were never a pleasant sight, and simply because he'd said no to a long weekend in the Lake District. It wasn't as if she didn't know about Cath; he'd been open from the start about his marriage, if only as a bastion against involvement. And context was everything; how many times had he told Esther that? Their encounters wouldn't feel the same somewhere else, somewhere neutral. There was a visceral thrill, he felt it every time, about being invited into her home, into her bedroom, into her bed. A series of penetrations, and isn't that, he told himself, what men are for?

He knocked again for the third time, trying not to sound over-peremptory, and wondering if she was asleep already. It was always possible; sometimes she seemed to want to close her eyes even before they started. He heard voices advancing from down the street, a couple of teenagers with cans of lager, or would it be cider? The former, probably, Special Brew. And a shared spliff; the perfume reminded him of that summer night on the beach in Brighton when he and Cath were fresh and new, and secrets were for another day.

He tried to recall Esther's number. It wasn't stored on his mobile, even though he'd long since learned not to leave the phone unattended when Cath was around. But he'd remembered correctly; he heard her phone ringing inside the apartment as soon as he finished tapping out the number.

Instead of his call being answered, the door opened. She looked smaller, as if she had shrunk like a mushroom being fried. Even her eyes seemed to have receded without their usual smoky make-up, and the oversized T-shirt was creased and stained as though she'd been sleeping in it since the last time they met. For sure, he should have let her know he was coming.

She took the flowers and looked at them as though she had never seen roses in plastic before. 'You'd better come in,' she said, and the smell of stale red wine and cigarettes seeped into the air between them.

When he replayed the day later, this part was always hazy, like the scenes in a dream which were there for no more than a few seconds after waking and then got lost in mist, leaving only the vaguest shapes. There was a kiss, there was always a kiss. And after the kiss there had sadly been no time for food, he remembered that, although along the way he had found some wine. They had gone straight to the bedroom and she had been... what had she been? Greedy, but disconcertingly absent at the same time. He couldn't remember any words, just noises in the dark; his, not hers. When they had finished she'd turned away from him, curled with her knees pressed against her breasts. He had taken the wineglasses to the kitchen and left them by the sink; there hadn't seemed any point in staying.

HE WASN'T ready to go home, even though he wanted a shower, but the need for another drink took precedence. Esther had unsettled him. It had been like paying for sex, which was something he'd only done once, for a bet. There had been an air of condescension about the whole business, and he got enough of that at home.

The King Billy wasn't the kind of pub he would usually use. Dark green paint peeled from the window frames and solitary men with scraggy cigarettes haunted the pavement outside the door. For some reason, this establishment hadn't been on the list for makeovers and he tried the door to the saloon, but it was either locked or stuck. Probably the latter, gummed from under-use. Not that the public bar was any better; he ordered a double Scotch and two grey pickled eggs and sat at a table by the window. Someone had left a Daily Mail on the seat in the corner and he enjoyed the forbidden, grubby thrill of reading it. The scotch turned into two, then three, and it was only when he rounded the corner on the way back to the car that he realised his keys were missing. And his phone. He knew immediately where they were, on the small bedside table next to her old-school radio alarm. It was a good thing about the keys. If it wasn't for them, he might have driven home and not noticed the missing mobile, and God knows what might happen if Esther called Cath. Which, of course, she could already have done.

He felt a sense of déjà vu as he stood by the dustbins,

banging on the door and waiting for an answer. No roses this time, and he was the one who was drunk. And his mobile was inside, so he didn't even have the option of calling her.

Still no answer. He'd have to use the kitchen window then, round the back, and thankfully her flat wasn't on the first or second floors. The sash window slid up easily enough, and he rolled himself inside and across the stainless steel sink unit, catching his belt on the taps and struggling to free himself for a few moments like a trapped beetle. Their two wineglasses from earlier were standing on the draining board, still unwashed with dregs of Chilean Shiraz staining the Ikea bowls like rust. Just where he left them. He listened for her movements but there was nothing, just that muted beat of music from across the street. It sounded different here – Acid House? Rap? Hard to tell, not that he would know anyway.

Light flickered through the open bedroom door, giving an illusion of movement. She preferred candles littered about her rooms; some were perfumed Yankees, others just tea lights in jars, and he sometimes wondered if she bothered to light them when he wasn't there. He sidled into her room but the bed was empty, the sheets rumpled and damp from their session earlier. Her smell was in the air, sweet and sour.

He felt like an intruder and realised that he was unconsciously trying not to make any sounds. Ridiculous, given his bellows and grunts of a couple of hours ago, but it would be nice if she made a few sounds too, sometimes, just to show willing. Still.

He collected his keys and mobile from the bedside table; the candles were all burned out except for one, the two foot high church candle he'd given her for Christmas. It was shorter than he remembered and must have been burning almost constantly. The thought made him smile; was that where the saying came from, keeping a candle burning for someone? Her favourite handbag, the green leather sack, still sagged against the wardrobe door.

'Esther – Esther!' There were no echoes in this flat. His voice soaked into the walls and in an apartment this size, there weren't many places to hide. He tried the small living area in case she'd fallen asleep on the sofa her parents had donated, but the cushions were in their proper place, plumped and angled and empty.

She always kept the bathroom door shut as if there were something faintly noisome inside, something to be ashamed of. He knocked first, out of habit, knowing how she hated him to see her unprepared. There were no shared baths or showers, not with Esther. Not that he particularly wanted to; she had called him gaunt once, the last time Cath had exiled him for a couple of weeks, and he'd preferred candlelight and covers ever since.

He pushed the door open slowly. The overhead light was off but two candles were burning, one at each end of the bath, giving the room a welcoming, golden glow. The small, warm space was filled with the scent of the geranium oil she always used in the water. It defined her more than any perfume, a mist on her skin when they made love. She must have used it tonight, the familiar scent around her as she climbed into the warm water while it was still clear, before it swirled and clouded red with the blood that had escaped from her wrists. He wished her eyes hadn't stayed open.

He said her name again quietly, as if trying not to wake her – *Esther, please* – as if she could change her mind. He wondered if he should feel for a pulse, but even though this was his first dead body he knew that the action would be futile and he could smell the blood now, like rust. Without warning, his mouth filled with acid and before he could turn away, his stomach spasmed and he threw up onto the floor beside the bath. He wiped his mouth and knelt there for a few moments while tremors ran through his body, like the aftershock from an earthquake. When they eased off he straightened up, unable to take his eyes off her, expecting her mouth to curl with a little moue of disappointment at his crass behaviour.

A thought struck him suddenly; his DNA wasn't only to be found among the contents of his stomach on the floor. There was bound to be a post-mortem, and they'd soon discover that she'd had sex not long before she died. In twenty-twenty retrospect, they hadn't always been as careful as they should. And what if someone knew about them? She said she had told no one, but women and their friends... okay, it wasn't as if he'd done anything illegal, but his business depended on reputation and he couldn't afford a scandal. And if Cath were to find out... He retched again, emptily, and felt a trickle of sweat rolling down his back.

He took a wad of toilet tissue and wiped his face, then cleaned the floor as best as he could, using the bottle of bleach hidden behind the loo. With luck the smell would dissipate before anyone found her, and he sat on the closed toilet seat, trying to focus his thoughts. The room looked different from this angle and he noticed something propped against a bottle of shower gel on the ledge behind the bath. There was no name, just the letter 'Q' neatly centred on the narrow envelope, with a single sheet of lined paper inside, torn from a pad. He recognised that handwriting, a slanting, confident script in violet ink that ran up slightly towards the end of each line. Almost elegant. He scanned the words - they were clear enough this time, as if panic had straightened them out - looking to see if he was mentioned. *Sorry*, it started, *but I never feel as alone as when I'm with you.* His hands were damp, smudging the ink and tinting the tips of his fingers. The words were beginning to shift about now, but that was because of the tears. He tried to focus; the note was nothing more than a brief message of regret and goodbye, and not a little self-blame, finished with a simple *Ex*, the way she signs her texts to him. Signed.

Blame; whatever else happened, he would be blamed for sure if anyone found out that he had been there. She was fragile, he'd known that from the start. He'd even welcomed her dependence, what had seemed a hungry need for his presence, even if she'd seemed indifferent to his body. But should he take the note? The envelope for sure, with its incriminating initial, but the note itself made it clear that she had done this to herself. That, at least, should stay. Nothing she'd written could be used to identify him.

His heart lurched and then slowed again when a siren dopplered past outside, fading into the night. As he washed his hands in the sink, Esther's body slumped down a little further into the bathwater and a gurgling sound made him realise the bath was emptying, a crimson whirlpool forming under the taps. Her foot must have caught the chain on the plug and dislodged it.

Already he could see a tide mark on her body as her breasts bobbed into view, and he reached back in to replace the plug, topping up the bathwater until she was decently covered again. He reached to tidy a strand of her hair that had fallen across her cheek, thought about trying to close her eyes, then stood back and looked around.

There was no more he could do here, but the rest of the flat needed checking - the bedroom for a start. He found a black bin liner in the kitchen, then stripped the bed and stuffed the bag with the duvet cover, the sheet and pillow-cases. But now it looked even more incriminating. He made up the bed again, with clean linen from the airing cupboard in the hallway, rumpled the sheets a little and made them look slept in, but only by one person. Then he made his way back out the way he'd come, through the kitchen window, remembering to put away one of the wineglasses and take the bin bag with him. He was back at the car before he realised his cheeks were covered with a sheen of tears. Before he realised he hadn't said goodbye.

TWO

T hree twenty-five in the morning, and what sounded like a party on the promenade behind the beach hut. Quincey sat up too quickly, feeling as if he'd left his head on the pillow; perhaps it had been a mistake to buy that bottle of Scotch on the way home. He could have gone back to the house, Cath was in London after all, but it had been hard enough to resist the temptation to climb into the car boot to shut away the world, and the hut had seemed like a decent compromise.

He lifted his hand to his face. The scent of blood still lingered there in spite of washing and scrubbing in water and whisky. If only he hadn't panicked about the mountain of files sent by Dr Dust. If only he had remembered his keys and phone when he left Esther's flat the first time. If only he had walked - run - away as soon as he saw the body in the bath. But no; judgement failure on a grand scale and now he was marked.

The nightmares had come as no surprise. Esther handed him a glass of wine, but it was the taste of rust that passed his lips. Then she was writing, page after page from her notepad, all with just one word that he couldn't read. He knew what it said, though. Quincey. His name, over and over. A whirlpool was spinning somewhere, oblivion calling; he was swimming, trying to get to the distant shore, to the beach hut, but the vortex was pulling him backwards towards Esther sitting in a boat shaped like a bathtub, tearing out the pages with his name and scattering them like giant leaves of toilet tissue. They turned into origami boats floating past him on the water, just out of reach, each vessel an accusation.

Through the beach hut window, striations of moonlight crept across the pillow to wake him again. The party outside had moved on and all he could hear was the sound of the waves. The spring tide was at its peak tonight, shrouding the beach. Then he must have slept again; the next time he opened his eyes, the small window was spattered with rain, pixelating the grey clouds that filled his view. He swung his feet on the floor and the movement disturbed the pent-up odour of his body from inside the bed covers. For a moment he wished he'd had a shower before he left Esther's last night, then remembered why that wouldn't have been possible.

He opened the door and looked out at the tide, already retreated across the muddy sand and grey as the sky. An early morning swim, salt instead of steam? But even as he looked, the rain redoubled its efforts, hiding the shoreline. There was nothing for it now, he would have to go home.

CATH's beloved BMW was parked outside the front gate; somehow dust and mud and bird shit instinctively knew to avoid the paintwork and tinted glass. Arrogance hath its privileges. His heart skipped a beat, but he knew that she would have taken a taxi to the station. As he opened the front door he heard the Dyson somewhere upstairs. He'd forgotten; this was a Wednesday, one of the days for Duchess to come and put their house in order.

The Dyson stopped as he shut the front door, and Duchess peered at him through the banisters. Cath swore she'd found the woman through an agency, but that was a patent lie. Duchess was not of this world, Quincey was sure of that. The eyes for a start, too wide-spaced to be human and a different colour each time she came round. Contact lenses, Cath had said, but he knew better. Of course, there could be two Duchesses, or more, working a rota system and sharing the money Cath left in an unsealed white envelope under the orchid in the hall.

Today's Duchess was wearing faded jeans that encased her thighs like denim-effect cling film. She came down the stairs towards Quincey, balancing the vacuum cleaner on one finger as if it weighed no more than a feather duster. 'Mornin', Mister Q,' she said as she shambled past, sniffing like a pointer.

He could smell it himself, this miasma that enveloped him like an invisible cloak. Before the early morning dog walkers were out he should have swum after all, run free and naked from the beach hut to the line of seaweed that marked high tide, let the sea cleanse him and wash away the reminders of Esther. But it was too late, the walk-in shower would have to do.

HE WOULD HAVE CHOSEN the cellar for his office even if Cath hadn't already appropriated the top floor for hers, citing a need for sunlight and space. *'It's either that or I spend all my time in London. And anyway,'* she'd said, *'a mole like you,*

you'll be in your element down there.' She was right; no distractions, no windows, just the blocked-up opening on the front wall where the coal chute used to come in from the street. Sometimes he fancied he could still smell the dust in the air, creamy and comforting as Guinness. Then again, he'd never been quite sure about Guinness.

A man could feel safe in a room like this even if the fluorescent tubes never lasted more than six months and a small tribe of mice occasionally dined on the outskirts of his files. They were far too fly for traps; the food always disappeared and the springs were sprung but there were never any bodies. Sharp teeth, mice, he'd kept one as a pet when he was a boy. He couldn't remember what had happened to it although his mother had looked uncharacteristically joyful for a few days after it disappeared. He vaguely remembered singing.

He'd tried the small plastic bowls of poison, persevering even though each morning he'd come down to find the trays overturned and the uneaten bait spread in Fibonacci spirals on the oak laminate. He'd given up the day he found one of the trays transported from the floor to the middle of his desk, still full of little blue granules. Surely not the mice; Duchess? Or more likely Cath, her version of a joke.

He wished he hadn't thought of the mice and their funerals. Had Esther's body been discovered yet or would it stay in the bath for days, weeks, deliquescing with decay?

If only, what if; life was littered with regrets. Work, that was the ticket, some displacement activity to keep the thoughts of Esther at bay. He fired up the laptop; the hard drive sounded more like a jet turbine every time, or was that the fan? And it was one of those days when the screen decided to display everything in shades of pink and green. Not that it was unattractive; he found it almost restful to see the world as a dichromate, like a dog. He'd suggested a spaniel to Cath once, a few weeks after the argument about children. It hadn't gone well; *If I don't want a squalling baby, what makes you think I'm going to want a foul-smelling animal dropping its fleas all over the house and pissing on the rugs?'* And then the clincher. *'Do you have any idea how much it cost me to import the Keshan in my office?*

'At least you wouldn't have to give birth to it,' he'd replied out loud, which hadn't been his intention.

He remembered that bruise, it had taken at least a fortnight to fade. And how could he explain to Cath that he needed a second go, another attempt to prove that he could father a proper child when she didn't even know about the first?

The hard drive settled down to an acceptable drone, the screen adopted a bearable colour palette, and he checked for messages. There were emails, there were always emails. It was easier to read when no one else was around. He could take his time, test different versions of the patterns he was seeing and plump for the one which made the most sense.

He scrolled through the usual items of correspondence from the office in Avonport, some of them dated almost a week ago. Everything sent to his accommodation address was supposed to be scanned and emailed on the same day it was received; *I'm a lawyer*, he'd said, *I can't afford delays*. Sometimes he suspected they held it up deliberately, especially when he'd complained about something. Or perhaps it was Wanda, attention seeking. He really would have to do something about Wanda.

Then he found the message from Dr Dust. Was it only yesterday morning that he'd attempted to read the files she'd sent? Geological epochs had passed since then, whole species had evolved and then become extinct. Esther had died.

He read the mercifully short message, a reminder of their meeting that afternoon in Avonport. For a moment he considered cancelling; how could he carry on as of nothing had happened? On the other hand, acting normally was probably a good strategy. He moved the message into the new 'Joanna Dust' email folder, disappearing it from his inbox. Action 1 - tick. It was a start.

The door at the top of the stairs opened and the silhouette of Duchess spoke to him. 'Finished, Mr Q. You pay now.'

'Cath leaves you an envelope.'

'No envelope. You pay, Mr Q. Please.'

He found his wallet, some small change and a crumpled £5 note. Surely there had been more? But of course, the pub last night and then the bottle of cheap scotch on the way back to the hut. And the afterthought flowers for Esther – his heart went on strike for a second. The flowers were still in her flat. What if they were traced to the petrol station? What if someone remembered him buying them? There would be CCTV, or did that sort of thing only happen in American crime dramas?

'Mr Q?'

'I'm sorry, no cash. Could we, I don't know, pay you double next time?'

'You have card, we go to cash machine. You drive.'

'I'm really busy... Sorry, you have to talk to Cath.'

The featureless shadow at the top of the stairs moved forward. 'You have card, we go to cash machine. You drive.' She shrugged. 'Or can call brother, he take you.'

He would have to fit a lock on that door.

. . .

THE ROLLING ROADWORKS on the motorway had reached the outskirts of the town and Quincey found himself funnelled by a contraflow onto the hard shoulder. The squeaking from the back of the car was bad today. It couldn't be the brakes; the noise disappeared when he slowed down. The first time he'd heard it, he'd imagined a squirrel in the boot, a stowaway hoping for pickings from the weekly supermarket trip. He'd even stopped and looked inside, but it was empty apart from the broken umbrella and the blanket that always felt faintly damp. One day, when Cath was out, he'd climbed inside and pulled the lid down as far as he dared. It was strangely comforting, if a little cramped, and he sometimes wondered about fitting a boot release on the inside so that he could shut himself in completely. A beach hut on wheels.

Cath had never understood why he wouldn't take taxis and trains. He hated travelling with her and her expectations; she carried her universe around with her and never seemed to feel out of place, whereas he knew, beyond doubt, that he was the unwelcome alien. '*Fuck off Radlett, you ginger wank stain,*' the Greek chorus of his childhood. In a car, though, even his 10-year-old Nissan with the key scratch on the side that he'd tried to fill in with one of Cath's nail varnishes – wrong shade, big mistake – he felt safe and protected. Ma might not have looked much from the outside, but there must have been something about her womb.

Twenty minutes later, he pulled into the unsurfaced car park between an office block and the station. The potholes showed up more after rain, tiny lakes of cloudy mud, and he had to drive around twice before finding a gap. Which of the other cars was Joanna Dust's, assuming she was here already, which he hoped she wasn't? Or was she a train woman too? He'd found it hard to tell from her voice and had tried googling her on the University website, but hers was the only profile without a photograph.

As if there hadn't been enough challenges already today, Wanda was on reception and he felt his body sag in preparation. As usual, he felt her eyes scan him as he walked towards her desk, starting at the hair and moving slowly down his body; not with desire, but as if she were checking to make sure that he'd remembered to wear all the essential items of clothing. She had the ability, shared with Cath and Ma - all women, come to think of it - to make him feel more than usually inept.

He needed to have a word with the management about Wanda. His money was as good as anyone else's, even if he only paid them to provide a business address and handle his calls and mail. And a meeting room, of course, when he needed to impress. It was all very well for Cath, being part of a fashionable set in Middle Temple, but he had to make do with the office in the cellar at home when he was allowed in, or the beach hut. From the sound of Joanna Dust on the phone, neither of those would have quite cut the mustard.

Something wasn't quite right; he could tell it from the way Wanda's smile was growing broader as she scanned the screen in front of her.

'Sorry, Mr Radlett, there's no room booked. You sure you called?' For some reason her voice always made him think of milkmaids.

'You know I did,' he said. 'Two hours, from three o'clock today. My client could be here any moment.'

Wanda sighed happily and hitched up a bra strap. Purple, he couldn't help noticing as she let it snap back against her shoulder. 'All the rooms are taken. We do require forty-eight hours' notice, it's in the contract.'

'But I gave you forty-eight hours' notice.'

'If you had, it would be on the computer.' She shrugged in sympathy. 'There are pills you can get these days, for memory. I saw them advertised somewhere. Or were they for "erectile dysfunction"? You should try them, Mr Radlett, could prove very helpful for a man of your age.'

'I'm 39, Wanda, not 93. And a little courtesy from you wouldn't go amiss.'

The air was disturbed as someone clattered through the revolving doors behind him in the lobby. 'Oh deary me,' said Wanda. 'This your client, Mr Radlett? Looks like she means business.'

THE SMALL GOD of provincial solicitors had decided to smile on him at last. They found a table for two in the café around the corner, even if she insisted that he sit on the fake leather sofa, which only seemed a couple of inches off the ground and released small trumping sounds every time he shifted his buttocks. He was already getting neck ache, looking up at her.

Most new clients, at a first meeting, turned up with some paper and a pen even though few of them ever made notes. The organised ones might have a ring binder or a laptop. Joanna Dust arrived with an airline bag on wheels, the contents of which had already been spread all over the table by the time he came back with a coffee for him and a glass of hot water for her.

'I need you to be quite clear, Mr Radlett, that this meeting hasn't started yet.' She was still stacking binders on the table, not looking at him. 'I don't recall a satisfactory answer from you regarding your costs. Fixed-price, Mr Radlett, I'm a university lecturer, not some highflying executive. My funds are limited. Do you understand?'

'Well, there are expenses...'

'What expenses? A glass of hot water? And what is all this nonsense about not meeting in your office? Not exactly professional, not what I was expecting. This is my career we're talking about.'

At last the airline trolley seemed to be empty. 'You asked for the documents, Mr Radlett, so here they are.'

'Please, Ms Dust, call me Quincey.'

'Doctor Dust. I worked hard enough for my Ph.D. and I don't see why I shouldn't get recognition. It's all about respect, Quincey, do you see?'

All he could see were the files and the words they contained. Thousands of words, tens of thousands of words. Millions, lying in wait like malignant centipedes. 'Perhaps it would help if you gave me a synopsis,' he said, 'a brief synopsis. The headlines, as it were.'

'Can you not read, man? I sent you a summary already... what is the point!' She sighed and opened one of the thicker binders. 'I've put together a chronology, cross-referenced to the other documents; here, I'll show you.'

And suddenly she was sitting next to him on the sofa, all legs and arms, smelling of soap and fresh air. Her long hair brushed against him, he was conscious of its weight even through the fabric of his jacket and shirt. He tried to concentrate on what she was saying, about how the new management team in the business school were discriminating against her because of her disability... Disability; he'd forgotten about that. Not surprising, she looked so normal. Did that count as woke or un-woke these days, the word normal?

The sofa was so small that her shoulder was touching his.

'Are you okay, Mr Radlett?' As if suddenly conscious of their closeness, she went back to her chair opposite him. 'You look very pale. I have Co-Codamol if it's a headache. Or was it the coffee? I never drink coffee in places like this, or anywhere come to that. Tea, that's a different matter, but they never make it properly. Might as well be in France.'

He realised he was staring at her. Like a cod, Cath would have said; she was always comparing him to a fish. 'Your disability, could you run through that for me – if you don't mind. Context is everything, as they say.'

'Whoever they are. "They" are the problem, Quincey, you do realise that. And ME is an impairment, not a disability. It is society that disables people; please tell me I don't have to educate you in the basics.'

This was going about as well as he'd expected. There were cases you simply shouldn't take on; how many times had Cath told him that? He was too greedy, a greedy fish. Bad fish.

'It was a figure of speech, no offence meant.'

'Figures of speech are signifiers of underlying thought patterns, dispositions to discrimination. I can't work with you if you're going to discriminate against me from the start. Carelessness, that's what it is. Starts with thoughts, gets translated into words and then into actions, and before you know it we're at a Nuremberg rally.'

He tried without success to replay the conversation so far, to see where he had taken the wrong turning that had exposed him as a subconscious Nazi. Did she really want him to hang for a figure of speech?

'I just thought...' What had he just thought? That the

beach hut would feel like The Ritz right now? The car boot wasn't far behind.

AFTER THE SESSION with Dr Dust, he was feeling rather peckish; the mere mention of a sandwich in the café had evoked a lecture on the perils of wheat, and after that the option of an egg baguette rather lost its lustre. He called in at Al's Plaice on the way home, not having the energy to cook for himself. It wasn't a success; the batter on the haddock tasted as if Al had formed it from plaster of Paris, and when he lifted one of the longer chips to his mouth it wilted disconsolately, away from his lips.

The 6 o'clock news on TV was almost over as he poked around inside the batter, looking for some vestige of protein and telling himself not to let them put the non-brewed condiment on next time. The local news reader, the one with the face that looked as if it had been left too long under the studio lights, announced that a woman's body had been found. In a bath. In a flat. In Uskmouth. Foul play not ruled out. So they weren't buying the suicide note; he should never have taken her those flowers.

ON THE RUN

Cerys wakes to the smell of smoke and frying bacon and rolls onto her back; the thin mattress on the floor might just as well not be there and she aches all over. It takes less than a second for her to remember where she is, an abandoned factory building near the railroad. Barely warmer inside than out, but at least it's shelter from snow or rain. And prying eyes. After the explosion, she doesn't want any welfare people coming after her. Or the cops.

She props herself on her elbows and looks around the dim space; the only light filters through high windows, grey with years of cobwebs and grime. About ten metres away, on the opposite side of the vast space, a young woman squats on her haunches, prodding a frying pan on a makeshift frame over an open fire. Kaley; she'd been watching as Cerys lifted a couple of cheap pies from a chiller yesterday evening and slipped them under her hoodie, then run interference when the shop-keeper tried to stop the girl escaping from his store. Kaley knew a runaway when she saw one and had offered a place to stay, for a while. Some offers are too good to turn down.

Another mattress nearby is unoccupied. A guy had been here last night when she arrived but had barely acknowledged her. Which is fine; as far as Cerys is concerned, most men are surplus to requirements.

Kaley calls over. 'You wanna eat? Bacon and bread. Pancakes are off the menu today, but there's coffee if you like it black. Noah scored it earlier.'

She's hungry. The two pies she'd stolen were all she'd eaten yesterday and they were the usual crap, thin pastry and air with a scrape of meat and onion. The chipped plate Kaley hands her is piled with thick rashers swimming in bacon grease, topped with a hunk of bread. Nectar.

She eats quickly, stuffing the bacon into her mouth, soaking up the fat with the slightly stale bread. And now what? Nothing comes for free, she knows that well enough.

'You're the girl from the trailer,' says Kaley, 'the one that exploded. It's all over social media, police are calling you a person of interest. They say your mom died.' She pauses and glances over with a questioning look. 'For real? My mom's shit too. If it was between me and the latest greasy bastard she decided to hang with, I'd be surplus to requirements. Not sure I would have blown her up, given the chance, but I'm not judging.'

'She was already dead,' says Cerys. 'One sex game too many and bad crack. I just saved money on a crematorium.' Somehow there didn't seem any point in denying it.

'Good point, well made. But there was someone else in the trailer, they said, one of the Lekkers. Earl. I guess you knew that.'

'He killed my mother.' As if her mom hadn't died inside a long, long time ago.

'Given a choice I'd rather take my chances with the police than the Lekker brothers,' says Kaley. 'Earl was bad enough, and Ches aint much better.' She sips some coffee, then shakes her head. 'It's Buck you need to watch, that man weren't made right.'

'You know them?'

'You don't? The Lekkers supply most of Fraserwood. They're based in their compound just outside town. Just the three boys and their ma; the father was put away years ago and died inside from a shiv in the back. I bet people queued up to be first to stick it to him.'

'What do they supply?' Cerys asked, as if she couldn't guess. She'd always kept away from anything harder than the occasional watery beer after seeing how her mom had spiralled down, doing whatever was on offer just to help her cope with the next sweaty bastard treating her like an object.

'Drugs mostly,' said Kaley, 'though they're moving into girls. Noah, the guy who stays here, he gets his gear from them. Ches been running things since Buck was put away a few years back, same place his Pa died. Can't remember what they got him for in the end but I know there was a killing they couldn't pin on him. Revenge for his Pa, people said. Not that the cops tried too hard, the Lekkers got friends everywhere. Tell you something, girl; you wanna hope he stays inside. If he thinks you had anything to do with Earl's death...'

This is not good. She has no regrets about what she did, the guy had been a stain, but the brothers sound like bad news. And if they have friends, all the more reason to stay out of sight. Perhaps she should have thought through the consequences before she lit the little pyre in the trailer, but who does that? Punishment, retribution, they have to be done quickly or what's the point?

Fraserwood is beginning to feel a little too small.

AFTER THE SMALL breakfast fire dies down, the vast space soon settles to the temperature of the air outside, freezing. Sleep last night had been fitful. Cerys curls up on the mattress and closes her eyes, but the events from yesterday keep replaying on a loop; the bodies on the bed, her mother's cold skin, Earl's fat neck, the smell of sex, the hiss of gas. The thrilling shock of the explosion. She'd smiled yesterday, but she isn't smiling now.

MID AFTERNOON. The door opens just enough to let a man squeeze through, as if trying not to be noticed. Noah, with sparse hair the colour of dying grass and a scrubby, half-formed beard. It takes a few moments before she realises he reminds her of the dog in the trailer park.

The man looks across and grunts, then unscrews a panel on the far wall, takes out a package and stashes it in his backpack. 'You're that trailer girl,' he says to Cerys. A statement, not a question. He stops by the doorway and turns to Kaley. 'Buck Lekker got out today. He knows whatever happened to Earl is no accident and he wants whoever did the torching. You know Buck; once he gets an idea in his head, nothing gets it out again. They're talking to everyone, trying to get a lead on the girl; they're pretty sure she had something to do with it.'

He looks back at Cerys. 'I was at their place earlier. They are fuckin' pissed with you. Buck's all for giving you a gasoline shower and flicking a match, and that's the good option. His ma thinks different; always was pragmatic, that woman. She wants to add you to their stable of girls and hire you out; they got customers looking for something different from the usual Colombians and Mexicans. A white girl like you, that's premium prices. And I heard some of their customers take a long time, a very long time, to have their fun with the girls. If that happens to you, you'll wish you were dead.'

This time yesterday she was a fifteen-year-old school-girl with a dumb ass mother, and no more worries than staying warm and fed. Now a family of psychos wants to kill or torture her. That get-out-of-jail-free card hasn't quite worked out the way she wanted.

Noah looks embarrassed. 'If they find out I know where you are and I aint told them, me and Kaley are screwed. You got till tonight, better be gone when I get back or I'm gonna have to call it in. I got no choice.' He sidles out of the door, and Cerys listens to his footsteps dying away on the metal stairway. The room feels even colder.

There's no point looking to Kaley for support. 'It's ok,' Cerys says, 'I'll go.'

'Sorry, hon, Noah's right; you can't stick around here. But where you gonna go? You need money and a place to stay.'

'Will he tell them where I am?'

'Not straightaway. Noah's ok. I known him since we were kids, he don't like hurting people and he's got this old-fashioned honour code around women. But the Lekkers can be persuasive if they think someone's holding out on them. And giving you up scores points... like I said, he's ok but he's no different from anyone else. When it comes down to it he'll look out for himself first. Still, you got some time. He said tonight, and he meant it. You gotta say off the streets till it's dark, though, or you won't last more than ten minutes before you get picked up. You see a black Toyota truck cruisin' around, you get outta sight, stat.'

ON THE ROAD into town yesterday, the smoke from the trailer a spreading stain against the clouds, she'd come up with the vague beginnings of a plan. Twelve years ago home hadn't been a stinking trailer in a frozen landscape, but an apartment - a flat, her mother always called it - in a low-rise block somewhere in the UK. She can still picture it; a narrow hallway, a living room draped with un-ironed clothes, a tiny bedroom, the bed kept level by a cheap paperback under one of the legs. A static memory, always the same. Or perhaps not a memory at all, just seeing in her mind what her mother had described. *'We're getting out of here, promise you babe, somewhere better.'* Those words were real even if the reality they promised never quite happened.

Life has never been easy, but at least it's been simple. Now, in less than a day, she's become a hunted animal. Prey, something she swore she'd never be. Part one of the plan now is to keep out of the clutches of the Lekkers and get far away from Fraserwood. How she's not yet sure, but fate hasn't given her much choice.

And then part two... Somewhere, thousands of miles away, is the reason her mother brought them both to Fraserwood. But how did she think this shithole ever going to be better than where they lived before? Cerys knows one thing; she's going to find whoever is to blame and make them pay for her mother's life, and her death. But between her and England are thousands of miles of mountain and prairie, and then an ocean. This will take some planning.

· · ·

SHE LEAVES before Noah gets back. There's no point staying where she isn't wanted, and she's in no hurry to make Buck Lekker's acquaintance. The fenced parking lot outside the derelict building is a desert of snow that has fallen, melted, refrozen and been re-carpeted by the next blizzard. A burnt-out car wilts in the middle, and the only light comes from floodlights on the railroad sidings a few hundred metres away, on the other side of the lot.

Cerys stands in the lee of the abandoned factory, checking to make sure that no-one is around, and then picks her way across the treacherous surface. Kaley had told her about a makeshift camp near the overpass on the southern outskirts of town. *'They're mostly ok,'* she'd said. *'Ask for Rafa, maybe he'll let you share his shelter for a day or so but then you gotta move on. He can be a tad touchy, just depends what he's on at the time, but he's better than some and he owes me. Remember, Fraserwood is the Lekkers' home ground, so don't let anyone know who you really are. Tell you what, use my sister's name. Aspen Collet - she lives in Quebec City, no-one around here knows her.'*

Most of her life she's felt invisible, now it's as if she's gone through the looking glass. Every person she passes seems to be staring at her and she hugs the sides of the buildings, constantly stopping and swivelling round at some imagined footsteps coming up behind. At the sound of a distant engine, she dodges into the doorway of a closed kebab shop and crouches down, watching from the shadows as a black Toyota pickup drives slowly by.

This is an unfamiliar part of town that makes the trailer park look like a holiday camp. She walks between piles of grey slush that line the sidewalks, and block after block of boarded-up shops. After nearly an hour, she sees the highway ahead, running way above the ground on concrete struts that straddle a collection of tarps, wooden crates and some tents. A makeshift village huddled in the shadow of the overpass, with a few campfires dotted about; the colours of the flames are a welcome shock after the monochrome world she's been walking through.

CERYS ASKS around and finds Rafa near the centre of the camp. A lean man in his forties, she guesses, with beads woven into his dreads. She tells him her new name, the words sounding strange, and that Kaley has sent her.

'How old are you, kid?'

'Eighteen.'

'Yeah, right. And I'm the fuckin' Pope. You in trouble? Runnin' from something?'

'Just need some space for a day or so, then I'll be moving on.'

Rafa starts to say something and then stops at the sound of a commotion from the edge of the camp. An engine revving, raised voices, and then the dry snap of a single gunshot. 'That don't sound good. Don't sound like coincidence neither. This been a peaceful place, then you arrive. Who knows you're here, apart from Kaley?'

'No-one. Maybe she told Noah, I dunno.'

'You want my advice, girl, you keep moving. I don't know your business and I don't want to, but if someone's looking for you, I'm gonna bet that's them.' He shakes his head, the beads clicking gently. 'Guns. Don't need no crap like that round here.'

'It's probably the Lekkers,' she says, 'Kaley said to stay away from them.'

Rafa stares at her. 'So you're *that* girl. Jesus holy Christ, you're in a shitload of trouble.' He thinks for a moment and then points to the far edge of the camp. 'There's a storm drain runs under the highway. On the other side there's a mess of brush you can lose yourself in.' He reaches under his poncho, pulls out a wad of grubby cash, and peels off a few bills. 'Never have liked those fuckwits and what they do to people, specially women. And their gear is mostly crap.' He pushes the money at her. 'Get your ass outta here. And don't worry, I won't say nothing.' He flaps his hands as if shooing away an annoying insect. 'Go on, fuck off. And good luck.'

———

SHE WATCHES from the other side of the highway, hidden in the scrubby undergrowth, unable to look away as a group of men wade through the camp, kicking and destroying the flimsy shelters and setting fire to the tents. After a while they give up, pile back into the black Toyota pickup and drive away. For a moment she considers going back to check on Rafa, but what would she say? People she doesn't know have had their lives turned upside down because of her. Maybe someone died. Time to turn around, walk away, and leave the mayhem behind. She has enough problems of her own.

CHAPTER
THREE

L ife, Quincey decided, had to go on. His, at least. Perhaps working would take his mind off Esther and the recurring images of her body in the bath, and judges never seemed keen on being ghosted by solicitors in the middle of a case.

The Employment Tribunal office had been designed to impress upon its victims the mundane bureaucracy of justice. A three-storey office block in concrete and glass, it squatted in a better part of Uskmouth like a cuckoo in the gap between a run of grey brick Edwardian semis. The street was a tributary from the main road, running through buildings which were mostly owned by the University, a procession of 1960s glass and steel boxes that were already slated for demolition. Uskmouth University, home of Dr Joanna Dust. Quincey had originally applied to the Law School there, and the rejection had been no less disappointing for having been expected, with a suggestion that he try the new University of Avonport, '*more practical, less critically academic.*' All euphemisms for less discriminating.

Parking was a pig, especially during the semesters.

Weren't students supposed to be poor and crushed by debt? The nearest multi-storey was a fifteen minute jog away and Quincey cruised the streets looking for an empty parking bay. At least the hearing today would be short, the unfair dismissal of a Somalian cleaner by the local health authority. He'd first met Amira a couple of months ago in the Avonport office, a shy woman wrapped in black and accompanied by a man who said he was her brother. In theory this was simple case, odds-on for an outright win, but you never could tell. If just one of the triumvirate of judges was on a bad hair day it could all go pear-shaped very quickly.

The claimants' waiting room was almost empty apart from a newly minted solicitor in a tight black skirt and not-quite-matching jacket. She sat next to a leaning tower of files, trying to explain something to her client, who looked like a refugee from a Twilight movie. Quincey had seen the girl before; she looked over and twitched a tired smile.

Still no Amira. Quincey checked his watch, then the clock on the wall, then went out to the clerk's desk. 'I was just about to come into you, sir,' said the man, 'they'll be ready for you in ten minutes. Room number four.'

He went back into the waiting room and tried the brother's mobile, but it must have been switched off or out of signal; Amira wasn't allowed her own phone. Being stood up by a client was one of his recurrent nightmares, something completely out of his control. Judges always seemed to think it was his fault, as if he had deliberately advised the clients to stay away solely to annoy the judiciary.

He noticed an unread text on his phone from Cath; urgent meeting in New York, wouldn't be back for a few days. New York? Why would she need to go there, unless it was it code for new lover. It might as well be for all the affection she showed him these days. He replayed conversations to see if there were any unfamiliar names she'd mentioned recently, but there was no-one he hadn't heard of before. He wasn't even sure that he cared. The therapist had once suggested, in her 'knit two purl one' way, that he saw Cath as his mother, which had put him off sex with anyone, including himself, for weeks.

The clerk came into the waiting room, which was now empty except for him and an ingrained, subliminal scent of resignation. 'They're ready for you now, Mr Radlett.'

MARCUS HAREMOUNTAIN WASN'T an easy name to forget. Quincey had always assumed the man came from somewhere in the Appalachians and was never far from a slightly out-of-tune fiddle. Not that Marcus would be thinking much about music in his cell at Uskmouth police station. Quincey heard the announcement on the radio while he was on his way back from the Tribunal hearing; a man was being held in custody for the murder of the student in the bath.

He hadn't liked Marcus, not from the moment that Esther first mentioned his name. For a start, why was a man who had once been a successful barrister teaching Philosophy of Law to students at Uskmouth Uni? And why was he giving Esther one-to-one tutorials at her flat? He'd wondered, sometimes out loud, if Marcus was trespassing on his own, exclusive, territory. '*What are you, the college bicycle?*' he'd said one evening after a glass of red too many, when Esther had been less than responsive to his attempts at romance. He'd regretted the words as soon as he said them, but the apology, instant as it was, didn't cut it.

She'd taken his mobile and car keys, run outside and dropped them down a drain. Cath had never bought the mugging story when he came home in a minicab. It hadn't been one of his finest moments; sometimes he wondered if he'd been entirely fair in their relationship.

A thought occurred like a lifeboat looming out of the mist; perhaps Marcus *was* involved and there was justice after all. Since that evening in Esther's flat he'd been working hard to find some reason, other than himself, for her death. '*It's not my fault*,' he had repeated to himself, a mantra from the therapy days, '*blaming myself is in my DNA.*' Perhaps, unusually, he'd been telling himself the truth.

He deserved a break today, after the fiasco at the tribunal, listening to Employment Judge Minchin lecturing him about wasting the court's time. At least he'd get another peaceful night at home, with Cath away. For the fraction of a second he thought - the rogue brain, tricksy as ever – *I could go to Esther*. It wasn't even a thought, just the recognition of a familiar picture which, as soon as he saw it, was overlaid with another scene; a cold, white body rising from the cloudy red water. Snow and roses, they didn't belong together.

He still had the envelope with his initial on the front. It was just the envelope, wasn't it? He hadn't taken the letter as well, Esthers's admission that she had killed herself, the passport to freedom? He fumbled inside his jacket pocket, swerving to avoid a motorhome that seemed to have appeared from nowhere. There should be a law. But even as he pulled the envelope out, he could feel that it was too thick. He didn't need to look; he'd forgotten to leave the letter behind and Esther's final exculpatory words were still inside, travelling with him, forever private. And now Marcus Haremountain was being held on suspicion of her murder. In the absence of a suicide note, a policeman's suspicions lightly turn to thoughts of homicide. Surely the professor had an alibi, surely the authorities would let him go? If they didn't, then a man who might be innocent would go to trial, and if they released him, the search for a killer would continue. But if he was guilty and set free, thought Quincey, then a murderer would be back on the streets, a murderer who almost certainly knew his name.

HE STOPPED off on the way home and picked up a fillet of wild Alaskan from the fishmonger on Bridge Street. Line caught, apparently, but how could you tell? Trust, everyone asking for trust. And what happens when you do?

After the failed haddock last night he'd planned a light supper of salmon en croute, samphire on the side and some home-made game chips, a small act of creation to counter the flashbacks of Esther, but the phone rang as he started wrapping the fish in a sheet of semi-thawed puff pastry. He thought of leaving it, but he was a Pavlovian dog at heart. And he was sure he'd put out a new tea towel yesterday but, typically, it had disappeared. Perhaps the Duchesses had a side line in recycled domestic linen. He wiped his hands carefully on his shirt and picked up the call just before voicemail kicked in.

'Quincey?'

Did women learn how to use that tone from girlhood, at secret classes from which boys were excluded?

'What is it Jennifer? I've just started cooking supper.' But he already knew there was only one reason his sister would call him.

'Is Cath there? Good, so you can talk, not that I care. You do know what the date is? You forgot completely last year, and even at Christmas which, God help us, nobody can forget, you left me to buy her a present. She's your daughter, Quincey. Three years old, she knows how to say your name, but otherwise you might as well be a stranger. Which you are.'

Three years – how could it be three years? More to the point, how did he end up with Poppy after a desultory affair with a woman who got back in touch months after they broke up, donated the baby to him in a hospital car park and then escaped child-free to live on a commune in Pembrokeshire? Not that he'd ended up with Poppy, exactly. Cath had no idea about his short-term lapse with Robyn and he'd driven to the only person he could think of, with the baby wedged on the front seat between his briefcase and a pack of Pampers. He couldn't remember the subsequent discussion with his sister - he'd read somewhere that the mind had evolved to erase memories of pain - or the scooping up of the child and her paraphernalia.

'Do you even know which day she was born, Quincey? Sometimes I wonder how she managed to get conceived in the first place. Did you consider a paternity test?'

The pastry would be drying out by now, going hard around the edges. Perhaps he should throw it away, pan fry the fish in a little butter and lemon juice. It would be a shame to waste food, but there was no point in doing something if it couldn't be done properly. And creamed potatoes rather than chips, comfort food. He didn't cook when Cath was around; *what do you think restaurants are for?*' rather than *'thank you darling, what a lovely surprise.'*

His sister was talking again. 'I don't suppose you've got around to telling your poor wife that you already have a child? No, didn't think so. Why I went along with this pathetic subterfuge I'll never understand... it's not that I don't like you, Quincey, it's just that you take up resources that might be better used elsewhere.'

'I'll get her something, Jennifer. What would she like? Tell me, I'll bring it up at the weekend.' He'd planned to take the bike for a spin if Cath were still out of the way, maybe pack the tent and camp somewhere in the Beacons on Saturday night. For a moment he thought of cycling to London, seeing images of Cotswold villages and pints of beer outside Oxfordshire pubs. And then he remembered the North Circular Road. 'What about Sunday – I could come for lunch?'

'One o'clock, sharp. And choose something for her your-self, just for a change. You're meant to be good at research, here's your chance. Girl, three years old, see what you can do. And try to look normal.'

He sat at the kitchen table with a mug of instant, his laptop and the Joanna Dust files, but instead of opening one of the binders he went to the photos synced from his phone; the new shots of the bike and a small gallery of Poppy. She'd smiled almost from the day she was born, as if she knew some secret about the world that was hidden from him and everyone else. Perhaps she did, perhaps it was the quid pro quo to make up for that extra rogue chromosome.

Robyn had blamed him, obviously, which was probably why she decided to try her luck somewhere more earthy. Jennifer had blamed him too, but at least she hadn't walked away. And in the absence of any better reason he blamed himself, it just seemed safer that way.

He wondered why he kept the photos on his phone; it wasn't as if he showed them to anyone. His secret, his dirty little secret. His broken daughter, given away like a bag of unwanted clothes. Because that's what you do when some-thing is broken and can't be repaired, you throw it away and replace it with something that works properly. Nothing wrong with that, surely?

He turned back to the files but a failed employment relationship seemed like an irony too far, and without making any conscious decision he found himself on Facebook, looking at Robyn's page, still surprised that laptops worked in yurts. He supposed that one day she would unfriend him and deny him this last access to her life. He said the word out loud – unfriend. To unfriend, to be unfriended. A public display of failure to maintain even a virtual relationship.

He scrolled down the page; how did she know so many people? None of the names were familiar and he wondered if she'd known them when they were seeing each other. But it was the latest photos that arrested him; her hair was shorter, almost military, the boots were construction-site chic and the tool belt, elegantly angled over her hips, was stuffed with implements waiting to be handled. And it might have been a trick of the light but was that the suspicion of a goatee beard?

He shut down the laptop. Too early for bed, nothing worth watching on TV, and the pub on the corner was full of people who knew each other. A time trial then, on the new bike, down to the docks and back. Shimano 27 speed shifters; they wouldn't let him down.

FOUR

The woman behind the counter seemed positive when he handed over the farmyard set to be wrapped up. '3 to 5 years' it said on the box, but with Poppy, who could say? The woman asked who it was for. 'My daughter,' he said, then wished he hadn't, then wondered why. 'She's a very lucky girl,' the woman said. 'We got the same one, well, the smaller set actually, not so many bits to get lost down the side of the sofa. My sister's girl, Sadie. She loves it, except she tried to bite the head off a horse. She's not much struck on cows either, come to think of it. Or sheep. Perhaps she's going to be a vegetarian – no, that doesn't work, does it? Or spend her time in an abattoir, like her dad. Funny, aren't they, children.'

Not the description he would have chosen.

The box was sitting next to him now, on the passenger seat of the Nissan. He'd been so pleased with himself that he had forgotten to write a card, stopped off at the newsagents round the corner, the one with a Kurdistan flag behind the counter, and bought a heart-shaped confection with glitter and a fairy on the front. You couldn't go wrong with a fairy, not for a little girl. And pink, even if it wasn't one of his favourite colours.

He couldn't understand where all the traffic had come from. It was a Sunday; people should be at home drinking beer and watching football, or whatever other people did to forget about their lives. They were down to fifty miles an hour on the M4, now thirty, now ten. It must be an accident. Quincey checked the time; he'd allowed himself two and a half hours plus ten minutes wriggle room. Counting down. No blue lights in the rear-view mirror yet, no sirens, and the lines of vehicles moved forward like soldier ants on a stealth mission.

The obstacle was ahead now, a lorry on its side. A single policeman, his motorbike on the wrong side of the central reservation, was funnelling the streams of traffic into a single line to get past. And the car with the crumpled bonnet, pointing the wrong way on the hard shoulder, looked like the Jag that had barrelled past him earlier. Two men, standing close but apart, were both speaking into their mobiles; the drivers, probably, it was surprising that they were both okay. So the dark stains on the tarmac were oil then, not blood.

He checked the dashboard clock again as he passed the wrecks and accelerated into the open road. Eight minutes, thirty seconds, so there was no need to call Jennifer; he wondered if Poppy knew he was coming.

As usual, there was nowhere to park and he used up the last of his safety margin cruising the back streets of Crouch End until he found a space rather too near an overflowing skip outside a house with no front windows. It was only when he was within a couple of hundred metres of Jennifer's front gate that he remembered the package on the passenger seat, swore quietly and jogged back. He couldn't have been gone more than a couple of minutes, but already someone had smashed the passenger window and the gift wrapped 'Farm Set, 3 to 5 years old', was gone, replaced with a brick half covered in cement.

He opened the door and saw the card lying in the footwell, the pink envelope showing a concertina tear across the top corner. The brick was on the passenger seat, sparkling with glitter on its edge.

He offered to show Jennifer a photo he'd taken of the broken window, but she wasn't interested. Poppy opened the card, sitting on his knee. She didn't seem to mind that there was no present, or perhaps she thought the card was good enough in its own right. He couldn't remember her being this heavy.

They put the card on the low windowsill next to the French windows, along with the others. Quincey wondered who had sent them; who were these people who knew his daughter, wrote in careful print 'To Darling Poppy', and remembered her birthday? He touched her hair experimentally as she rearranged the cards, flattered when she leaned into him, and then turned and smiled as if he were a friend. He had, he realised, no idea what to do with her or what to say.

They had almost finished lunch when the doorbell rang. 'That will be Taylor. It's alright, Quincey, I knew you wouldn't be able to cope for too long, so I asked one of Poppy's friends round to keep her occupied while we have a chat.'

Sometimes he looked at Jennifer and saw his mother, even now. Heard the same sharpened flint in her voice as she instructed the girls upstairs in their play duties. It was a shame her husband wasn't home, Fenton; not that they were close, but at least he was a man and that counted for something. Just what, he wasn't sure.

He was examining the picture on the place mat, a cathedral surrounded by sheep, when Jennifer walked back in. 'The man calls himself a professional and still he thinks Harry Potter is real. Dirty crockery jumping into the dishwasher of its own accord? Place mats flying through the air and into a drawer? No, leave it now.'

Her hair had more grey than he remembered, not in fashionable streaks but evenly distributed, watering down the auburn. And bags under her eyes; you could do something about that these days, surely Fenton earned enough. Or perhaps he didn't see them or didn't care.

'I spoke to Robyn last week,' Jennifer said. 'It sounded like she was in Mongolia. She wanted to see Poppy on her birthday, but I said you were coming.' She toyed with the half drunk beaker of apple juice. 'The girl is her daughter too, Quincey. She has some rights.'

'She walked out on us, Jennifer. You realise she lives in a yurt. In Wales.' He thought better of mentioning the goatee.

'Nothing to do with the fact that you have a wife, god help her? You men, you leave your sticky fingerprints on everything you touch, like a three-year-old with a jam sandwich.' His sister picked at a half eaten chipolata from the green, plastic plate that matched the beaker. 'She's talking about having her back, Quincey. Full time. She wants to take her away from me.'

His sister was crying and he couldn't remember when he last saw tears on her cheeks. It wasn't that he didn't know what to say, he didn't even know what to think.

Jennifer looked over at him. 'She said she was going to call you. Did she...?'

He shook his head. Typical Robyn. Wait until the messy, smelly stage was over and then stomp back in. 'She can't do that, surely. Social services, it was all agreed, you got the residence order.'

'And now she wants custody, Quincey. Said we can do it the hard way or the easy way. You know Fenton, he's on a good whack these days but Robyn's her mother. How would we stand a chance against her if she takes it to court?' She wiped away a tear, leaving a smear of ketchup under her left eye.

He wished she'd messaged rather than waiting to tell him in person. He'd never been good with tears, not even when they were tomato flavoured. And it would have given him time to collect his thoughts and form an opinion. It was one of the reasons he didn't like court appearances, having to think in front of people. Never a good idea, too many traps.

What would it be like if Robyn took the girl? He'd still be able to see Poppy; surely her mother wouldn't be that cruel. On the other hand... And there was the voice inside that he didn't even want to hear, whispering that it was a good idea. With a single bound, Jack could be free; no more obligatory visits, no more complaining calls from Jennifer about his failings as a father. No more visits to hide from Cath.

But what if he were to confess all? *Darling, I have a daughter, only slightly damaged.* Perhaps Cath would understand; they could decorate the spare room, Poppy wouldn't need much space. And a childminder – how much did they cost?

No, perhaps not.

A sudden thump sounded from the bedroom above, along with the sound of a child, half screaming, half crying.

No, definitely not. He wondered if he could get away while Jennifer was still upstairs.

A TEXT ARRIVED from Cath as he was passing Swindon on the way home, wondering when he could get the window fixed. '*Back Tuesday*,' it said, '*we need to talk*.' And then another, a few seconds later. '*For the avoidance of doubt, that was not a request*.' And the hits just kept on coming.

AT LEAST THIS TIME, he had confirmed that there was a meeting room available at the offices in Avonport. Joanna Dust was waiting for him in reception; he stood on the pavement outside and studied her for a few seconds through the plate glass wall of the atrium. Was this how university lecturers always dressed, he wondered? His law tutors at Avonport Uni had favoured an unstructured wardrobe in shades of beige and grey. He should have taken it as a warning sign but he'd been so delighted at being accepted on the law conversion course after a scraped 2.2 in geography, and the freedom from decision-making for another couple of years, that he wouldn't have minded if they'd dressed as Death and passed round bubonic sandwiches at lectures.

Dr Dust – he was still learning not to think of her as Joanna – sat posed under some kind of palm tree arrangement. Her colour scheme for the day was red and black. *She's come for a fight*, he thought, and wondered if he could get to the lavatories by reception without her noticing. Probably not, especially with Wanda lurking behind the desk with a piece of pre-planned abuse. Oh well, time to gird his loins, whatever that was supposed to mean.

The revolving doors caught his flight bag on the way into the building, and as he pulled it free one of the wheels came off and careened in an elegant loop across the floor towards his client. She looked up from the file she was reading as the wheel hit her foot, and her sigh reminded him of his mother.

THE ROOM that Wanda had assigned was, he guessed, probably the smallest in the entire building. A five minute trek through corridors transported from Knossos - where was Ariadne when you needed her? - no windows, a door that got within a couple of inches of shutting but no further, and opposite the ladies' loo.

'You certainly know how to show a girl a good time.'

He looked for signs of a smile, but she was busy arranging papers across the table, leaving no space for him.

'Shall we start then?' she said. 'We agreed an hour, I'll pay for no more. It would have helped if you'd emailed me your comments beforehand, as I asked. Time, Mr Radlett, it flows only one way.'

He knew he shouldn't have come, but she had agreed to pay on receipt of his fee note and the bean jar was running a little low at the moment. 'Please, I'd really rather you called me Quincey.'

'And I'd rather not. Boundaries, Mr Radlett, boundaries. So, to business. In the absence of advice from you, I did a little research of my own. Employment Appeal Tribunal cases are all published online, as I'm sure you know. You do agree that the Jelic judgement is relevant to my case? I have been persecuted, Mr Radlett, persecuted beyond endurance, and I shall not go back to work for my torturers. Find me a new job they must, and find me a new job they shall. Did you draft something to the Vice-Chancellor, as I asked?'

The damp patches under his arms were spreading, and his bladder was already full again. Perhaps the organ was shrinking, or becoming less elastic. How would one cope with an ossified bladder?

'Jelic, yes, excellent case,' he said, 'just run through your view on that again.' He wondered if he could make an excuse to go to the gents, then effect an escape and phone her from his car and claim a medical emergency.

Before he could move, she tapped the table in front of him. 'I would have thought your view was of more importance; you are the lawyer, I am the client. I have got that right, haven't I? And to make it easy, I sent you the link to the Tribunal's decision. Tell me, please tell me, that you read the case, Mr Radlett.'

He had a vague memory of an email blizzard from her after their last meeting, all the messages still unread on his laptop. But there had been so little time, what with one mistress killing herself, another growing a beard, his secret daughter about to migrate to a Welsh hinterland and his wife making veiled threats.

'My brother is a barrister, Mr Radlett. I asked him to recommend a solicitor and one of his people came up with you, although I'm beginning to wonder how. Hugo's not like me, he gets quite tetchy when things go wrong. And he will take this personally, if you under-perform to the extent you seem to be doing so far.'

Women should be banned from having brothers. Ok, maybe that would be a little difficult, but perhaps he should make it one of his questions each time a new client got in touch. Family history, the need to get a full picture - there would be a way to put it without making them suspicious.

And far from being ossified, his bladder was going into contractions like a pregnant woman whose waters had broken.

'I do have the right Quincey Radlett, don't I? I haven't made some ghastly mistake and ended up with a building janitor who happens to have the same name as a professional solicitor? Just say if this is a case of mistaken identity - it could happen to anyone, I'm sure. We'll call it quits; you go back to the mops and pails with which you feel more comfortable, and I'll find myself a real lawyer.'

She was smiling, he was sure that's how most people would define her facial expression, but there was an abyss of pain awaiting him behind those dark eyes. He wondered if she knew Cath. From somewhere he heard the sea rushing across the shingle and smelled the salt spray. All he wanted was to sink beneath the surface of the water, where it was quiet and calm and no-one could see him. He opened his mouth to reply, but nothing was happening. He had become mute. Dumb fish, stupid fish.

HE WAS ALONE in the room. She had seemed almost compassionate when she left. 'I'll tell reception to send someone,' she'd said, 'get well soon.' And at the door, 'No need to bother sending a bill. Quincey.'

IT WAS STRESS, of course, he knew that. He'd gone home, changed his clothes, locked and bolted the front and back doors and hidden in his office in the cellar. The smell of coal dust was strong today, as if he were slipping back in time.

He wanted Esther now, so badly. Not for sex, just for comfort. A warm, soft place to hide, candlelight and geranium oil. With her beside him he could sleep without dreams, or none that mattered.

But what about the man who had been arrested, Marcus, what about his dreams? Quincey realised that he had no idea what his competitor looked like; how could you imagine a man's dreams if you had never seen his face? The first result on Google was a link to Marcus's profile on the University's website, the same place he'd checked out Joanna Dust. The photograph was a surprise, a man in his early fifties with a chin and nose curling round to meet each other like Mr Punch. The cheeks were shadowed hollows and his hair was flat, as if the top of his head had been sliced off, with wisps around the ears. Was this the best image the man could find? And what could Esther have seen in this creature? Perhaps, after all, the affair had been in his imagination.

He'd heard nothing more about the arrest, so perhaps it was already yesterday's news. He looked at the photograph again; an ordinary man, if a little ill-favoured in appearance. But who was he to talk? Earlier, in the office with Joanna, when the words refused to cross the chasm between his brain and his mouth, he had felt his eyes beginning to bulge. Another stress reaction; when he was a teenager he used to examine his face in the mirror, trying to will his eyes to sink back into his face and not thrust out between the pale, ginger eyelashes. He sometimes wondered if amphibian DNA had got mixed in with his, an ancestral frog hidden somewhere in the family tree.

The roses still bothered him. Why had he taken such a pathetic gift? CCTV footage, a credit card receipt, his car number plate, all of them would be recorded somewhere, waiting to be checked. They would have held a post-mortem and by now they must have realised that whoever had made love to Esther just before she died, it wasn't Marcus.

And then there was the suicide note. He'd been carrying it around for nearly a week; he might just as well have signed his name in her blood on the bathroom wall.

His brain was surely beginning to swell, pressing on the skull.

Of course, he could always send Esther's note anonymously to the police, minus the envelope with its incriminating Q. But that would simply be the proof that someone other than Marcus had been there. Everything he had done in her flat since he found the body had been a confession of guilt. And even if he hadn't taken the razor blade to her wrists, he was guilty; how could he not be? He had been guilty since the day he was born.

VANCOUVER

Aspen looks at her watch, then double checks by the clock on the wall behind her reception desk. 2.30am, another four and a half hours before her shift ends. She folds over a corner of the page she's reading, places the book on the counter, stretches and stands. A quiet night so far, no guests complaining about noisy aircon, no drunks stumbling back from late night clubs.

She shakes her flask of coffee; at least one cup left to see her through until the day shift arrives to set her free at seven. Then back to her room for a few hours of broken sleep, followed by more studying.

Greg had threatened to drop by in the afternoon. Tutor, and lover. A bit fucked up, but that's always been the pattern of her life, so why should anything be different now?

A limo draws up outside the door, and a gaggle of teenage girls tumbles out. Aspen pushes the button to open the door and they totter in, all short skirts and high heels and smudged eyeliner. Probably not much younger than her but they seem like children, innocent and naïve.

Unformed dough. Lucky. They make it to the elevator without throwing up and pack themselves in, leaving a haze of stale smoke, cheap perfume and deodorant in the air. With luck, they'll make it to their rooms before anyone is sick, which they will be. That will be the cleaners' problems, not hers.

Four o'clock, just three more hours until she can shrug on the coat that's too thin for a Vancouver winter and go out onto the streets lined with half-melted snow. She pours a coffee and unwraps a cereal bar. Caffeine and sugar, what's not to like?

She turns back to the book, an introduction to criminology. Greg had persuaded her that if she worked hard enough, she could get into university as a mature student. A degree would mean a better job, a better job meant more money. And more money would speed up the time until she could put her plan into effect.

Who would have thought? High school had been a stretch, always trying to keep people from discovering that she was rough sleeping when she couldn't persuade someone to let her sofa surf. But she's sure of one thing; she won't end up like her mother, whoring herself out to put food on the table and ending up bruised and broken in a barely liveable trailer.

She realises she's been reading the same sentence for the third time, puts the book down and takes the note from her bag. It was waiting for her when she came on shift, from Jeanne on days. '*A couple of guys came in asking for a Cerys Morgan. I said I didn't know anyone with that name, but they had a photo of you. I said nothing. One of them was kinda creepy. Watch yourself.*'

It's seven years since she left the burning trailer behind, along with Cerys Morgan, and became Aspen Collet. A made-up name for a made-up person and it has served her well so far. No sign of Earl Lekker's brothers; she's almost forgotten about them. But who else would be looking for Cerys? In a twisted way, she feels proud for them. She knows what the need for revenge feels like, a deep-seated itch that nothing can scratch; nothing pleasant. The note is worrying, though, and not something she can ignore. She sighs and looks around the hotel lobby for the last time. It's time to move on again. With luck, Jeanne has bought her a day or so, and then she'll leave Aspen behind and get back on the road.

She's sitting by the window in her apartment, looking down onto the street, when she sees Greg's Prius drive past and park a block away. He walks back towards her building with the easy assurance of a man on his way to a lover, a long apricot scarf wrapped around his neck and his stubble carefully groomed. Every inch the second division academic with pretensions. He'd messaged earlier and said he wanted to talk about something. That's not a good sign; Greg talks at, never with, and she isn't in the mood for a lecture. She wonders, vaguely, how he would sound without a tongue.

Sleep had been as broken as expected, especially after seeing the note Jeanne had left for her. The hotel job has only ever been temporary and study was always a stupid dream. She knows she's been lazy these last few years, hiding away; there has to be a better way to make money quickly. She isn't greedy, but her plan calls for a lot more cash than she's put by, and as far as she's concerned, nothing is off the table. Crime, as she's learned, is a subjective concept. Not to mention addictive.

. . .

GREG POURS himself a glass of Merlot - he always brings a bottle and a jar of stuffed olives - and settles back into the only easy chair, still wearing the scarf and maintaining the image. She'd dodged his kiss when he came in, just a scrape of stubble on her cheek, and his disappointment is obvious in the droop of his thin, pale lips. At the same time, she can sense his excitement about something.

'I'm tired, Greg. It was a long night and I'm behind on my reading. You said you had something to talk about?'

He pops an olive in his mouth, then takes the toothpick from his beloved Swiss Army knife and dislodges some detritus from between his teeth. Building up to the big reveal. 'You, Aspen, are looking at a free man. I know you thought I'd never do it, but I told Francoise about us and said I wanted a divorce.'

She doesn't bother to stifle the sigh.

'It was almost as if she was expecting it,' he says. 'She didn't even cry, just packed a bag and said she was taking Theo to stay with her mother.' He beams as if he's given her a prize.

'I never asked you to tell her,' Aspen says. 'You and me, we're nothing more than a bit of fun, something to pass the time. You know that's always been part of the deal.'

'I know you were just being kind,' says Greg, 'not putting pressure on me.' He tosses back the wine and pours another glass. 'Now there's no need to hide anything we can make plans. I thought we could go away for a few days, maybe fly south for some sun. My treat.'

How has she got to this point? Step by small step. She'd started out babysitting for him and his wife, nothing unto-ward until the day she turned up and he opened the door stark naked. Drunk, of course, and Francoise was out. She'd pushed him away and left, but something had changed between them, as if a boundary had been breached, and eventually she'd given in. And now he's left his wife for her. Prick.

A few more weeks to get her exams out of the way and he would have outlived his usefulness. His devotion has been draining for some time, and the thought of actually being shackled to him - any man - is unsupportable. Sometimes she wonders who's doing the using.

She watches from the window as he walks back to his car, head down, dragging his feet. What had he expected from such an unconsidered announcement? He'll get home and his natural arrogance will reassert itself, but no matter. Greg was never going to be part of her future, other than as a stepping stone.

Time to slip into another skin. And soon.

ASPEN DOESN'T GO BACK to the hotel. She messages Jeanne but her pursuers haven't been back, although that doesn't mean they aren't watching. She asks what the men looked like and if there had been any doubt, there isn't now. Two men, probably brothers, one with a scar and a lazy eye. The creepy one.

The apartment still feels safe enough. If they knew where she lived, they'd have been here by now. Maybe, though, she can shift the balance of power. They might have an old photo of her, but she has the clearest image of Earl and they aren't going to look that much different from him, apart from Buck's eye and his scar. On the winter streets, with a hat, scarf and coat, she could be anyone.

SHE SPENDS TWO DAYS SEARCHING. A freezing wind bites through her coat but she keeps moving to keep warm, scanning for black Toyota pickups. Men and cars, they wear them like armour. At last she finds one parked up on Main Street outside a cheap diner. She watches for a while from across the street, huddled in a doorway. The truck's empty so they must be inside, fuelling up. She walks down a block and then back, just in time to see them come out and drive away. They pass right by her without a second glance, but there's no doubt - it's the Lekkers. Still, she might as well set a hare running. She messages Jeanne again and tells her she's moving to Chicago to stay with an aunt. If the Lekkers get back to her colleague, they'll buy themselves a wasted journey, and her a few more hours. At least, that's the plan.

CHAPTER
FIVE

The wisps of cloud were pink and purple on the horizon, the sea a grey line below. When he'd arrived at the beach, the mud and sand had stretched almost to the edge of vision, but the tide had turned and the water hadn't so much flowed back as seeped up, appearing all at once and then deepening, rising up the dark wooden lattice of the pier. The seaweed that coated the thick posts was mermaid hair, lifting and floating like someone called back to life. He hadn't even noticed the water covering his shoes, plastering his trousers to his legs. Walk forward, why not? Find that calm, quiet rest beneath the surface. The ultimate hiding place.

'Quincey Radlett, what the hell are you doing man?'

He turned with difficulty, his feet already sunk into the muddy sand, feet of clay. It was the woman and dog from the other day, standing by the edge of the water more than ten feet away. They must have been watching him for some time.

'Have you lost something? Won't find it now, tide on its

way in. Come on man, out of the water now. That's right, there's a good lad.'

It was harder than he thought to wade back, as if the sea were trying to keep him like a spurned lover who can't let go.

'That's a pair of trousers for the dry cleaners. Just let 'em dry and they'll be sticky as hell. All the salt, God's own business to get out. Take them to Ledbury's, up by the Church. My cousin runs it; strange woman, but every family has one. Mention my name, you won't get any money off but at least she won't lose them.'

The dog had lost interest and wandered off along the beach. The woman started to follow and then turned back to look at him. 'Very seductive, the sea. Stood there myself once, long time ago. But seducers never have an answer, not one worth having. Go home, man, get dry. I find a nip or two of gin usually helps.'

HE SPENT the latter part of the morning at a mediation session, which didn't go well. If he was honest with himself, the whole morning hadn't gone well. He'd made himself a boiled egg and Marmite soldiers for breakfast, but watching Marcus Haremountain making a statement of wounded innocence on the local news as he was released, followed by an inspector with an Estuary accent announcing that they were following up other promising leads, had led to a yolk that was crumbly rather than runny and no dunking.

As for the judicial mediation; the gods had foisted Employment Judge Minchin on him again and the fiasco last week hadn't been forgotten. The client was little better, a spherical man with skin like dough who had worked in the same gentleman's outfitting section of a local department store for over seventeen years. And then decided that he'd really rather not deal with customers any more. Preferably not with colleagues either. A hernia precluded the warehouse job he was offered, and a conviction that computers were the dung of Satan meant that the admin offices were mere temples to sin. Possibly true, but not germane, as Quincey had tried to point out more than once.

While he was sitting with the man at the Tribunal offices in Uskmouth, Joanna Dust sent him four emails, two texts and a voice note. He decided to save them until he got home, rather than suffer while he was in public. Deferred pain, like deferred gratification. His parents had never understood how he could put some Christmas presents aside to open on Boxing Day, or the day after, or the day after that - a small package in reindeer wrapping paper had lasted until Easter on one occasion. The anticipation was invariably better than the resolution; a bit like sex, in his experience.

There was more joy awaiting him; Cath would soon be back from the States. Not that he was sure when her flight was getting in, or even where. Heathrow, probably. Avonport airport had started flights to Newark a couple of years ago, but Cath had always been strangely phobic about New Jersey. Probably something to do with The Sopranos. This time she hadn't told him where she was staying, not that he would have contacted her. It was a long time since anything in his life had been of interest to her.

THE NOTE WAS on the hall table, where the Duchess money was usually left. He could tell that Cath had been in; a pair of her heels were stashed neatly by the front door and a trace of her perfume hung in the air; Jasmin Noir, the one she never wore when they were together. The bottle had appeared on her dressing table one morning, but he hadn't asked, not wanting to risk the answer.

He took the unread note into the kitchen, made himself a coffee, left it on the table and went up to the bedroom to check the wardrobes. No, her clothes were still mostly there as far as he could tell; he'd lost touch with her appearance. He made his way carefully back downstairs, conscious that his legs felt disconnected. His body seemed almost weightless as he held onto the banister to stop himself from floating free.

Esther's handwriting had been like an elf's, spiked and elegant, always moving forward. Cath's letters were squat, almost carved. Two notes inside a week; lucky Quincey. He read the note through twice, threw the lukewarm coffee away and made another cup, wishing he hadn't given up smoking.

Cath had never been one to mince words. '*We need some space,*' she'd written (and who were the '*we*'?), '*stay somewhere else for a while. Not the beach hut, people will talk. Get a room or a flat. A few months, see what happens. I'm in London until the end of the week, be gone when I get back. No need to leave key, just call before you come round in future.*'

And there was a PS. '*Call these people, I think they could help.*'

Quincey looked at the name, Avonport Avoiders, with a local phone number. They sounded like an American football team who didn't trust their body armour. And help with what? Right now he felt beyond the assistance of anyone.

The house was hers; she had never seen the point of joint ownership. At the time, it hadn't seem to matter. Now, in the space of a few seconds, he had become deracinated. Rootless of Kilvercombe; a battered Nissan, a couple of suits, a beach hut and a bank account that would rattle if you shook it. Not much to show for thirty-nine years.

THE MAN behind the counter in the newsagents remembered him. 'Your daughter, she liked the card? She's a very lucky girl. Some fathers...'

Quincey took a packet of extra strong mints; one of his back teeth was making a bid for freedom and he wasn't sure about the quality of his breath. A local paper too, might as well look for somewhere else to stay. The last time he'd done this was when he was a student, sharing rooms with a group of undergraduates in their second year while he was the eminence grise, the mature student trying another throw of the dice in the hope of a better score this time around.

A large cat was asleep in the shop window, under a set of postcards advertising plumbers, electricians and French teachers. And at the bottom, written in green ink on a tangerine background, was an advert for a room to let in central Kilvercombe. There was a name – Tansy – and a mobile number. A room was definitely less permanent than a flat, less threatening. You could own a room, it wouldn't own you. He stood by the doorway and called the number, watching as the cat stretched, turned a hundred and eighty degrees and curled back to sleep.

. . .

THE WOMAN's voice had a transatlantic twang. Yes, the room was still available, why not come round now? She gave him the address, an avenue of double fronted Edwardian villas running down from the church.

It was only a five-minute drive and he pulled in behind a Volkswagen camper van decorated with a pattern that reminded him of the only time he'd ever taken acid, by mistake, and watched Highway to Hell erupt in fluorescent streams from the speakers at a party in St Pauls.

The door of number five Rathbone Avenue was painted the same tangerine colour as the card in the newsagent's window, and the small front garden was a shrine of Buddhas; some obese, some ascetic, some merely contemplative. The wooden porch was curtained with a web of dream catchers in stained glass and silver, wood and feathers. He looked down at his salt stained trousers and wished he owned a pair of jeans, just to fit in.

A small brass bell hung on a bracket, but before he could ring it, the door opened. 'You must be Quincey. Come on in, honey, I don't bite. Not during the day.' Mid seventies, he guessed, and still living in the age of Aquarius. Her grey hair was braided into two plaits that reached the waistband of a full-length turquoise skirt which wouldn't have looked out of place at Woodstock. 'You okay, hon, you look kinda shell-shocked. You want tea? I have chamomile, let's go talk.'

The scent of incense – jasmine, at a guess – didn't quite cover another smell from the days when life had seemed a little richer with possibilities. The last joint he'd smoked was the one Robyn had passed to him on the first night they spent together in her cluttered bedsit. She could have told him it was skunk – he'd made it to the bathroom with seconds to spare.

The woman sat him at the kitchen table and handed him a mug of something that the cat wouldn't have disowned. 'A man your age, looking for a room, you don't have to tell me something's wrong. It's okay, not going to pry, a person needs secrets sometimes.' The freckles on her hands were gradually morphing into liver spots and the lines on her face were proudly free of makeup, but she had been a looker once. Still was, in a disconcerting way. 'You want a cookie? I baked some this morning.'

'No, thanks. The room?'

'Oh, that. It's yours, honey, I make quick decisions. Soon as I saw you I thought, that man needs Tansy's help, needs to lighten up a tad, find some peace.' She smiled like one of the statues in the front garden.

'I just thought,' he said, 'perhaps I could see it first?'

IT WASN'T HOME, but it would be more comfortable than the truckle bed in the beach hut. A double bed, a wardrobe, a chair constructed from woven tree branches, some still mottled with moss. The bay window looked onto the street; not too much traffic, he could sleep here. Just before he left to go back for his clothes and files – between the beach hut and the room he'd manage without an office for a while – Tansy had shown him the other rooms downstairs. 'Mi casa es su casa, yada yada. There's broadband and beanbags, no TV though. You okay with that? Who needs it anyway; God was on a high the day he invented the Internet.'

'And in there?' He was standing by the door she hadn't opened, opposite the living room.

'Don't you worry about that. I'm still struggling with attachment, but then doesn't everyone? You go through life, you collect crap. Either you leave it along the way or you store it somewhere. I keep mine in that room and one day I'll learn to let go – just not yet. Like St Augustine, huh? Make me chaste and celibate, God, but just not yet. Between you and me, honey, chance would be a fine thing.'

CHAPTER SIX

The next morning, Quincey went through the files in the cellar at home and realised how few he needed to take. A good thing, given the circumstances. He paused at the top of the stairs and looked back down on his room; the desk, the office chair he had bought second-hand on eBay, a sprung mouse trap on one of the bookshelves, bereft of mouse, and a half-empty mug of cold coffee. One of the Duchesses could see to that.

He felt a tightness in his chest as if something inside was curling into a ball for protection, his inner hedgehog. Would he see this room again? This house? It already looked alien, and he had the sense of never having really belonged here as if he were no different from one of the rodents hiding away in the skirting boards. Tolerated, sometimes hunted, never safe. And now he was running away to his own hole in the wall.

He piled the portable property by the front door; two suits, a suitcase with the least objectionable underwear and some socks, the two shirts Esther had bought him for his last birthday, the ones with the pastel stripes that he'd had to pretend he'd bought for himself when Cath asked, clearly not believing that he would have had such good taste. His two spare pairs of shoes which, now he came to look at them, seemed like something one might find in a skip or a charity shop. The Burberry coat that Cath had given him for Christmas, in one of her absent-minded fits of affection. Or guilt. The one-wheeled flight bag packed with papers, and a selection of bags-for-life containing box files. And the gold Cross ballpoint Ma had given him for his sixteenth birthday, with his name engraved in italics on the side. That had been a good day.

An earlier drizzle had turned into insistent needles of rain. He filled the boot of the car with the bags and laid the suits on the back seat. Then remembered the bike. Suits moved to the front seat, front wheel off, both front seats pushed forward, bike jammed into the back. It was only when he started the engine that he noticed the sheet of paper slipped under one of the windscreen wipers. He turned them on, hoping to dislodge the flyer, but it arced gracefully backwards and forwards across the glass without any sign of leaving. The needles had turned to bullets, drumming on the roof of the car.

Quincey left the engine and the wipers running, opened the door and tried to stretch round to catch the paper as it swung in his direction. He missed it the first time, tore a corner the second and then scored a catch. He was about to let it drop to the ground when he realised that it looked different from the usual '50p off your first pizza delivery'. Not so glossy, monochrome.

Water dribbled down the back of his neck and into his ears (Bates, the school swimming instructor, ex-Royal Marine, holding him under at the deep end with a boat hook). He slammed the car door a little harder than he'd meant to and replaced the handle without help from the perished elastic band he'd used the last time it fell off. And then he looked at the crumpled and torn paper. Despite the rain, the printed letters on the sheet of white A4 hadn't run. A decent printer then, not using the cheap ink cartridges that he'd been reduced to. He forced the words to behave themselves, and as he read the hedgehog inside curled tighter and tighter, a ball of spines puncturing his viscera.

There wasn't much; a couple of lines, marks on a page. Of course, it could have been meant for anyone. There was no address on it, no name. No salutation. But whoever left this knew what he – or she – was doing.

'Tomorrow at eleven, Uskmouth crematorium. It's possible Esther wouldn't want you there, but her wishes don't count any more. Neither do yours.'

It was a week today that Esther had died, a week in which everything had changed. In the back of his mind was the constant worry that the police would find him and blame him, but not this. Going to the funeral was out of the question. There was no connection between him and Esther; he had told no-one about her and she'd kept his existence secret as far as he knew. So who was this person? How had they found him? Even Esther had never known his home address.

Quincey read the note again. It was innocuous enough, read objectively, but who could be objective in a situation like this? Perhaps – another lifeboat in the mist – it was simply a neighbour of Esther's who had noticed his car on one of his other visits and done a little well-meaning detective work, being a good Samaritan. But the mist closed quickly and the lifeboat disappeared; if that were the case, why be so cryptic? And what was that about wishes?

Something told him this note wouldn't be the last, so

perhaps Cath had done him a favour after all. Unless someone were to follow him now through the streets – a possibility, but not one he wanted to entertain – then the move to Tansy's could throw the mysterious writer off the scent. He could go to Bruford's in the High Street, buy one of those car covers and travel by bike as much as possible. With luck, there would be no more unwanted epistles and the inner hedgehog could unwind and go back to bumbling about in the undergrowth of his life.

HE HAD HEARD cocks crowing before, but not outside his bedroom window at 6:30 in the morning. Who would have thought a bird could make so much noise? And the smell of jasmine and dope from yesterday had been replaced by a melange of something sweet and sickly with high notes of burning insulation. It reminded him, for reasons that he couldn't quite place, of the time the council rat man had come round to the house. At first he had thought the sound above the bed was the mice, setting up an outpost in the attic, but after a couple of weeks even he had to admit that it sounded more like a 24-hour construction site above the bedroom ceiling, and the sight of a rat in the fruit bowl, balancing on an apple like an elephant in a circus, had tipped the balance. He hadn't told Cath.

Quincey swung his legs out of the bed and collected a splinter from the unvarnished floor boards. The curtains were tie-died blue cotton, dotted with cigarette burns and thin as bible paper. He pulled one aside carefully, worried that it might crumble in his hands, and looked down on a cockerel the size of a small spaniel, perched on the low wall of the front garden. While most of the body was white, with a red comb and wattles, the tail feathers glowed a vivid, chemical blue.

The bird looked up and crowed with a self-certainty that made the French connection seem ever more likely. Quincey opened the window and thought better of throwing his least prepossessing shoe. The bird paced backwards and forwards along the top of the wall as if weighing its options, then stopped in front of him and crowed triumphantly at full volume .

The shoe was still in his hand when he heard the door opening.

'You met Sarkozy, then,' said Tansy. 'Didn't wake you, did he? I couldn't make up my mind whether you like to rise early or late – I said to Sarkozy, go easy on the boy, but he never listens to me. On the other hand, he keeps the hens happy. You want eggs for breakfast?'

She showed him the chicken coop after a three egg omelette and coffee that should have been reclassified as a Class A drug. 'I call them my girls, hate to think what Sarkozy calls them. When you don't have children in your life you need something alive to care for.'

'Wouldn't a cat have been easier?'

'You ever seen a cat lay an egg? No, me neither. Anything in my life has to pay its way. It's win-win, good karma all round.' They wandered through the garden back towards the house, past raised beds of various vegetables and fruits. 'I eat organic when I can, who knows what they put in food these days. Tomatoes with fish genes, potatoes related to a squid. Don't get me wrong, I like progress but I also like to recognise what I eat.'

'There's something I forgot to mention yesterday,' he said. 'I have a bike, I wondered if I could keep it round the back here.'

'No problem, hon. Didn't have you figured that way —
what is it, Harley? Indian? I used to ride Herman's Moto
Guzzi after he passed, but it got too heavy and I sold it a
couple of years ago to a man from Hebden Bridge; what a
beard! I still miss it – the bike, not the beard. Any time you
want to take me for a ride, I give good pillion.'

'No, just a push bike. Twenty-seven speed gears,
though. Shimano.'

'I take back the pillion offer. There's kooky and there's
just plain weird. You can store it in the lean-to by the chickens, should stay pretty dry there.'

AFTER PACKING AWAY the few possessions in his room,
Quincey found the note that Cath had left him. It was like
her to be enigmatic; he'd complained once about her lack of
clarity in marital instructions and she'd told him that as a
good husband, he should pick up her intentions by osmosis.
What was he, a plant?

He looked at the name again; Avonport Avoiders. So
what were these people avoiding and what if they wanted
to avoid him as well? He called the number on his mobile
but hung up as soon as it was answered. A woman's voice,
rather perky, which wasn't what he had been expecting, not
that he could have articulated his expectations in any
coherent form.

He tried again on his laptop, googling the name, but
there were no hits. Very queer. He considered ignoring
Cath's injunction to get in touch with these people but he
was a solicitor and a husband, and both roles involved
taking instruction. Back to the phone, then.

ON THE ROAD

The Lekkers might buy her fake news about travelling to Chicago but she can't take any necessary risks, so she sets the alarm on her cell for five in the morning. Packing will take no time; she's long since learned to travel light. No attachments makes life so much easier. When you have nothing, you have nothing to lose.

She wakes to a sound from her phone but it's still dark and too early for the alarm. It's a text from Jeanne who'd taken over on nights. *'They came back. Had to give your address, sorry. They had my son.'* Aspen moves from asleep to fully awake in less than a single breath. She swings out of bed, wishing she'd replaced the knife that some cunt stole last year when she was sleeping rough, but it's already too late. She hears more sounds on the other side of her bedroom door; someone is in the apartment and the place is scarcely a palace, so they'll be in the bedroom any second. One person or two? Two, at least. She can almost feel the pull of their presence through the walls, and there's nothing she can use as a weapon.

The door handle turns slowly. For a moment she

considers the window, but it's three stories down onto concrete. Not good odds either way. Back against the wall, then, behind the door. Her only plan is to slam it into whoever tries to enter and then run past them. Or will it be better to let them come into the room and then try to escape?

Decision time. The door starts to swing open and two men step in cautiously, focussed on the bed opposite. As they move forward she darts around the door but it would never have worked. Before she's halfway across the living space, someone grabs one of her arms, almost dislocating her shoulder. He swings her around and then she feels the almost muffled crunch of something hitting her head as everything turns dark.

A JOLT BRINGS her back to consciousness. She tries to move, but her hands and feet are tied together and thick tape covers her mouth. At least she can breathe. She calms herself, forcing her heartbeats to slow, and takes stock. She's on her back in a vehicle, probably under the hard top on the pickup she saw them in earlier. Her feet and hands are numb with cold and her head pounds where her attacker knocked her out.

After the jolt that brought her back to consciousness, the truck is travelling more smoothly. It's hard to judge their speed, but it's steady, so that means they're on a highway, not in a city. After a few minutes, the speed drops and the truck sways as they turn a corner, then another, and come to a stop.

The boot opens with a soft, expensive swish of servo motors. Against the poorly lit backdrop of a motel block stand two men, looking down at her. The Lekkers at last, just not the way she'd wanted to meet them.

'I told you,' says the one with the scar on his cheek. Buck. He's high on something, his voice teetering on the edge of a crazy giggle. 'We'll just leave her in here overnight. She can't go anywhere and not like she's gonna be screaming for help.'

'We should carry on back to Ma. We're wasting time.' Ches, the businessman.

'Lighten up, bro. We got her at last. I'm celebrating tonight. Maybe come back and have some fun with her later; maybe knock her around a little first. Always wanted to have me a redhead... feisty little bitches.'

Ches shakes his head. 'You know what Ma said, no touching till we got her home. But maybe you're right, I could do with a drink and we can't risk getting pulled over with her in the back.'

She's already just an object to them. They'd talk like this about a dog.

Ches pushes a button on a remote. The boot doors fold shut, and she hears the men walk away. If she can roll onto her side she might be able to sit up; it takes a few minutes but eventually she props herself against the side of the truck. She tries to flex her wrists and feet but the ties are too tight, and from what she can see there are no convenient sharp edges to let her cut herself free. The Lekkers aren't that dumb, even if they hadn't locked the truck.

She sits back for a few minutes, her heartbeat rising again. How could she have been so stupid? As soon as she saw the note from Jeanne, she should have run. Packed her gear and left the city within the hour. Now it's too late, and she tries not to think about what will be waiting when they get her back to Fraserwood.

She tries to rotate her injured shoulder. Thankfully it's just pulled, if painful, and then she hears footsteps scuffling around the back of the truck. Surely they're not back already, or perhaps they've decided to have some fun with her after all. The truck rocks slightly on its suspension as she hears a scraping sound by the rear doors, metal on metal, and suddenly one of them jerks open to show Greg with the tire iron he used to lever the boot open. He lifts his finger to his mouth, as if she could make any sound, then pushes the lower door down and clambers in next to her.

'Don't worry,' he whispers, hunkered down in front of her. 'I got this.' He doesn't even sound ridiculous.

She'll never laugh at a Swiss Army knife again. He cuts through the zip ties and peels the tape from her mouth.

'Can you walk?' he asks.

She nods, not trusting her voice yet, and lets him help her out of the truck. He carefully pushes the boot doors shut, as well as he can, and supports her along the row of curtained motel rooms to his Prius waiting in a small car park at the side. He's about to help her in when she stops him and whispers.

'You should slash their tires. It won't stop them altogether, but it will slow them down. Be careful.'

As he trots off in a half crouch, she decides that this has been a very weird day.

THEY DON'T TALK until the motel disappears behind a curve in the road and they reach the on-ramp to the highway. 'I couldn't sleep,' says Greg. 'I came back and parked near your apartment. I meant to call you to see if we could talk, but I guess I didn't have the balls, not after what happened yesterday. Then I saw the truck draw up and two men go into your building. A few minutes later, they came out with you between them. You didn't look so good.'

'Why didn't you call the police?' she says.

He pauses for a couple of seconds before replying. 'I've known you for a while, Aspen. You've always been closed down, private. I knew there were things in your life you didn't want to talk about and I told myself that was ok. Perhaps it was one of the things that made you so attractive, that sense of mystery. I know I'm pompous, but I'm not stupid. My life has been so sedate. Boring, if I'm honest. You brought me fireworks, whoever you are. Is Aspen even your real name? It doesn't matter, you don't need to say. But I guessed you'd rather not get on any official radar, so I followed the van rather than call anyone. I didn't have a plan, I just thought... To be honest, I didn't think. I just reacted.'

Her head's throbbing, and when she tests the place she was hit she can feel that the hair around the bruise is matted with her blood. She looks over at Greg, still wearing his apricot scarf. She's rarely surprised by people, but he's managed.

He overtakes a sedan, pulls in and smiles at her. 'What now? You want me to take you back to the apartment?'

'No. As soon as they realise what's happened, they'll call someone. They'll be waiting for me if I go home.'

'But your stuff?'

'There's nothing there I need. Except money. Can you let me have some? Anything?'

'No problem,' he says. 'We'll find an ATM. And then what? I can take you anywhere you want to go.'

A few hours ago he'd offered to shackle himself to her, now he's her ticket to freedom. 'You're a kind man, Greg, but it's best I don't tell you where I'm going.' As if she knows herself. 'I know it's a cliché,' she says, 'but just forget you ever knew me.'

AT THE ATM in a small town a couple of miles off the highway, he gives her one thousand dollars. 'I can't take this,' she says, but lets him persuade her.

The sky is already beginning to lighten. 'I'll get a bus from here,' she says, 'I'll be ok now. And do me a favour. Call Francoise, tell her you had a breakdown and didn't mean it about the divorce. Ask her to come home, with Theo. Families should stay together.'

SHE STANDS and watches the car drive away until the tail lights fade into the distance, then turns and makes her way towards the centre of town. Time to head east.

CHAPTER
SEVEN

The early evening air was soft and welcoming and there was no sense in tempting fate, so he took his bike rather than the car and padlocked it to the railings outside the address he'd been given. He was early for a change, and not the only one. This part of town was usually empty after the offices shut, and the University Hospital kept to itself these days now that the A&E department had shut down.

Avonport Avoiders; the five people littering the pavement were living up to their name. Four of them were smoking but in isolation rather than the usual companionable huddle of addicts. The fifth, a woman who clearly had insufficiently caring family and friends or they would have warned her about the leggings with the short tee shirt, was pacing up and down, examining the screen of her mobile phone every five steps or so, and sighing audibly.

One of the smokers, a woman whose face reminded him of his first rabbit, glanced across as he finished removing the front wheel from his bike, and essayed a smile. A white van drew up, driven – as far as Quincey could see – by an ex-Archbishop of Canterbury. Perhaps the beard was protection against unchaste thoughts; who in her right mind could feel amorous with that crawling towards her across the pillows? A woman in hessian bounced herself out from the passenger seat, said 'see you later Terry' – not the Primate of All England then – and came across to the fissiparous group.

'Hello Tina, Jerry, Lakshmi. Is that Toby over there – he's never talking to Gorinda! And you must be Quincey. We spoke earlier, you changed your mind then.'

She'd sounded younger on the phone, less homely. No beard rash so maybe Terry was just a neighbour, or her vicar. Or were they married but in a brother/sister relationship? So many options, no wonder he sometimes felt confused. The woman whose name he was trying to remember - Gaynor, he seemed to recall - pottered down the fire escape steps to a door in the basement of the building.

The smell from a half-empty bag of ketchup-drizzled chips lying by the bottom step made him both hungry and ashamed at the same time. He should have eaten before he left Tansy's, but he wasn't sure of the food protocols yet. And now he was about to spend a couple of hours sitting in a circle with a group of social phobics while his stomach played atonal symphonies. He thought of going back to the street, but rabbit girl was so close behind that they collided as he paused by the door. No whiskers and her scent was a mixture of tobacco smoke and ginger beer, which he found disconcerting if reassuring. Jasmin Noir would have been quite out of keeping with the time and place; he tried to imagine Cath as part of the group, but he knew she would rather bathe in bleach than lower herself to this diminishment. Another reminder, as if one were needed, of where he fitted in the hierarchy of life.

The space was vast, some kind of storeroom with chairs stacked against the walls, collapsed collapsible tables and a cluster of exhibition screens with a bedraggled foliage of posters hanging by their corners. At the far end was a makeshift stage; surely they wouldn't be asked to perform.

The others seemed well practised at the rigmarole, each fetching a chair and arranging themselves in a punctuated circle.

'Come on now, cwtch up a bit,' said Gaynor. 'You too Gorinda, you won't catch anything nasty.' He hadn't noticed the accent before, Welsh-lite with just a hint of a melody underneath the words. 'And now we're settled, I want to introduce our new member - Quincey, is it?'

There was an inchoate murmur from the others, which he interpreted as some kind of welcome, and then one of the men started to sob, a small, private sound that seemed out of place in front of other people even though the others ignored him. Quincey was used to having this effect on women, but not usually on men. An inducement to despair, his therapist had called it, which had struck him at the time as rather unkind, not to say unfair.

The structure of the meeting soon became clear, with each person relating their successes and failures at personal interactions during the preceding week. The sobbing man had managed over ten minutes in Lidl, a heroic effort for anyone in Quincey's opinion, Tina the rabbit girl had managed to speak for long enough to hold a conversation with someone in her office, Lakshmi had sat on a park bench without being hit by a falling asteroid.

Quincey wondered what he was doing here. Wasn't he a professional used to working with people, holding down a relationship, sometimes more than one at a time? He wasn't like this collection of misfits, so proud of their tiny achievements. So why had he come? Why had Cath, not known for her empathy, suggested this?

As Gorinda described how she'd taught a class for the first time in a year without a Valium to cushion the anxiety, Quincey rehearsed his contribution. Mistress killed herself, wife thrown him out, an attack of muteness during a client meeting, dreams of living in a beach hut or a car boot. No, he'd have to invent a different story, or they'd think he was weird.

After an hour, Gaynor called a break and Quincey followed the others outside. He seemed to be the only one not smoking and almost accepted when Tina offered him one of hers, a shy proffering of the crumpled packet. 'You came by bike,' she said, 'looked like a posh one. I used to have a racer till my dad sold it one day while I was at school. I loved my bike, not sure I'd have the puff these days. Red, it was, and gold. Wouldn't mind a better look at yours.'

He followed her up the steps and they both stared at the empty railings where he'd chained the bike. 'Oh dear,' she said, 'scags everywhere these days. Not far to go, have you?'

What would anyone want with a one-wheeled bike? Once again, the goblins of spite were pissing on him from their shadows. He collected the abandoned front wheel, told Gaynor he had to go and called Tansy from the street, not knowing what else to do. Within ten minutes, the camper van arrived like a floral rescue chariot.

'Not your week, is it hon?' The passenger seat in the

front was upholstered in red velvet and speckled with large grey and white dots. 'Don't mind those, I cleaned the worst off so they shouldn't stain. It's Lili Marlene, she gets excited whenever I go over thirty. I try to get her to stay in back, but I might as well be talking to myself.'

As if on cue, something landed on Quincey's shoulder and he yelped with surprise as a horny beak gnawed at his left earlobe.

'Lili, get off the man! Damn that bird - Lili! If I told you once; any more of this and we're off to the fjords. And I tell you, girl, only one of us is coming back and it aint gonna be you.'

The gnawing stopped as Quincey turned to look. He caught a flash of blue feathers and then felt a raking burn down his nose.

'She likes you, knew she would. Here, you want a Kleenex for the blood?'

TANSY ASSURED him that the waterproof plaster on his nose didn't make him look like a complete tosser. He was glad there was no-one else to see him, although it would have been worse five minutes ago when she was rubbing the wound with a crushed clove of garlic. 'Beats TCP any day. Anti-viral, garlic. Great for earache - put a clove in each ear, go to sleep. You wake up smelling like salami, but the pain's gone. Trust me.'

He decided not to mansplain the difference between bacteria and viruses. 'Why didn't you tell me you had a parrot?'

'I only use the P word when I'm cross with her. She's a macaw, blue and gold. Never forget the gold, she's kinda proud of it.' They were sitting in the kitchen, with the bird perched on a cabbage, preening. 'Lili kinda freaks people out, but she's a sweetie when you get to know her. I just thought I'd let you settle in first before making the introductions.'

She rolled a joint, a thick carrot in liquorice paper. 'It's age, honey, your tastes get more sophisticated. That's what I tell myself. Home grown, I grew up with mellow, don't need trips any more.' She looked thoughtful for a moment. 'Shrooms, though, they're different. But without a desert, the visions are crap - Kilvercombe just ain't New Mexico, the spirit guides like it warm, and why not?'

Lili swapped the cabbage for Quincey's head. 'See, I told you. Just keep the movements slow, she don't like surprises.'

The bird was heavier than he'd imagined and he remembered a picture in a schoolbook about the Spanish Inquisition. It showed a man with his head encased in a steel helmet and a torturer tightening screws to crush his skull. He'd always thought that the torturee seemed remarkably unconcerned, as if this were an everyday occurrence.

'I think she's hungry,' said Tansy 'You want ice cream, baby?'

Lili started a stately jig on his head, in what he assumed was a display of psittacine joy.

'I make it myself,' said Tansy, 'low fat, obviously. Hey, Lili, you come here, let the man go get you a treat.'

With a last kneading of her claws, the bird jumped across the kitchen table and turned to face him. It looked rather sombre, he thought, as if it had given up trying to categorise him and found him a disappointment. Just like all the other women in his life.

'You mind, honey? The freezer's in the conservatory -

look for the margarine tub, left-hand side. Here, have a drag of this - sweet, huh?'

Tansy handed him the joint, and he inhaled carefully before handing it back. Not so bad, and he suppressed the worst of the coughing until he was out of the room.

The freezer was a chest model, like the one his parents had at the back of the garage. He remembered the discussions about how much of a pig to buy, then the delivery of chunks of dead animal wrapped in polythene. What would a vegetarian freeze, apart from Ben & Jerry's for parrots?

He lifted the lid, looked down into the glazed eyes of a frosted weasel that appeared to be relaxing on top of a sack of frozen peas, and dropped the lid again. Tansy had said mellow, hadn't she? He lifted the lid again, slowly, but the weasel was still there. Jammed in against the peas was something else, this time with feathers and a beak that could have gone ten rounds with Lili's. On the plus side, the margarine tub was where she'd said.

Back in the kitchen Tansy was blowing smoke into Lili's face, and he could swear the parrot was smiling.

'You wanna feed her? You sure? They say it helps with the bonding.' She opened the tub and excavated spoonfuls of the mixture with creamy lumps and black specks. The parrot waddled across and began to pick delicately. 'This is her favourite, I don't often get to make it. Me, I prefer Cherry Garcia, but what would the world be if we were all the same?' She handed him the spoon. 'Your turn, I need to go pee.'

Only one puff of the joint and already he had the munchies. He scooped a spoonful and tasted it - a gritty vanilla - before giving another to Lili who had squawked angrily when he fed himself rather than her. He was still thinking about the weasel.

Lili had given up with the spoon and held the margarine tub with one claw while she raked furrows in the surface of the ice cream with her beak. Quincey looked around; Cath would hate this room with its archaeology of accretions, he thought, with its posters and photos and lists blu-tacked to the walls. He left the parrot and went over to one of the larger pictures, just above the fridge. The colours reminded him of TV programmes when he was a boy, as if everything had been filmed through a brown filter, but there was no mistaking a teenage Tansy - the skirt was almost identical to the one she wore every time he saw her - although he guessed her breasts could no longer defy gravity in quite the same way as they so evidently did back then. She and the girl she was embracing were both topless. From the look of the crowds in the background, they weren't the only ones.

'Vanity, I know.' Tansy was standing next to him, smelling of patchouli. 'I told you I had a problem with attachment, but who wants to let go of the good times. I was sixteen, Lori was a year older. I worshipped that girl, more fool me. Year later she went to Bryn Mawr, I heard she married a dentist. Sometimes I wonder, what if?'

'Where were you when this was taken?' he asked.

'Woodstock. If I could go back in time...' She reached out to the photo but stopped as if to touch was forbidden.

He was sure she'd said she had a husband once.

'One thing I learned early was that you gotta take affection where you find it, don't matter what body parts it has,' she said. 'There's little enough love in this world, not the right kind. You find someone warm and willing, you don't turn them down, never know when the next chance might come.'

Tansy shooed Lili away from the half empty tub. 'I told

you, girl, when that batch is gone you gotta wait till I find more maggots.'

'Maggots?'

'Ant and Maggot Surprise, she likes the protein. You sure you're not sickening for something?'

H e retrieved the front wheel from the back of Tansy's camper van. How many times had he ridden the bike? Three times, max, he hadn't needed to wash the Lycra shorts yet, and it probably wasn't even covered by insurance now that he was an itinerant lawyer unprotected by their home cover. And even if it was, he would have had to report the theft to the police. Moving above the radar, not really optimal given the circumstances.

He walked through the kitchen, skirted the freezer in the conservatory - why hadn't he asked Tansy about the weasel? - then past the vegetable beds to the shed. For some reason, it felt proper for the wheel to go to its own resting place, even if it had been a rather short-term accommodation. The door was slightly ajar and as he pulled it fully open, he saw the bike propped against the far wall; 27 speed Shimano shifters, Reynolds frame, Schwalbe tyres. Tyre, singular, the other was in his hand. No sign of the padlock.

He turned and looked out at the garden for a reality check, then back into the half-gloom of the shed with its smells of wood and oil, earth and rubber. The bike was still there, looking rather forlorn, with its empty front forks resting on a frayed plastic sack. He felt as if he might cry.

He replaced the front wheel and lowered himself to sit next to it, looking out at the garden. Someone was playing games. First the note, then the bike. Acid surged up into his throat as he realised; he had been found. Surely it was only a matter of time before he would feel hot breath on his neck and handcuffs around his wrists, and after the shenanigans in the bathroom with her body, who would believe he wasn't to blame?

Today was her funeral, the last goodbye, the last opportunity to be close to her. He couldn't go, how could he go? On the other hand...

He levered himself up and rested his hand on the narrow saddle, resisting the impulse to close the shed door and relax into the safety of the shadows. This could be his chance to smoke out the game-playing stalker. His heart was racing as if he were about to perform in court. But did he even want to know? Wouldn't it be better to move on and leave this Quincey behind? Shed his skin, like a serpent.

But the idea wouldn't leave him now. Eleven o'clock at Uskmouth crematorium; it was too far for the bike, but just doable if he drove. He could pretend to visit someone else's plot of ashes in the garden of remembrance and there would be no need to join the service, he could simply lurk like an anonymous ghost under the cypress trees for a silent, private farewell as her coffin passed by. But for safety's sake, a little disguise might be in order and a hat might help.

. . .

HE MADE it with fifteen minutes to spare, parked a couple of streets away and checked his appearance in the rear-view mirror. Not an image that really worked for him and the striped wool of Tansy's bobble hat, lifted from the coat hooks by the front door, smelled of stale parrot, but along with sunglasses and stubble he didn't resemble a hotshot lawyer and lover. Provincial lawyer and philanderer? Every inch an Avonport Avoider, though. Perhaps he always had been.

Clumps of people in shades of sadness were standing outside the main crematorium building. He knew he should walk past, head for the Garden of Remembrance and watch from a place of hiding, but that woman must be her mother, standing like a black sun orbited by a cloud of minor planets. That's how Esther would have looked, given another quarter of a century of life; tamed hair defying grey, quietly encapsulated in her own isolation. Someone was talking to her and she was smiling the polite acknowledgement of grief, but even from here he could see that the words were failing to reach their target. He had done this. He was the thief of life.

He wondered how many people would come to his funeral. Cath, probably, if only to complain over his coffin about how thoughtless he was to die while she was in the middle of an important case. Robyn? Even if she did, he wouldn't recognise her. Jennifer would be there out of a sense of sororal duty, shepherding his daughter if Robyn hadn't effected her escape by then. And a priest of some sort, he supposed, sadly describing the purgatory that awaited him. Or had purgatory been banished in some encyclical that had passed him by? It didn't matter. Only venial sins could be washed away in that waiting room of judgement and his were surely mortal. Hell would be his destination, if it existed, eternal separation from whatever called itself God these days.

He shambled past, trying to look as if he didn't belong, but as he got to within a few yards of Esther's mother, heads began to swivel in his direction like a field of dark daisies seeking the sun. Was it the bobble hat? Had he missed the wanted posters with his face staring out?

And then he realised that they were staring past him, not at him. The hearse had arrived. He looked back, unable to stop himself, as the coffin - pale wood, white lilies - was hoisted onto the shoulders of the undertaker's men. Someone detached himself from one of the clumps of mourners and joined them, a last chore. An old lover, perhaps, or a brother, not that she'd ever mentioned one. But he'd never asked; her family was none of his affair, and he wondered how many other secrets had died with her that day.

The space was emptying as the groups nodded and dabbed and filtered inside. Quincey let them go and then followed the path through the beds of pink and yellow roses until he reached the line of trees and bushes, a liminal space bordering the lawn of ashes. He was conscious of trying not to breathe. He'd watched a TV documentary once, when he was young. A middle-aged man with a domed forehead and hipster trousers stood up to his calves in a Polish swamp outside Auschwitz, a soup of human remains. *This is what happens when men aspire to be gods*, the man said. It was hard enough aspiring to be human.

Traffic hummed from behind the high fence, which kept the world of the living at bay. The shrubs had deep green leaves that looked almost artificial and he wondered what would cost more; a gardener to keep the plants growing, or a cleaner to housekeep the dust and rain spots away? Surely a crematorium wouldn't have plastic shrubs; he picked surreptitiously at a nearby stem, feeling slightly relieved when it snapped in his hand, moist with sap. No sap in Esther.

Of course, they didn't burn the bodies straight away. He remembered an RE field trip to a crematorium when he was at school; religious education taught by an atheist had its quirks. Other kids went to Lourdes, you had to wonder. There was a talk by a humanist celebrant who had shown them the button on the lectern that activated the conveyor belt under the coffin, to take it behind the blue velvet drapes to where there wasn't, apparently, an instant drop into a furnace but a filing system of bodies in their pine and mahogany caskets, queuing for eternity.

After the talk he had wandered away from the main group being shown how the giant crucifix at the front could be substituted by a star of David, or nothing, and found himself behind the heavy curtains that divided the living from the dead. On one side of the room were the shelves of ashes in their plastic bottles, and then the ovens, two of them. One was cold and empty, filmed with fine grey powder, the other was glowing through the glass; *the fat ones take so much longer*, a voice behind him said, *really screws up the timetable*. The bureaucracy of death; maybe there was no other way.

He wondered why he was here in a garden of ash. What had he expected? Some sort of catharsis, a puncturing of the bubble of guilt? The space outside the building was empty, while inside they were replaying Esther's life; the edited highlights, the bits they knew about. They would tidy her up and put her away and go back to their lives, and no-one would know about her last night except him. Him and the person who had left the note.

There was no point in staying here any longer. He felt vaguely nauseous, not an acid bile but the empty sickness that comes with the loss of... Hope? Direction? Self? Just loss, perhaps. Surely that was enough.

He made his way back to the entrance gates, taking the perimeter path past the miniature plaques. He thought, on balance, that he preferred graveyards.

THE NOTE under the windscreen wiper was no surprise, which surprised him. He considered not reading it, as if that would somehow negate the spell. What power would the words have if they weren't assimilated? Could imagination be any worse than the reality? All the same, he took the folded paper and stuffed it in his pocket. There would be time.

THE PARROT SNATCHED the bobble hat as soon as he let himself in through the front door, and perched on the newel post with the scrap of wool hanging like a trophy from one claw. How many ants and maggots could a parrot eat in a day? He would have thought seeds would be preferable, if asked, but live and learn.

The door from the hallway into Tansy's private room was slightly ajar. Quincey knocked, a questioning, hesitant tap that really didn't want an answer, and was rewarded with silence. He pushed the door open a little more and peered in; the curtains were half drawn, giving the space a cool and attenuated air. What was it she had said about attachment and possessions? The room looked like the inside of a Victorian junk shop and seemed to stretch out of sight as if it had no walls other than those formed from shadows. A number of glass display cases were interspersed with chests and tables, some of them covered with decorated rugs like an Amsterdam living room.

Inside the case nearest the door, bordered by mahogany and brass edges and staring into an empty eternity, was a static weasel, its front feet raised slightly on a posed branch covered with moss, a golden-throated mouse curled below it like a sacrifice. Was this the one he'd seen in the freezer yesterday? Surely not, although perhaps he ought to check later, just for peace of mind. He began a circumnavigation of the room, and as he rounded a pine tallboy he saw, leaning over a table littered with the bodies of small songbirds, a man holding a scalpel, peering through the spectacles perched on the end of his nose as he prepared to cut into the belly of a robin.

Quincey heard himself squeak, a girlish ejaculation which surprised him almost as much as the shock he felt when he backed into a wooden dressmaker's dummy, dressed like Fay Wray, which surely wasn't there a moment ago. The two of them fell to the ground in a failed tango, the dummy's string of jet beads wrapping itself around his neck as if in some strange lover's ritual. He fought with the jewellery to disentangle his limbs, only just remembering not to apologise as he pushed himself upright, using Fay's left breast to steady himself.

Perhaps the man by the table was deaf? There had been no movement – in fact, he was still in exactly the same pose, scalpel hovering above feathers.

The dust from the fall hung in the air and a sneeze was coming; he could feel it whipping itself into a frenzy in his left nostril. He tried to hold it in, but the emission set the chandelier above his head tinkling like crystals in a summer breeze.

He made his way over to the tableau. The man was a marvel of taxidermy, with eyes of glass and two ears that didn't quite match, but the texture of the skin was a masterpiece. He couldn't help himself; he reached out to straighten the spectacles on the man's face and the left ear fell off. At least his reflexes were still okay; he caught it mid-descent and fielded it straight back onto the table where it rested next to the robin like the model for a Dali painting.

'I never did get that ear right.' Tansy had come into the room without him noticing. 'I think that was about the tenth attempt – it's like painting, always wanting to add just another dab of colour. You just have to say 'enough' and let it go.' She picked up the ear and held it against the man's head. 'He always had selective hearing, Herman. Said it was a man thing, they just couldn't hear women's voices properly. Damned biological reductionists, what do they know? He could hear just fine when we were under the blankets and I was asking him what I could do to make him happy. Still, he's the one ended up getting stuffed.'

Quincey resisted the urge to back away again in case another dummy was lying in wait for him, as Tansy laid the ear back down on the table. 'Quincey Radlett, meet Herman McInerney. My husband, as was. We had what you might call an alternative lifestyle, he was one of the Hells Angels at Altamont in sixty-nine, Oakland chapter. That's where I met him; the Stones were playing Under My Thumb and I was a couple of feet from that boy when he was stabbed. Meredith something; I couldn't wear green for years after, and the sound of Mick Jagger's voice brought me out in hives. Herman hustled me away – I was so high I thought a dark angel was taking me down to hell. Wasn't quite that bad though sometimes I've wondered.'

Lili Marlene swooped from nowhere, picked the ear from the table and glided off into the shadows.

Tansy sighed, took Quincey's arm and walked him towards the door. 'This ain't a room for the living. Come on honey, you look like you could do with chamomile tea and chilli chocolate brownies, just baked. How was the funeral, by the way?'

HE CYCLED to the beach hut just to prove that the bike was real, not to mention the rest of the world; he was beginning to suspect the hallucinogenic quality of the air in Tansy's house and the brownies were a little too more-ish. A couple of teenage boys were attempting to launch a small sailing dinghy with a white monocoque hull and red mainsail. One wore a wetsuit decorated with zigzags in fluorescent yellows and greens, the other shivered in knee-length shorts and a T-shirt.

Quincey took the note from his pocket, felt the texture of the paper, lifted it to his nose in case there was a trace of a scent, and put it unfolded on the small table. So innocent. He was suddenly thirsty and made himself a coffee, then watched the boys pushing out into the water. He could do that; point the bow at the horizon, set the sails, and never look back. All he needed was a boat.

They were under way now, wetsuit at the tiller, shorts handling the jib. A gust caught them and the little boat keeled under the weight of the wind as wetsuit sat on the side and leaned as far back as he could to stop them capsizing. The sound of their voices, excited and laughing, floated across the beach.

Quincey picked up the note. Words, only words. How could they hurt him? A stupid question; his life's work was about words, such a strange choice of profession for a man who couldn't bring them to order.

Before he could unfold the paper, another gust pulled it from his hand and carried it, bouncing in the air, towards the edge of the sea. It dipped down for a second as if examining the ground for a safe landing place and then jerked back upwards again. For all that he had tried to ignore it the note now felt like his most precious possession, and losing it would be a tragedy. He scrambled down onto the beach and raced towards the water; outrunning the wind, what hope of that?

The note hung lazily in the air, twisting slowly before sinking down to fall at the feet of a woman who was watching the dinghy, goose winged now, heading towards the end of the pier. She stooped to pick it up just as Quincey arrived.

'Is this yours? Oh Christ, it's you.'

Out of context he didn't recognise her at first, with her long hair tied back in a ponytail and no makeup, assuming the dark smudges under her eyes didn't count. Her feet were bare, dusted with sand, with unexpectedly bright red polish on the toenails. 'Joanna, I mean, Dr Dust - this is... unexpected. I thought you lived near Uskmouth.'

'I see you've recovered the power of speech.' She smiled to soften the words and handed him the note. 'Things have moved on. I wanted a change of scenery for a few hours and then I remembered the pier that you'd talked about. What's your excuse?' She seemed in no hurry to walk away; life was full of surprises.

'Would you like a coffee?' he asked. 'My beach hut is just up there, the turquoise one. I have chairs.'

What on earth had possessed him to say that? She tried

to control a laugh by turning it into a cough, not entirely successfully.

'I'll pass on the coffee but I could do with somewhere to sit; this isn't one of my better days.'

HE GAVE her the canvas chair with the fewest stains from seagull shit, feeling as if he were entertaining an aunt. He hadn't really seen her in daylight before; her skin was so pale he wondered if there could be any blood beneath the surface, and lines curved in arcs from the corners of her eyes as if gravity was winning the fight. She looked at him once, as she refused the coffee again, then turned towards the sea.

He didn't know what to say, or where to look. Perhaps she had already forgotten that he was there; he sensed a tension in her body as if every muscle was on notice. If this was relaxing, no wonder she was always fatigued.

'Are you married, Quincey?' She was still looking towards the water and he wondered if he had misheard.

'Or a partner,' she said, 'a significant other? Anyone?'

'A wife, Cath.' It felt strange to say her name.

'Do you love her? Does she love you?'

'She's my wife...'

'Your wife... your possession.' It was as if she were talking to herself. 'It must be so easy for people like you. Husbands, wives, all those words sanctified by tradition. Signifiers of concepts that are so ingrained you don't have to articulate them, or even think about them. But they exist, these concepts, you make them concrete in the way you live. Are you a good husband, Quincey? Do you meet the requirements of the job spec?'

Perhaps she was drunk. It would explain why she was still in his company.

'I'm not sure I...' He stopped, not knowing what he meant to say.

She turned to face him; did the woman ever blink?

'Husband,' she said, 'master of the house. Wife, someone who turns away, a veiled one. Etymology matters.' She paused. 'I'm being impertinent, forgive me. I said this was a bad day.' She tucked a strand of hair behind her ear and turned back to the sea. 'Lisa moved out last night. Nine years together and then this happens, totally out of the blue, no warning. Just the day before we were discussing whether to try a different brand of muesli this week, and then she's in the hall with her cases packed and her front door key on the table. Said she'd be staying with a friend until she could get a place of her own. Said she was too exhausted to carry on with me and my malarkey. I think I screamed. I know I hit her. She just stood there while I tried to drag her away from the door. She didn't fight back even though I must have hurt her. When I ran out of anger, she sat next to me on the floor and held me - I thought she'd changed her mind, I was so happy - then she kissed me as if we had never been lovers and was gone. What do I do now?'

The strand of hair had escaped again and lay against her cheek, black on white, moving gently in the breeze against the statue that her body had become. Perhaps the Greeks and Romans hadn't been masters of sculpture, perhaps their gods simply turned people to marble. And was that a reward or a punishment?

He felt cheated somehow, as if she should have made a declaration when they first met. Worn an off-limits sign, to prevent possible embarrassment. Or perhaps there were other indications, subtle markers that he had missed. A dress code? At least it explained her distance from him and he felt relief that it wasn't his fault.

Joanna stood, blocking the sun. 'I should go; I'm sorry for bothering you. Please forget what I said; I didn't sleep much last night. And thanks for the water.'

He watched her walk along the beach, not looking back, until her shape shimmered as it merged into the haze from the sea. And then he read the note.

OTTAWA

Aspen turns off the road and waits for the gates to open. Someone has cleaned and polished the bronze letters on the entrance arch: *Disciples of the Risen Spirit*. A crap task, but not as bad as some given to the acolytes. It's been a long time since she's been one of those. She guns the black G-Wagon down the mile long track, through the campus with its dormitory and mess huts and on towards the main house.

Lev must still be out somewhere. His Rezvani Tank-X is missing and Aspen pulls in next to his space. If you're going to join a cult, she thinks, it might as well be one that pays; at least for those at the top. And she's very good at climbing. She nods at the guards by the front door and makes her way to the office on the second floor. She might be on the top team, but she still has responsibilities. Tonight is important; an induction for new wives and acolytes, followed by a group consummation. And then her favourite ritual - a discipline, when malefactors get what's coming to them. Even though she doesn't deliver the punishments herself, the spectacle is always a turn-on. Some people go to boxing matches; what's the difference?

It could hardly have been better timed; tomorrow is her birthday, halfway through her twenties, and she wonders what Lev has bought her this year. For her twenty-fourth it was the Merc, and he's the sort of man who always bids himself up. A complete cunt, of course, but he serves a purpose and this iteration of her life has proved to be more than a little fun, even if her sixth sense is right and it's nearing its natural end.

She uses her personal password, logs in to the encrypted system and pulls up the list of new wives. All of them are under nineteen years old, all part of the community for at least a year to prove their suitability. All virgins, theoretically, not so easy to find this close to Ottawa. She needs to pair each one off with a new acolyte before tonight, ready for the group consummation after the mass wedding. Last time had been a fiasco with three of the men overwhelmed by the occasion and unable to perform; from husband to sacrifice in less than an hour. Harsh, but as Lev always says, failure is not an option for the Disciples of the Risen Spirit. This time there will be no failures, with a little help from the fully loaded pharmacopeia at the Disciples' disposal.

Aspen looks through the head shots next to each bio. The community maintains high standards when it comes to physical attributes, and although she's indifferent to sex herself, she likes to watch other people fucking in front of her. That part of tonight will be fun, too.

The next task is to look through the new acolytes being inducted into the community. This will be their first time on the campus; while they serve their probationary month, they stay in the satellite site, thirty miles away. There have been attempts before at infiltration; journalists, police, private investigators looking for missing persons. After one so-called exposé, Lev had introduced the quarantine system, a chance for the Disciples to do some investigating of their own.

She scrolls through the names and photos, skimming over the usual vapid and credulous faces, until she arrives at one that makes her heart skip. In the ten years since that day in the trailer park, she's discovered more about the men looking to revenge the death of their brother, the miserable roach she exterminated. The men who abducted her from her apartment and planned to hire her out as a sex slave until Greg freed her. Such an unlikely hero, Greg, someone else she hasn't thought of for years. Did he ever get back together with Francoise? Families; sometimes she thinks they're just not worth the trouble.

She pictures the men standing by the open boot of the truck where they'd thrown her. Even though it had been dark she'd seen enough to know who they were. Ches and Buck, Earl's brothers. The photo she's looking at must be Ches, even though the name above the image is different; she knows what Buck looks like, scarred and imperfect, not up to spec for a Disciple. So somehow they've tracked her here. Coincidences are for other people, this is deliberate. After escaping from the pickup, she'd hoped that they'd give up, especially if she dropped off the radar. But no, the little fuckwits really want payback for their brother and they clearly have more nous than she'd given them credit for.

Someone, somewhere must have talked. It had to be Kaley, giving away the name she's been using. It's a shame; she's rather liked being Aspen Collet, but now this identity is probably compromised. Of course, it's always possible that Ches is just fishing, following rumours. Sadly for him, though, he's not in Kansas anymore. This is her turf, and she's not the naive girl from a few years ago. The discipline ritual tonight just got even more interesting.

Revenge, she's long since realised, really is a dish best served cold. She'd been precipitate with Earl and let her emotions get the better of her, but in her defence she had been quite young. He would hardly have suffered; such a waste of retribution. She only hopes that a merciful god allowed Earl to survive the explosion and smoke inhalation; to live long enough to wake from his stupor and feel the flames charring his flesh and sucking the oxygen from his lungs.

Now it's Ches' turn to pay for his temerity in pursuing her for so long. And all of this, she reminds herself, is nothing more than an amuse-bouche, a practise run for the pain she plans to exact on whoever condemned her and her mother to exile.

It's mid afternoon when Lev finds her, still in the office. She might not like men, but they have their uses. From the moment three years ago when she saw him and a group of Disciples handing out pamphlets near the National Gallery, she knew they'd be useful. A cult; what better place to lose herself, just in case the Lekkers picked up her trail.

Lev had realised within a couple of days that she wasn't buying the Risen Spirit bullshit, but he knew a fellow chancer when he saw one. He fixes himself a coffee and wanders over to see what she's working on. 'You ready for tonight?' he asks. 'It's been a good month, but I'm still thinking about upping the tithes.'

She really will have to divert some of the Disciples'

money into her own hidden cache; revenge doesn't come cheap. She'd suggested helping Lev with the accounts, but he always keeps a tight grip on finances. There had been a treasurer for a while, but he ended up being terminally disciplined for taking a slice. If you're going to steal from the boss, get it right.

Talking of discipline... 'After the marriage and consummations, we have three for the pit tonight?' she asks.

'Sure. As I'm in a good mood, I was going to let them go with a beating and a fine; what do you think?'

That won't work for her at all. 'You could, but don't you think it's time we laid on some serious entertainment? It's been a while since the last show and it won't hurt to reinforce discipline. We don't want people getting ideas, especially with a new batch joining us.'

The way he looks at her, as if he's seeing her for the first time. 'You're in a feisty mood. But ok, you have a point.'

Now for the kicker. 'I want to add someone,' she says. 'It's a bit controversial... he's one of the new guys being inducted today.'

She shows Lev the photo and the man's record.

'Are you sure?' he says. 'We found nothing on him; he seems genuine enough if a bit old. Good physique, though, keeps himself in shape.'

There hadn't seemed any point in telling Lev what happened back in the trailer park or about the kidnapping. Why say more than you need to? Truth is a commodity, just like anything else, not to be given away lightly. But she knows Lev will need a reason to lose an income stream. A story he can believe.

'I'm sure,' she says. 'This bastard tried to rape me when I was younger, back in BC. When something like that happens, you don't forget the face.' She enjoys the challenge of making up stories on the hoof, and this one is believable enough, almost the truth. There's no need to reveal Ches's real name just in case anyone does a little digging.

Lev runs his hand over the blonde stubble on his head. Aspen knows that rape in the abstract doesn't bother him, except when it's done to his property. Lev doesn't like damaged goods. 'You say he tried. Did he succeed?'

'What do you think? No, I got away and left him wishing he hadn't tried. It's a long story; I haven't thought of him for years. Then I saw his photo, and it all came back.'

'I'm surprised he's still alive,' Lev says, frowning 'It's not like you to let disrespect like that go unpunished.'

'I was thirteen when it happened. Anyone tries that these days, there won't be anything left to go to the pit. But you know me, I always play a long game.' That, at least, is true. 'Trust me, Lev, tonight will be all the payback I need.'

'If you say so. Put him on the list, you choose the sentence. And happy birthday.'

After Lev leaves, she moves Ches to the discipline list and deletes him from the acolytes. He'll already be here in one of the dormitory huts, being prepared for tonight; the new acolytes are kept isolated until the ceremony. She could probably persuade one of the guards to let her see him, but what would be the point? He'd realise that his cover had been blown and might try to escape, and a shot in the back isn't quite the outcome she has in mind for him. Better to let things unfold as they should and stick to the plan. Ches will find out soon enough that his life has been diverted onto a very short, unpleasant track.

. . .

THE DISCIPLINE PIT hides behind a line of sugar maples, a few hundred metres from the main house and silhouetted against the sunset's afterglow as the favoured members of the community assemble. There are no seats here, apart from one for Lev as judge and jury. Once everyone is in place, the floodlights flare on, bathing the pit in brilliant blue light and hiding the spectators in shadows. Several large metal rings, set into concrete blocks, surround a steel table glinting in the light, with a wide centre slit running almost the entire length.

After a few minutes of waiting, a squad of guards lead four men into the centre of the arena, chained to one another by their ankles. They shamble and stumble as they make their way down, unencumbered by shoes or clothes. With the tape over their mouths and the zip ties around their wrists they're already broken, less than human, heads down and focussed on the uneven ground. As they reach the centre of the pit, the last man in the line lifts his head and looks up. At least one of them still has some spunk left in him; Ches Lekker.

Aspen stares at him and he seems to look directly at her, but it's impossible to read anything in his expression. In any event, she's hidden in the shadows and he must be blinded by the lights. The roles have been reversed. Although she's the hunter, and he's the prey, he seems unconcerned as if he's the one in control. Perhaps he's expecting Buck to swoop in with a rescue plan; men like him always expect to win. In a way, she wishes Buck would try. It would be a bonus to get two for the price of one. But one will do, for now.

A guard unchains the men from each other and refastens them to the thick metal rings as Lev holds up a hand to quieten the low murmuring that ripples through the spectators. 'The Disciples of the Risen Spirit are merciful,' he says. He rarely shouts and his voice carries across the clearing. 'But mercy must be tempered with justice. Mercy must be bought with sacrifice. To give sinners the chance of eternal light, their spirits must be cleansed.'

Another susurration around the crowd, as if they buy this bullshit.

'Al Malone.' The first man looks up, shaking with a combination of shame and cold and fear. 'You are guilty of defiling one of our sisters and this is my sentence. The part of your body that offended must be sacrificed for the salvation of your eternal soul.' He nods at the guards standing by the side of the pit. They walk towards Malone, lift him onto the table, strap him down with his legs splayed apart, and then rip away the duct tape covering his mouth.

This is the point where they either scream for mercy, or weep, or shout abuse. Aspen always has a bet with herself; Malone, she thinks, will beg, and she isn't disappointed. It takes him a few moments of swallowing and making small animal sounds before he finds his voice. Pathetic, as it always is, as if apologies and abasement at this stage will make any difference. Once they're in the pit, there's no turning back.

She quite likes amputations. Simple, clear cut, and given the nature of this punishment it will be a knife day, an opportunity for a virtuoso performance. Hands, or sometimes even whole limbs, are removed either with an axe or a chainsaw, which always seems crass by comparison. No elegance, no finesse.

Lev is in a merciful mood; someone gives Malone a rubber dog bone to bite on. At a discipline session a couple of months ago, the pain had caused one victim to bite off his own tongue; two amputations for the price of one.

Tonight's executioner does his job quickly and efficiently. It's always pleasing to see someone take pride in their work. Malone sinks to the ground once they unstrap him and throw him off the table, scrunched into a foetal crouch as if to hide what's been done to him. She's always been impressed to see how the will to live stays till the end, even when they know it's hopeless.

The next two are guilty of stealing and both lose a hand to an axe, and then it's the turn of Ches. Lev turns to Aspen. 'He's yours. If you want to say anything, make it quick. I missed lunch.'

She's been wondering what to say to the man who planned her torture, but the three writhing bodies next to him have satisfied any desire for gloating. She must be losing her touch. All the fine words and speeches have evaporated, and she wants this to be over now. She cheated Ches of his revenge once and now he's about to pay for the sins of his brother and for pursuing her. Harsh it may be, but she can do without the complication.

'I'm done, Lev,' she says. 'You know what needs to happen to him so let's end this and get something to eat.' She watches without emotion as Lev pronounces sentence - castration. Ches is strapped down, not even trying to struggle. He's seen what happens, and he must have realised by now that there won't be any rescue. The knife flashes in the floodlights, Ches is dumped with the others and then Lev signals to one of the guards, who steps forward with an assault rifle over his shoulder. This is the real mercy. A couple of bursts and all four men lay sprawled in growing pools of blood, not moving.

Aspen walks next to Lev as they leave the small arena. Oysters and tequila tonight; she can't wait.

He read the text from his sister; if Jennifer felt unable to say something in person, it was bound to be bad news and he wasn't disappointed. Robyn had been in touch again, still wanting to take Poppy. *Talk to her*, Jennifer said, *make her see how ridiculous that would be.*

He supposed she was right. Robyn had always seemed only half in the world; perhaps that was the attraction. He'd always felt that she was searching for something, but didn't know what it was. Not him, that had become clear. And not a child either. Robyn had dumped Poppy at the first opportunity, so why take her now?

He turned from his phone to the note left on his windscreen at the funeral, looking at it again for clues. '*Would she be alive if you had stayed?*'

Why ask him? It had always been the same, people trying to make him feel responsible for things that were outside his control. It wasn't fair.

The writer had to be Marcus Haremountain. One way or another, the man was involved, even though he'd talked his way out of the police station. What on God's green earth had Esther seen in him? Quincey tried, and failed, not to think about them together, talking about him and laughing about his failings as a lover. Or had Esther kept him a secret? Perhaps Marcus found out that she had another lover, watched until he left that night, made her murder look like suicide, and then forged the note.

He'd read about people sent mad with jealousy, and didn't they say that after the first murder, the rest become so much easier?

TANSY INVITED HIM TO SUPPER. Casserole, she called it, which seemed a little vague, and he still hadn't checked on the freezer weasel.

'Anyone meeting Herman for the first time, they need sustenance,' Tansy said, ladling a few more gobbets of meat onto his plate. 'Not so bad as it used to be; I tell you, when he was alive that man was a career option all in himself. I like him better now, more manageable, the way men should be - present company excepted. Lili, she never understood him, feeling was mutual. I caught him once; he'd tied her feet to the handlebars of his bike and was about to go for a run down to Exmoor on the M5. He said she needed the exercise to stop her wings from getting weak. A macaw remembers things like that.'

He detected a distinct gaminess to the casserole that even the chunks of turnip couldn't hide.

'I was thinking about you today, while I was mucking out the chickens. Man like you deserves a new start. Whatever's going on in your life - and I don't need the details, honey, I never was one to pry - you need to move on. Maybe that funeral you went to is a sign.'

Quincey pulled a whisker from the gravy and laid it on the side of his plate. Moving on, it rather implied somewhere to move to. But the thought was enticing. A new start, to be born again and become someone new, someone with better luck.

'I got this friend across town,' said Tansy. 'We met at a taxidermy conference in Huddersfield. She does rebirthing - could be just what you need. Even Herman went, though he should have been more honest about his asthma beforehand. Still, me and Romola hauled the body back here between us and as he'd never got round to being in the country officially, as it were, we decided not to trouble the authorities. Bureaucrats, they don't know the meaning of the word "flexible".' She speared the last piece of meat from his plate and swallowed it whole. 'You'll like Romola, very motherly. I'll make you an appointment.'

HE'D NEVER BEEN to this part of Avonport before. He wouldn't have been surprised to find replicants hiding here in what seemed to be one enormous chemical factory, miles of giant pipelines joining storage tanks and steel chimneys. Even through the car's aircon, there was an acid tang to the air that reminded him of leaking fume cupboards in the chemistry lab at school. H_2SO_4, HNO_3; funny the things you remember.

He wondered if Tansy had given him the right address - surely no-one could live around here - until he turned up a side road and found himself in a fragment of 1930s suburbia left behind from a gentler time. The row of pebble-dashed semis seemed transplanted, normality juxtaposed with dystopia.

How had Tansy described her friend - motherly? The

woman who opened the door filled the frame and creaked like a failing house as she led the way along a narrow hallway. The two downstairs rooms had been knocked through and the windows onto the street replaced with a single sheet of plate glass, while someone who never suffered from hangovers had designed the Axminster carpet. Perhaps it was all part of the therapy, to disorientate him and break down his defences. They sat at the far end of the room on either side of a wooden desk that looked as if a small husband had knocked it up under duress.

The woman handed him a business card: *Romola Anastasia Romanoff - Rebirthing, Channelling, Interior Design.* 'I'm a traditionalist, I don't do rebreathing,' she said, 'I have to make that clear. I leave that to the Buddhists; in, out, in, out - all that counting. Did we count when mummy popped us out? Nonsense. Our task is to recreate the delicious trauma of birth.

Did she know that the mole on her cheek had a two inch long hair like an aerial curving out? He remembered the whisker from last night's meal and felt a little nauseous.

'Compression, that's the ticket,' said Romola. 'Relive the journey through the birth canal but without the fear. Sign the disclaimer here, here... and here, and we can begin. Pop your clothes off and I'll get the rug.'

He'd been lax on the laundry front since moving in with Tansy and was reduced to the maroon Speedos under his trousers. When Romola reappeared with an orange shag pile under one arm, she shook her head in sorrow. 'Those are quite unnecessary. How can we be reborn if we cling to relics of the past? Were you wearing undergarments when you were expelled from your mother's body? No, today we leave shame and the past behind. Trust me, it will be a relief.'

She pulled all the curtains, stretched the rug on the floor and made him sit at one end. The sound of a woman moaning emanated from a pair of speakers on the mantelpiece. 'You surely don't imagine your mother sang lullabies as she forced you out?' said Romola. 'This was the soundtrack to your birth. This is what you heard as you came into the world.'

She manoeuvred to her knees next to him, more creaking, and before he could resist she'd gagged him and pushed him onto his back, the red silicone ball on its faux leather strap stretching his mouth wide. 'In the womb you had no voice,' she said. And then, with a strength that shouldn't have surprised him, she rolled him up as if he were the innards of a giant spliff. He tried not to grunt with pleasure, but couldn't help himself when she clambered on top of him, her weight crushing his chest. She was saying something, but he could hear nothing over the sound of his blood pounding through his brain. And the orange nylon pressed around his ginger-haired bollocks - the appositeness of the colourway hadn't escaped him - had given him the biggest erection of his life, straining against the rug like a dandelion trying to displace a paving stone. Wasn't this what happened to men when they were hanged, the body's last defiant attempt at self-propagation?

She was shifting about just enough to allow him an occasional breath, moaning in harmony with the background soundtrack, and he realised he was going to come. There was nothing he could do with his arms and legs pinioned; there was no escape. He couldn't remember this happening the first time around. Any second now if he didn't suffocate first; it would be a close-run thing.

Too late. With serendipitous synchronicity, she ripped the gag from his mouth as the first spasm started, unrolled him with a single tug, and they both watched as he pumped helplessly over the shag pile.

QUINCEY STOPPED the car by a park bench next to a small patch of grass at the corner of the road. All things considered, £200 for professional cleaning of the rug had been a small price to pay.

Something had shifted inside him. Behind was the chemical plant, in front a view over the estuary stretched towards Uskmouth, and he felt as if he were on the edge of a borderline in his life. Not far from the opposite side of the old bridge, and surrounded by the swirl of the incoming tide, stood the ruins of a building, a tumble of stone on a small lump of rock and mud just above the seaweed line. A man could be safe on an island, cut off and unreachable. Invisible. Perhaps that was what he needed; not just to move away, but to disappear. Sever the ties and set himself free. The new self, a rebooted Quincey 2.0. He didn't know where to go or how to do it, but it sounded like the start of a plan.

CHAPTER
TEN

There was no sleep for him that night. The bedclothes felt too tight and he lay on top of the quilt, scared even to scratch himself. He wondered if Tansy would know what had happened, but she was in her private room when he got back and he spent the evening sitting on his bed with a damp hummus and carrot wrap.

Something had happened yesterday. He felt his blood effervescing and couldn't remember feeling so alive. Esther, Cath, Joanna, Marcus – even Poppy (more than a twinge of guilt); here was his chance to leave them all behind. At some point he drifted off and woke from a dream of Romola, dressed in Axminster and perched like an owl on the mantelpiece in her living room, her head thrown back while she crowed like a triumphant cockerel.

The crowing continued after he opened his eyes; Sarkozy singing to the dawn. Quincey considered his face in the bathroom mirror and put the razor down, unwetted. A new life, a new look. Who was there to please now, apart from himself? No mother, no sister, no clients, no wife. He ran his hand over a chin which looked and felt like coarse sandpaper. He could start with stubble and move on to a beard.

Tansy didn't ask him about the rebirthing. 'What happens with Romola, stays with Romola.' But she seemed unsurprised when he said he'd be going away for a while. 'Don't reckon I'll be letting your room again so leave whatever you want here, honey. Me and Lili will keep it safe, won't we baby?'

The macaw perched on the back of the chair at the head of the kitchen table, a materfamilias in blue and gold clutching a small rodent in one claw.

'She doesn't eat them,' said Tansy, 'more like a furry security blanket. She'll carry it round for a while till bits fall off, then I get her a new one. She's kinda picky; last week only pygmy shrews would do, now it has to be voles. It's like living with a child.'

Lili lifted the trophy and rubbed her beak along its flank, then shook it vaguely in Quincey's direction until the head fell off.

'Oh honey... that was new only yesterday. You gotta make them last or you go without, we talked about this.'

HE DECIDED NOT to take the car, or the bike. Tansy lent him a rucksack; 'Herman kept his stashes in there. I used to say to him, that stuff will mess with your brain, but he was going through a Grateful Dead phase. You know what it's like.'

Quincey wondered if this was another reference to ice-cream but decided not to ask. Sometimes Tansy's world and his had the slimmest of intersects.

. . .

'ARE YOU SURE THIS IS YOU?' asked the cashier, studying the photo in Quincey's passport. 'We have to be careful when customers withdraw large amounts. It's for your own protection and security.'

'But it's my money.'

'I think it's the hair,' said the cashier. 'Are you wearing a wig, perhaps? Lord knows I make no judgements about vanity. My wife, you should have heard her when I got a tattoo. I'd been watching too many war movies, mind, always was easily influenced according to the missus.'

'For god's sake man, just give me my money.'

'Please don't raise your voice, sir.' He pointed to a notice attached to the security screen: '*Offensive behaviour towards our staff will not be tolerated.*'

A deputy manageress led him away from the cashier and into a small room by the end of the counter. She sat opposite him, protected by a table that would not have impressed Romola's imagined husband, and gave him the sort of smile usually reserved for recalcitrant children. 'How would it be if we gave out money to every Tom, Dick or Harry who came in and asked for it? We wouldn't like that, would we, Mr Radlett?'

'But you know me. You opened my business account. I've banked here since I was at University, and you were at Oxford with Cath. You invited us to your house for dinner.' Admittedly, just the once.

'We have procedures, Mr Radlett, and you are asking me and my staff to rely on our judgement rather than evidence.' She studied the passport, then his driving licence. 'These images are rather generic, don't you think? Amorphous features, not at all helpful. She took off her spectacles, polished the lenses on the hem of her skirt and sighed. 'I never wanted to be a banker. The church called me, I always fancied myself as a priest once they opened the door to women. High church, obviously, bells and smells or what's the point? And a secret knowledge, something to believe in.' She put her spectacles back on and peered at him. 'But what is knowledge, Mr Radlett? How can we ever truly know anything? Surely knowledge is no more than true justified belief and then, inexorably, we come like supplicants to the definitions of "true" and "justified", not to mention "belief".' She drew a breath, still looking at him, and breathed out again slowly. 'Are you sure you want it all? May I ask if it's for an investment? We have advisers...'

'Please, I beg you, just give me my damned money.'

'If it wasn't because I know you so well, Mr Radlett, I'd be calling security right now. Your mother, God rest her soul, would be ashamed.'

HE STASHED the cash at the bottom of the rucksack, and on the way to the station he threw his mobile under the front wheel of an approaching dust cart. No traces, isn't that what Romola had said? No way to be traced, either. Perhaps this is what it really felt like to be reborn.

He bought a one-way ticket to Paddington, remembering just in time to use real money rather than a card. Tansy had asked if he had any plans - *'yes or no will do, honey, don't need the whys and wherefores,'* - and that's when he had realised that for the first time in his life, he was free.

He had vaguely warm memories of London. Hamleys had been a traditional Christmas treat, tacked on to the end of his mother's shopping trip for herself. *'Your father has no idea what to buy, he's a man. I suppose he has strengths of his own, although God knows what they are.'*

He'd long since blocked off his memories of the time around Pa dying and no-one ever talked about it, another of those parts of his past that were always out of focus. But one vague image that stuck was at Pa's funeral, when he was twelve years old. He'd noticed a woman sitting at the back with a child next to her, a small girl with wisps of ginger hair escaping a baseball hat. They must have left before the end and didn't come back to the house, and when he'd asked his mother who they were, she'd slapped his legs and told him he was imagining things.

THERE WERE BARELY any seats free on the train even though it was a weekend, and he had a choice between a man who lived the supersize-me dream and a woman reading an old Penguin paperback. It was only when he tucked the rucksack under his knees that he realised her legs were barely long enough to reach past the end of the seat cushion. As the train slowed down for Swindon and the refreshment trolley arrived, she pulled a couple of packs of sandwiches from her bag.

'You want one? I can never decide so I buy them both, then have the choice of looking like that guy over there - which would be weird - or throw some away. Brie and gooseberry on oatmeal, or prawn cocktail on white. Or we could have one of each, share the joy. Mine's a coffee, by the way, white, no sugar.'

He chose the prawn, bought two coffees, and wiped mayonnaise from his chin.

'Of course,' she said, 'we could cut out all the crap in the middle and decide to get married right away. You know how tiresome it is, all that relationship foreplay; meals out, cinema, theatre - you'll understand why I wouldn't suggest ballroom dancing - and life is so short. That was a joke, you can laugh.' She pushed the lunch detritus away and picked up her book, a slightly foxed copy of The Critique of Pure Reason. 'You know Kant? He never had a wife and I can understand why. Donald Rumsfeld would have liked him, a great man for unknown unknowns was our Immanuel.'

The day was feeling like a conspiracy of philosophers.

'Me, I prefer Schopenhauer,' she said. 'He saw the world was crap and wasn't afraid to say so. Not hot on chance, either; everything has a cause if you know where to look. And without Schopenhauer, Wagner would have been just another failed revolutionary who couldn't write a melody to save his life. For the school play one year I suggested we do Die Walküre with me as Brunnhilde - I'll give my parents that, they didn't hold back on my education - but Miss Rothstein said there were too many spears and the boys would get over-excited. She was probably right.'

AT PADDINGTON she moved surprisingly fast and was halfway down the platform, arm-in-arm with a man who could have been her twin, while he was still manoeuvring the rucksack through the carriage door.

Why was everyone walking so quickly, and on a Sunday? The tide of people flowed around him as if he were that island in the estuary; he was already acquiring invisibility. But more than that, he needed to acquire a base; a room, a bedsit. And some food; the prawn sandwich was already in another life and he craved something hot and greasy that would give Tansy an apoplexy. Even the food bars on the station concourse looked too worthy and he found a café a couple of streets away, populated by cab drivers and tired-looking blondes dressed for warmer weather.

He ordered a double cheeseburger and fries and was still deciding between the plastic ketchup and mustard bottles on the table, when a ukulele appeared next to the vinegar.

'You mind? It's the girls, they go around in packs, makes me bollocks shrink just to see them. Feral, they are, you'd think after the nights they have they'd want to go home and have a kip. Makes me glad I never had daughters. Never had boys neither, come to that. That's the multiverse for you, never know which version of your own life you've won in the draw.' He took one of Quincey's fries and dunked it in his coffee. 'Oops - sorry, mate, got into bad habits lately.' He stretched out a hand. 'Name's Jack but friends, such as they are, call me Prof.'

'Quincey...' Damn - he'd already forgotten that he was supposed to be someone else.

'Nice moniker - comedians for parents, was it? Or classicists? Has a sort of Virgilian ring to it. Play for the other team, do you? Not that I mind, live and let live, I say, and some of my best friends etcetera etcetera. Never seen the attraction myself - mind you, come in here and see the harpies, makes you wonder.'

He picked up the ukulele and rubbed away a spot of grease. 'Not seen you in here before.' He nodded at the rucksack on the chair next to Quincey. 'On your travels? Come to see the sights? Man like you, I would have expected a briefcase. Let me guess - accountant? Am I right?' The man's drooping moustache was fringed with coffee, which he wiped away with elegant, yellow-stained fingers.

Quincey tried to think of what to say. He'd been given a second chance to weave a new life for himself, but accountant was too close. He should have worked out a life story beforehand, but it was clear that planning and serendipity didn't go well together. Then he remembered a documentary he'd watched a few weeks ago about dying local trades. Go large, he thought, why not?

'I'm an eel catcher,' he said, 'a family tradition. Avonport estuary.'

Prof didn't seem fazed. 'I had thought tax inspector if you weren't an accountant, so I suppose eel catcher is pretty close. Both trying to catch slippery customers, eh? As for the jolly old anguilliformes - wrong side of town for them. There's a nice little place near Aldgate, serves pie and mash with liquor. Can't abide it myself, I have a delicate constitution and green sauce makes me puke. Cod in batter I can manage, on a good day.' He took the last chip and winked at Quincey. 'Must be a woman then, brought you up to our fair city. Tell you what, me and the lads are playing tonight, the Toad and Teaspoon just round the corner from here. Nine o'clock, bring her along and you won't hear a better version of Like a Virgin by a uke band and operatic tenor. The beer's crap, mind, but after a couple who cares?'

'I'm not sure where I'll be tonight - I need to find a place to stay for a while.'

'There's more to you than meets the eye, my friend. But you're in luck as it happens. There's a spare room at my gaff; bloke I shared with, Pashtun - don't ask me why, probably the beard - he got involved in a minor dispute, failed to make a convincing argument to the constabulary concerning his whereabouts one evening and the discussion is now continuing in Pentonville. Thanks to a little truth bending by m'learned friends - now there's slippery for you - he should be out in about nine months but he never quite assimilated the concepts of agency and responsibility, and the notion of time off for good behaviour is a phenomenon that has always given him a wide berth, so who knows?'

ANOTHER DAY, another bedroom. Prof removed the obvious takeaway cartons, the contents of which seemed well on their way to evolving into new life forms, but from the smell there were possibly more to be discovered.

'Make yourself at home,' the Prof said, 'Pash was about your size, a natty dresser even if his eating habits left something to be desired, always had a crease in his Levis.' He waved at the wardrobe. 'Feel free to rummage if you feel the need for a change of style. Never a man to bear a grudge, Pash, and a flexible attitude to property. He'd have those trousers off your legs without you noticing, should he find himself enamoured of them, which would require a stretch of the imagination given Pashtun's sartorial predilections.'

Quincey found a pair of jeans after the Prof had left him and tried them on; thirty-nine years old and this was his first essay into denim. Ma had never been keen; '*Do you seriously want to look like the spawn of a tradesman?*'. The only mirror was fixed to the wall above a small washbasin in the corner of the room, and he balanced on a chair with uneven legs, bobbing up and down to get a sense of how he looked. Sagging was the word that came to mind, and one bob'n'twist left the jeans halfway across his buttocks. In the bottom drawer, he found a belt with a plastic buckle in the shape of a fried egg. Unusual and at odds with his received image of Pashtun, but strangely satisfying and possibly de rigeur for an evening of entertainment at the Toad and Teaspoon, even if he would have to disappoint the Prof and turn up alone.

. . .

'WE'LL BE ON AROUND NINE,' the Prof said. Quincey fell asleep on the bed and slept with no discernible dreams. When he woke it was already a quarter to, and with armpits like Brie and no stomach for a shower he found a t-shirt in one of the drawers to complete the new ensemble - primrose yellow with a picture of a dinosaur and the words '*I am, are you?*' Cath would have complained that it clashed with the yolk on the belt but then Cath wasn't here, and if she had been, the colourway would have been the least of her problems with him.

The Toad and Teaspoon was smaller than he'd imagined, just another shop front sandwiched between a greengrocer advertising cheap calls to Africa, and a launderette. He negotiated a couple of battered yams on the pavement, deciding not to get involved, and entered the pub. He wasn't sure what he'd expected, some sort of stage, perhaps, but there was no sign of any entertainment other than the Prof, ukulele in one hand, pint in the other, laughing at the bar with a blonde man, twenty-two going on fifteen, wearing lederhosen.

'Quincey, my man! Get your arse over here and some beer down your gullet. Meet Rupert, our vocalist. Don't be fooled by his etiolated exterior. Lungs like a whale, this boy, I swear one breath lasts all evening. Angels weep when he sings, and not just from the pain.' He finished his drink in one gulp. 'Better go and earn our crust for the night; come on my lad, time to give those tonsils an outing.'

The rest of the band coalesced from the crowd of drinkers; five ukuleles, one of them a woman who reminded him of teenage lust, and Rupert, clustered in an alcove at the far end of the bar. The Prof stepped up to the mike stand; 'Guten abend, meine Herren und Damen. We're going to start tonight with a number for all our swivel-eyed friends, whichever political rock they're hiding under at the moment.'

The on-the-spot goose-step rather took him by surprise, syncopating with the ukuleles as they launched into a ragtime version of Springtime for Hitler, but on balance Quincey thought it worked, artistically speaking. Cath would not have approved.

WHEN THE FIRST set ended Quincey made his way to the loos at the back, and as he washed his hands the Prof came in with Rupert.

'Thought I might find you here. I swear I'm getting arthritis in me fingers. It's the strumming, the fan stroke plays havoc.' Rupert had gone into one of the cubicles but left the door open, and the Prof went to join him. 'Just us girls powdering our noses. The lad here manages to get some decent gear from someone at that fancy musical college of his, though I don't ask how he pays. You want a couple of lines? Call it a welcome present, now we're living together - wipe that smirk, Rupert, some of us still bat for the right side.'

It would have been churlish to refuse, something the old Quincey would have done, but he hadn't expected such an immediate hit. His brain felt as if it were fizzing and he noticed that Rupert had rather good legs, tanned and epilated. He wasn't sure whether Cath would have approved or not.

· · ·

HE REALISED, during the encore of Tomorrow Belongs to Me in the style of a Johann Strauss waltz, that he had no idea how to get back to his room.

'No problem,' said the Prof as he joined him at the bar. 'Gotta get some decent kip tonight, working for the man tomorrow.'

'You don't do this for a living?'

'I wish. When I jacked in the day job, I had no idea what I'd do - anything as long as it didn't involve standing on my hind legs in front of a bunch of lazy gits who went to Uni because they couldn't think of anything better to do. Be different these days, student loans and all that crap. Didn't help that the powers that be closed the department I was in - "not relevant in the current economic climate," they said. Bunch of bean counters.'

'What did you do?'

'Assistant Professor of Experimental Ethics, University of Hounslow - it's a long story.' He toasted Quincey with the dregs in his glass. 'Me dad never understood; he worked in a warehouse for Homebase, fancied himself on a forklift. Me mum, that was a different matter. She graduated with a first in PPE from Oxford and then became a local organiser for the Communist Party of Great Britain (Marxist Leninist). I think she married me dad in an effort to raise her class consciousness, but in reality she thought he was a prat. Bit harsh on the poor bugger, all he wanted was a couple of pints every night and weekends pottering amongst the peonies. He once told me he always voted Tory, she never knew. Wouldn't have crossed her mind that he could do something off his own bat but still, that's the proletariat for you.'

They started to walk back; the yams were still there,

along with a squashed plantain. 'How do you get by now?' Quincey asked.

'Tell you what, unless you got something better to do why don't you join me tomorrow, come along for the ride? Coco Pops at eight, wheels up at half past. Don't be late.'

MANHATTAN

Six a.m. The bacon is crispy and the breakfast pancakes are just the way she likes them, stacked high. She prefers eating at this time with the street cleaners and transport workers, before the office crowds and their skinny decaf soy lattes. The diner suits her; just a few minutes from her small apartment on E13th street and en route to her job a forty-minute walk away at Shadow Security Solutions, a deliberately nondescript office on W38th and 7th. The walk gives her just enough time to clear her mind, prepare for the day ahead and get some exercise. And who wouldn't want a daily commute that takes her along Broadway? Winter in Manhattan might be cold but it beats the frozen wasteland of Fraserwood Trailer Park, hands down.

She hadn't got home last night until past midnight, and sleep had been shy. Too much coffee as she worked through the latest reports from one of their investigators and time, as Feroz is always telling them, is of the essence. At least this time he's right. Her first job today is to send out the aptly named Advisor teams to talk to witnesses in a major financial fraud. She'd gone out with them a few times when she first started; on-the-job training, Feroz called it. She's still amazed at how stupid people can be; the witnesses think they're safe and hidden but no matter what they've been told by police or prosecutors, no witness protection program will keep them hidden for long from Shadow's investigators. Once they're found the Advisors weave their magic to persuade them that their memories are a little more vague than they'd led the prosecutors to believe.

She'd questioned this precarious strategy; surely memories resurface if the incentives are attractive enough, she'd said to Feroz, or the threats too weak. But as he pointed out, the Advisors are very good at their jobs and witnesses are never left in any doubt what will happen if they remember the wrong facts. Memories are what you decide they should be; back to that marketable and relative commodity, truth.

Feroz is out today and she'll have time to indulge in a couple of her own projects. One is almost complete, now that she has the resources of Shadow to call on. A little unfinished business, dealing with the last remaining Lekker brother. Buck is still out for vengeance, doubled up now that he's lost Ches as well as Earl. They have long memories, the Lekkers. It's seventeen years since she blew up her mother's killer, seven since she gave the signal for Ches to be emasculated and gunned down and Buck still won't let it go.

As Aspen walks north along Broadway, her mind drifts to her last days with the Disciples of the Risen Spirit. Barely a month after Ches died in the discipline pit, Lev started to edge her out in favour of someone new, someone fresh. She always knew it would happen one day. Lev liked his women young, and she knew how the game would end. Either she would give in gracefully and accept her reduced status, which was never going to happen, or Lev would find a reason to have her taken to the pit, something that definitely wasn't in her game plan. Add to that the fact that her identity as Aspen might have been compromised, and she really had no choice.

She left the G-Wagon behind in a back street in Montreal - all the cult cars were fitted with trackers - and made a convoluted trip, long planned, across the border and down to New York. It had been an earlier change of scene than she'd wanted and without as much in the way of funds as she'd hoped; Lev had been generous with things, not so much with hard cash.

But leaving the cult had been a blessing, in a way. She'd remembered enough of her criminology studies to blag her way into working with with Feroz and she's learned a lot since, better than from any book. It's been a perfect way to hone her investigative skills, as well as giving her time to build up the coffers for her next trip to the other side of the Atlantic. Security pays well.

But first she needs to take care of Buck. As soon as she got the job at Shadow, she set up some online triggers to let her know what he was up to. Luckily he hasn't had the sense to outsource his search for her to anyone else, or to change his identity. Lesson One: if you want to be invisible, become someone else. As far as the people at Shadow know she's Rosie McKenzie, from Toronto. From Cerys to Aspen to Rosie; who will she be in the end? Perhaps identity is like truth, she thinks. Malleable and controllable, able to be whatever we want it to be.

To be fair, she can afford to let Buck go. She made sure to cover her tracks after she left the Disciples and the likelihood of him finding her is remote. But it's possible; he's still looking and she doesn't like loose ends. Messy, you never know when they'll trip you up.

Hacking into the Lekker security system was child's play. It's become addictive, almost as if she shares Buck's home at the family compound outside Fraserwood. She sits in her apartment at night, watching him come and go, almost always alone. Ches had been the brains behind their business, and since his sad demise things have clearly gone south for Buck, with his crew deserting like the proverbial ship's rats. Failure, after all, is an unattractive trait.

She briefly considers whether to use one of Shadow's enforcers to finish things, but she knows she'll have to sort it out herself, and under the radar; Feroz isn't keen on his employees going off piste on personal projects, especially if it involves his assets. And anyway, it will feel more fitting to close the circle herself. Tomorrow is Saturday and she's due a few days off. Enough time for Rosie McKenzie to get to Fraserwood and take care of business.

She sits by a window in the bedroom on the second floor of the main house in the Lekker compound, looking across miles of empty land. She knows this landscape; in summer the clouds of dust kicked up by any visitor will be visible from the horizon, but from the beginning of November the track will have been ice-hard, the fall's mud ruts cemented in until the spring thaw. No matter; her eyesight is perfect, and she wants to see the pickup long before it registers on the security cameras. The hire car that brought her here is tucked out of the way behind one of the barns.

Funny the way things work out. The man who killed her mother grew up here along with his brothers. As far as she's concerned, they shared his guilt. Their mother probably sat in this chair, still grieving for Earl and watching for Buck coming home from jail to the rest of his life. Now it's another day, another homecoming, but a different welcome.

The blanket of cloud seems to be sinking, and the grey light is fading fast. There will be more snow before the night is out, that's for sure. She bends down to pick up the mug of lukewarm coffee, and when she looks back at the landscape, a pinprick of light is moving down the track towards the house. Even through the gloom, she makes out the shape of the truck; time to go downstairs and get ready. There won't be any dramatics, no explanatory monologues to give him time to plan an escape. This is real life, not entertainment.

The pickup's engine noise fades to silence and the front door opens. No voices, which is good, even though she hadn't expected him to be with anyone. She knows the pattern of his life. Not that she's squeamish, but she is efficient. There's no need to kill any more than necessary and she tries to be an ethical executioner. It's a matter of pride.

She already knows he'll come straight into the kitchen, the warmest room, and she waits in the corner opposite the door, cradling one of the older AKs that she liberated when she left the cult. There are no neighbours out here to complain about the noise.

The gamble pays off, not that she had any doubts. The door opens and there he is, the first time she's seen him in the flesh since she watched him as he discussed her fate by the back of the truck where she was lying bound and gagged. He looks thinner than his on-screen images showed, and the grey skin of his face hangs loose, as if it's barely attached to the underlying flesh. He's older and worn. *Pig ugly*, her mother would have called him in the

British accent she never lost. But the puckered scar on his cheek is as livid as if it's fresh, and one eye droops so badly now she doubts he can see much with it. Enough to see her, though.

'What the fuck!'

'Stay right there, Buck. I mean it.' She keeps her voice calm and level, and waves the AK as a reinforcement. 'I heard you been looking for me so I thought I'd help you out, seeing as how you've been so crap at it. Your brother fared better, not that it did him much good. Two down, one to go.'

She should have finished him by now the way she planned, but maybe there is something to be said for drama after all. Who doesn't like to take the stage once in a while?

Buck takes a couple of steps into the room but is still ten feet or more away on the other side of the large kitchen table. His eyes flick from side to side like the cornered animal he's become. 'Whadya want, bitch?' he says, with a tremor in his voice. 'You ain't gonna make it out of here. My guys are on the way.'

She quite likes threats, even clichés, she's always found them calming. Someone who threatens isn't the one in control. 'Your guys?' she says. 'They all jumped ship after Ches disappeared and they realised you'd be running things alone. Been watching you, Buck, living your lonely life. No family, no crew. Not exactly a born leader, are you?'

She watches him shifting from one foot to another, not sure what to do. 'You remember Earl?' she says. 'That shit-head brother of yours killed my mother. What was I supposed to do, give him a fucking prize? I was within my rights to end him, what you might call restorative justice.'

She pauses, aware of his smell of tobacco and whiskey and sweat. 'You had a choice, you and Ches. You should have accepted what happened and let it go, an eye for an eye. You know how that works. I only did what I had to do.' She shrugs. 'I would say it was quick for Ches, but in truth it wasn't. I don't reckon you would have given me an easy ride if I hadn't got away. You were even crap at kidnapping me; bet your Ma was pissed.'

He's sweating harder, giving his face a satin sheen. If I were him, she thinks, I'd throw myself onto the ground under the table and try to use it as a shield. Might work, might not, but worth a try. She watches as he assesses the possibility, and as he tenses his body to move she squeezes the trigger, remembering to steady herself for the recoil. The burst catches him at the start of his dive and he collapses in a cloud of splinters from the edge of the table, blood pooling around him. Part of his face has been shot away, including the lazy eye. Her ears are ringing as she moves forwards carefully, skirting around the table, but there's no way that mess of flesh and bone is getting up again.

She wipes the gun clean even though she's worn thin latex gloves every time she handled it. No hostages to fortune. It can stay here; all the weapons used by the Disciples are untraceable. But it's time to move; she doesn't want to take any more risks than necessary.

She stops for a moment by the kitchen door and looks back at Buck's body. After so many years, this chapter is finished, and a debt has finally been paid. In full. She's often wondered if killing Buck would leave her with a sense of loss; the burn for vengeance has been a powerful motivator. But now that she has the freedom to move on, all she feels is satisfaction. With the surrogate gone, she can move on to the real thing.

SHE STILL HAS a family to find and one last obligation to play judge, jury and - perhaps - executioner. There's been little to go on, just the photo of her mother and a man on a beach. And a date, the year before she was born. She's been putting it off until all the other obstructions were out of the way, but now the Lekkers are gone it's time to do some digging; the UK keeps records of births, deaths and marriages online. With a bit of luck she'll be able to discover what disaster made her happy, pretty young mother take a two-year-old over four thousand miles away to a shithole in Canada, forced to earn their food and rent on her back for creeps like Earl Lekker. Someone is to blame, and she's going to make someone pay, even if the original perpetrator is gone after all these years. What does the bible say about visiting iniquity onto the third or fourth generation? Religion might be for fools, but its words work for her.

CHAPTER ELEVEN

The Coco Pops were cornflakes and a mug of coffee was cooling by the side of the bowl. 'I usually take a thermos,' said Prof, 'don't exactly get invited in for a cuppa and a hobnob. There was this woman, mind you, asked if I'd take the kids as well, and the husband. Lovely place, it was. Who would have guessed? You always know something is wrong, though, when they don't do their roots.'

Quincey had vaguely registered the van yesterday, parked a couple of doors down the street. Off-white, with a streak of rust all along the off-side panels.

'It takes them in different ways,' said the Prof as Quincey searched in vain for a seat belt. 'Third time I went out, this guy keyed the van. Little chap, he was, like a pocket Mussolini. Called me a fascist, which is ironic. I should have had it fixed but you know how it is, the little tasks get away from you. I've always thought that's what a wife is for, a combination of outsourced memory, alarm clock and cattle prod. Do this, do that, I didn't hear the lawnmower dear. I tried it once; as experiments go I have to say that it failed to produce the expected results. She ended up joining Médecins Sans Frontières, mucks around in deserts now.'

They joined a queue of traffic on the Westway; a light drizzle misted the windscreen and Prof turned on the wipers, which juddered backwards and forwards, adding an arc of bird shit to Quincey's view. 'Good thing I met you. Pash used to help me out on the bigger jobs, and after his little mishap Big Mary was usually game for a laugh, but she got a hernia trying to carry a Smeg fridge by herself. I told her to check if they'd emptied it.'

THEY PULLED up behind a red Vauxhall Corsa on a wide, leafy street in Ealing. 'Should be simple, this one,' said the Prof, checking something on his phone. 'A plasma telly, 50 inch. You'd think they'd moderate their expectations if money was tight, but everyone has rights these days, no responsibilities. They think they can have whatever they want, regardless. Take sofas. Once upon a time they were like overgrown armchairs, these days everyone has leather corner units with motorised foot supports. You have any idea how heavy those things are? I hate sofas.' He led the way to the front door and pressed the bell. 'Let me do the talking. You just stand there looking vaguely menacing, which I admit probably doesn't come naturally, but do your best. A scowl might help get you in the mood.'

The door was opened by woman who, Quincey guessed, was probably in her late thirties. The papoose across her front was overflowing with baby and another child was jammed, feet first, under her left armpit. An off-white poodle trotted out from the hallway and sat in front of Quincey, staring up at him with an unreadable expectation.

'Fucking great,' said the woman. 'What is it this time – washing machine? Cooker? Go on, take the fucking lot. What do I care? I told them, give me another week or two and I'll get straight, but do they listen? No, they send round bastards like you to take the food out of my children's mouths.'

'We've come for the TV, my love,' said Prof. 'Six months with no payment, it says here. Let us in, there's a good girl, and we'll be gone before you know it.'

'Don't you fucking good girl me.' But she backed away and Quincey followed Prof down the hallway towards the sound.

Every surface on the corner unit leather sofa was covered with piles of un-ironed laundry, and the small poodle overtook them to lay claim to a half-eaten sausage in his bed, a large cardboard box lined with what looked to Quincey like old pairs of knickers. The TV perched on an empty plastic storage box, the lid bowed under the weight, and as the Prof pulled out the plug the sound of the cartoon was replaced by a wailing from one of the piles of clothing where another infant was nesting amongst the all-in-ones of its younger siblings.

This could have been his life; nappies and baby-sick and plastic toys and the pervasive odour of a life without hope. Although it would never have been his but his woman's, whoever she was. Robyn had opted out early, and as for Cath... They had been at a party in the days when she wasn't ashamed to be seen with him and someone in her chambers had announced that she was pregnant. *'Don't get any ideas,'* Cath had said in the taxi on the way home. *'If you think I'm letting some parasite feed on me from the inside then think again. Children are nothing more than socially acceptable vampires. Maybe when they find a way to implant wombs in men, then we can talk.'*

He helped to carry the TV out to the van, and the Prof gave him a clipboard. 'Get her signature if you can manage it without personal injury. Keeps the paperwork tidy but don't worry if not, no-one ever checks.'

The front door was still open and Quincey found her on the sofa, staring at the gap where the TV had been.

'He bought me that as a present,' she said. 'Guilt, I suppose. Week later he was off with someone he met at a sales conference in Basildon. It wasn't even as if she was younger than me - must have been good in bed, whatever that is. I suppose if you don't know what it means, you're not any good. God knows I did my best by him, the bastard.' She found a tissue stuffed into the papoose and wiped the tears from her cheeks. 'He said he'd see us right but after the first payment - late, of course - nothing. He never answers his mobile, the company says he got another job but they don't know where. If he wants to shit on me, fine, but these are his kids, you'd think he'd care about them. I always assumed we could afford this sort of life but it was all done on tick, not that he told me. And now I watch my world being disman-tled around me; take lumps of my flesh, why don't you? No-one cares - what will we do when all the rooms are empty?'

She signed the paper and passed back the clipboard. 'Do you enjoy doing this, destroying people? A man like you, surely you could find something more honourable?'

At the gate he turned to see her and the poodle, watching him from the front door. Honour was a concept that had never troubled his thoughts; he wasn't even sure if he knew what it meant. But running away, no matter what you called it, he was pretty sure that didn't count.

· · ·

HE SPENT the afternoon experiencing smartphone withdrawal symptoms. It was one thing to start a new life, another to realise that he was isolated in a city of strangers. Even Cath's voice would be welcome now.

The Prof asked him out again that evening, back to The Toad for a drink with a couple of people from the band. 'Not Rupert, he's singing in the chorus at ENO tonight. I think it involves dressing as a tramp, de rigeur for opera these days, so I'm told. I can just about cope with Les Mis when I have to seem caring, more of a Glasto man myself. Dad rock, someone called it, suppose he was right.'

In the end there were just three of them; him, the Prof and Janine, the woman who reminded him of teenage fumblings. After half an hour on the arcana of sweet spots and bending - Quincey was beginning to wonder if Freud had a point - the Prof got a text, winked and left them. 'Don't wait up matey, I'll be home with the milk floats if at all.'

Janine finished her third pint, one ahead of him, and asked if he wanted to share a curry at hers. 'We can pick it up on the way back, just stay away from the goat vindaloo cos my U-bend blocks to spite me and quite frankly, I don't have the time.'

WHILE HE SEARCHED for plates in her kitchen, she locked her mother in the back bedroom. 'Safer that way, she has a tendency to explore and usually gets lost between the bathroom and the stairs. Knows how to use her mobile, though. Three times last month she called out the fire service to rescue her from the loo, now we're blacklisted. God help us if she leaves the gas on again.'

He hadn't realised that the curry was for dessert. Holding her, first on a sofa, then on the floor, was like wrestling a Labrador puppy. Everything about her body was taut, as if all the tendons and ligaments inside had been tuned to breaking point. There was no question of him orchestrating or possessing. He was nothing more than a stage prop for her self-absorbed performance. It was almost liberating to realise that she had no expectations of him other than to be there for the heavy lifting.

She tasted, disconcertingly, of geranium.

Afterwards, over the sag bhaji and lemon pilau - cross-legged on the floor, he should take more exercise - he looked at the drape of her over-size tee shirt hiding the small breasts. Esther used to read him Leonard Cohen poetry and now he knew what was meant by the upturned bellies of fallen, breathing sparrows. There was a dissonance about her, as if she had slipped over from another reality and hadn't quite mastered the rules of this one.

She finished the last forkful of rice and leaned back against the sofa. 'Thanks for that, wasn't talking about the food. It was a bad day today; sometimes sex is the only thing that helps. That and alcohol. I stay off the weed; I need to be anchored, not set afloat.' She rearranged the tee shirt with a modesty that seemed a little late, and her smile was old porcelain.

'Help with what,' he said, to show he was listening.

She shrugged. 'In your life, when you eat food, you smell and taste it. When music plays, you hear it. In my life it's different. I hear smells, like bird songs in my head, but usually out of tune and full of discords. And I don't just hear sounds, I see them. On good days it's no more than a sense of colour, but when it's bad...' A small tear glittered in the corner of her eye. 'When I play in the band, it's like throwing myself into an ocean.'

He wondered if he should touch her or take her hand.

'It's called synaesthesia,' she said. 'Great name, huh? And mine has to be one of the rarer kinds. This doctor, he said "Now you have a diagnosis you'll feel so much better." I said, your voice is still yellow pebbles, what's changed? I think he felt unappreciated, I felt betrayed.'

'But doesn't that just make every experience richer?' he said.

'You kidding? I tried to kill myself when I was fourteen. Some days I was completely trapped in this web of colour, I could barely move. It's like everything is connected and there are no spaces in the world. No isolation. Silos, I want silos, somewhere to hide where I can be alone. Nothing to see, nothing to hear, nothing to feel.' She looked up at him. 'Could you get me some water? I don't want to move yet.'

She held the glass in both hands, like a child learning to drink. 'I used to go to Sunday School, United Reform. Mum thought it would be less intimidating than a high church. You'd think they'd realise; religion, intimidating? Something wrong there. But in those days I didn't question it. I even wanted to be a nun - Sister Act has a lot to answer for. They told us that God was everywhere, in everything, and in my mind he was like a rainbow of music.' She paused for a moment and took another sip. 'It used to be under control. Then one day I woke up and I realised that there was no God, that if he had ever existed, now he was gone. I sometimes think, if I could find belief again, maybe my life would go back to normal, but belief is an act of faith and I have none. Why should I? What loving God would do this to me?'

. . .

SHE SAID he could sleep on the sofa if he wanted to stay, but at that moment there was a wavering shriek from the stairs. 'Damn, but she's good,' said Janine. 'Picked the lock again. I'll have to fit a bolt.'

THE PROF HAD EITHER NEVER COME HOME or already left by the time Quincey surfaced the next day. There had been no talk of rent or contribution to the food, and as the cornflakes were down to the last crumbs and the coffee jar was empty, he decided to go hunting for provisions at the yam shop near The Toad.

On the other hand... The sky was clearer than it had been for days, with just a few clouds like the cotton wool balls Esther kept in a jar in the bathroom. Used to keep.

The shop could wait. He began to walk, forcing his steps so that he was out of breath, almost running. He'd borrowed a hooded sweatshirt from one of the drawers in his room and some navy sweatpants, and done the chair balancing act again; with the stubble he could almost persuade himself that he was unrecognisable.

This wasn't a part of town that he knew; Jennifer had lived in North London since she married and moved away from Kilvercombe, and his visits to her had been rare enough even after she took on Poppy. He'd made a couple of trips to meet Cath at her chambers in Middle Temple, but she hadn't been keen; cramping her style, he'd always thought.

The streets smelled of spice; what would it be like in Janine's head, with no boundaries between the senses?

The scale was increasing, the buildings growing. Eventually he reached a main road with a park on the other side. Such an expanse in the middle of a city; Hyde Park? Kensington Gardens? He knew the names but realised that he was a little hazy on the locations. He dodged the traffic and made his way through the iron gates towards a marble portico at the end of a formal stretch of water. Urns and fountains always reminded him of his honeymoon in Naples; Cath's choice, she had a thing for volcanoes, he'd discovered. He'd thought she might have mentioned it before, but even then he was realising that Cath treated personal information as if it were her heart's blood.

He sat on an empty bench, looking out across the water as a cluster of bright African women swayed past without so much as a glance. Although the sun was out, a cool breeze skewed the jets from the fountain and he pulled up the hood.

He noticed a woman walking quickly towards him from the other end of the lake. Her urgency made him think she was about to accost him but her eyes were unfocussed, eyes, he noticed, that were the same deep blue as her long, tailored coat. As she passed the bench she stumbled, tried to right herself and then fell to the ground, sprawled like a supplicant in front of an altar. Her shopping bag - Waitrose, reusable, the sort Cath preferred - knocked against his leg. Whatever she had in there was heavy; he'd have a bruise on his calf by morning. He reached down to help her up, but she pulled away from him as if he were contagious; there was just a moment where she looked directly at him, those eyes again, and then hurried on.

She slowed as she reached the portico and stopped under the middle arch, a Madonna against the white marble. For a moment her shoulders seemed to droop, as if the weight of her jacket was too heavy for her body to bear. Then she turned and faced back towards him, looked around, reached into the shopping bag at her feet and spread some sort of sheet on the ground. She smoothed it carefully, tweaking the edges as if making a bed, and then positioned herself dead centre. Street theatre, perhaps? If so she wouldn't have much of an audience.

She stood with her eyes closed and her arms hanging loose, as if waiting for something. A minute passed, two, and then she reached into the bag at her feet and pulled out a large green plastic bottle. But instead of drinking, she unscrewed the cap and doused herself in the liquid, shaking it over her head and arms and splashing it on her chest. If this was meant to be entertainment, thought Quincey, it needed more work before she was ready for the big time. But that wasn't what made him feel uneasy; there was something about her actions that made him think of ritual cleansing.

He was a couple of hundred yards away, but the faint sound of her voice carried on the breeze; singing? No, it was more like a chant or a prayer. And now he caught the perfume of the petrol, sweet and almost exotic.

He hadn't been conscious of getting to his feet, but now he was standing, watching the woman as she anointed herself. No-one else had noticed. A man and a dog at the far end of the water were jogging together into the distance. The Africans were nothing more than a flicker of colour at the edge of the park.

Without any conscious thought he began to run towards her, an unfamiliar feeling, wondering if he should shout at her to stop and wondering if it would make any difference. She was clicking something, a cigarette lighter that kept blowing out in the wind; another fifty yards, twenty, ten. And then the breeze dropped, the lighter caught and suddenly tendrils of flame were dancing across her, almost teasing, appearing and disappearing as if not sure whether to bother. But then they made up their mind, and the blue of her coat turned to orange as she became a pillar of fire.

He pulled the sweatshirt off as he ran the final few yards with some inchoate notion of using it as a shield while he rolled her over and put out the flames, but already the heat was too intense as he flapped ineffectively and he realised that - semper idem - he was of no consequence.

By now she had fallen to her knees, almost as if she were willing herself to melt. Why was she so silent, no more than a dark shadow inside the flames? He heard himself shout something, some meaningless denial, and for a moment the shadow seemed to lift its head as if to look at him, the last person she would see. A few sparks landed on his bare arms and chest, an acupuncture of heat, and even the air he breathed seemed to be on fire.

He had never thought death could take so long but at last she was still and now he was the one on his knees, sobbing, his tears blurring the charred, fœtal shape smouldering on the ground in front of him.

'Holy shit. You alright, mate?' A few feet away a small crowd had materialised - where had they all been a few moments ago? - and half of them were pointing mobile phones towards him. 'This'll go viral, no worries,' said a man at the front. 'You'll be a fuckin' hero.'

Quincey felt for his own phone, forgetting that he'd thrown it away, and winced with pain; both hands were red and sore. 'Did anyone call the fire brigade or an ambulance?' he asked, trying to catch his breath.

'Woulda missed it all.' The man again, looking round at the others for support. 'Citizen journalist, me, gotta stay detached. You any idea how many hits this'll get?'

'For Christ's sake...'

Quincey stopped at the touch of a hand on his shoulder. 'I called one, they're on their way for what it's worth. And the police.' The woman took off her jacket, perfumed with the scent of roses, and put it around his shoulders. 'Sorry, not quite your style but you're shivering. It's the shock, the blood vessels in the skin shut down. And you probably need to get those hands seen to although it looks like you were lucky, not too much damage.' She glanced over at the smouldering figure on the ground, then turned back to Quincey. 'No, don't try to get up, not yet. As for her, best wait for the medics, there's nothing more you can do for her now.' She squatted in front of him, the stubble of her hair dyed pink, her left eyebrow sequinned with gold piercings. 'So this is what a hero looks like,' she said, 'who would have guessed? You tried, that's what counts. More than that bunch of losers. And remember, whatever caused her to do that it was her choice. Judging other people never seems to work out well.'

For a moment Quincey thought she was going to touch him again, but she bounced back to her feet - expensive trainers, matching her hair - and looked down at him. 'I'm late already or I'd stay, sorry. You did a good thing.'

'But your jacket...'

'Never suited me anyway. Maybe it will fit Lois.'

'Lois?'

'I have to run - sorry the woman didn't make it. And remember to take care of yourself, Superman.'

HE TOLD the policewoman that his name was Dirk Gently and gave an address that Jennifer had lived in years ago. No, he didn't know the woman who tried to turn herself into a torch. No, he'd never seen her before. No, he had no idea as to her motives.

A paramedic came for him then, after helping to load the body into an ambulance. 'You're lucky you didn't get any closer, if you can call it luck. Superficial burns, these, but you should come in with us and have them checked.'

'What about her?'

'Do you need to ask? Bad way to go, if you ask me. You have to hope that she asphyxiated quickly. Did you know, when people were burned at the stake the richer ones would pay the executioner to strangle them first? Damn sight better than burning. So why would someone deliberately torch herself? If you want to kill yourself, there are easier ways to go; they never think about who has to clean up the mess afterwards.'

HE DECLINED the offer of hospital, not wanting the attention. The sweatshirt smelled of smoke, with small holes where sparks had burned their way through - he'd never go near a bonfire again - and he dumped it in the nearest waste bin. The jacket was tight under the arms but black and relatively un-tailored, good enough to get him back to his room without too many glances. He felt in the pockets; a crumpled tissue in one, a lipstick in the other. He pulled off the gold cap, turned the base and drew a glittering pink streak on his wrist. His skin had lost sensation, the sounds of traffic were muffled.

This body wasn't his.

At the yam shop he picked up a loaf, butter and some milk, added a jar of Marmite on a whim, didn't remember the cornflakes until he got back to the apartment. There was still no sign of Prof and he sat in front of the small TV in what passed for a living room, dripping melted butter from the slices of toast. He'd never eaten a loaf in one sitting before. Cath insisted on seeds and worthiness, he'd grown up with Mother's Pride. You knew where you were with white sliced.

He found a news programme reporting something about cuts to the health service, barely listening until a picture came up of the park he'd been in earlier. He recognised the pavilion, now cordoned off with police tape, with a dark shadow on the ground where the burning body had fallen. Ashes to ashes. Not a body; a person, a woman, his second death in as many weeks. Tomorrow, unbelievably, it would be exactly a fortnight since he had seen Esther for the last time; both alive - warm and in his arms, murmuring his name with what he had imagined was love - and dead. Two women who had chosen him as the witness to their deaths; what bad karma had led him to that fate?

The scene shifted. For a moment he feared it would be footage of the flames but it was no more than a zoomed-in image of a man kneeling on the ground, bare-chested, looking at something out of shot and then turning to the camera, his face streaked as if from some Iron John initiation ceremony. How could he have ever thought that no-one would recognise him? Even with the unkempt hair and Z-list stubble, even without a suit, there was no doubt that he was looking at himself.

And now the gods were laughing at him; no, pissing all over him again. The next item was a picture of Esther, younger than he remembered, from an image he'd never seen. *'The police are keeping an open mind on the cause of death,'* said the newsreader. *'Another man was seen in the vicinity of her flat on the evening she died, the authorities are appealing for him to come forward.'*

Anyone could have seen him that night and given a description to the police. Not that it mattered. With no suicide note, it was a murder investigation and someone was toying with him. Someone knew exactly who he was.

His hand felt as if it were still in a fire, but in spite of the pain he closed his eyes, suddenly overwhelmed by exhaustion. He fell asleep where he sat, dreaming of the sea.

HE DIDN'T WAKE until the sound from the TV disappeared. He ached everywhere; the numbness had been replaced by a hyper-sensitivity as if the skin had been peeled from his flesh. While he was asleep, his eyes had seeped and the lids were gummed together; it was an effort to force them open.

Prof was watching from the other side of the room. 'I thought I'd had a hard night! I might be getting too old for these carry-ons, I really should stick to women my own age. They may be martyrs to gravity, but they have more realistic expectations. As for you, my friend, you really look like shit. Nice jacket, by the way, not sure it's your colour. Could move up a size, perhaps? And what the fuck happened to your hands?'

Quincey forced himself upright on the sofa, feeling as if he'd drunk a bottle of Bells in one session. His hands were swollen and red, the left not so bad, the right streaked and stained dark; perhaps, he thought, the marks were part of her, molecules of her body vaporised and condensed on his skin, fused to his body.

'If you're going to puke,' said Prof, 'I'd rather you used the bathroom.'

· · ·

At least he could hold a mug of coffee; the caffeine hit was like the coke he'd sampled in the Toad. He stared at the surface of the kitchen table, seeing figures in the abstract patterns of the yellow melamine and listening to Prof bustling around. He didn't trust his voice, not yet.

'You want pizza?' asked Prof. 'There's more than enough for two, thin base Margherita from Tesco with my own toppings. Sliced salami, Stilton, couple of eggs, baked beans. I tried Spam once, not a success. Trying to reach my inner child, but not sure he's still there. Probably a good thing, given my childhood.'

Death, Quincey decided, makes you hungry. As long as it's not your own.

After supper he sat in the living room watching something forensic on the TV, while Prof hunched over an old laptop that was as thick as a brick. The paracetamol had kicked in and Quincey felt as if his hands belonged to him again. He knew he should change out of the sweat pants but didn't have the energy; it had taken a while before he had realised why the smell of burning was following him around. Had Prof noticed? And would it matter?

'Shit, did you see this? I wondered what was going on in the park, there were police cars all over the shop. Thought it might be a bomb or something, but this...' Prof stared at the computer screen for a few more moments and then sat back slowly and looked across. 'You should have said something, you dumb bastard, unless you're gonna tell me you got a mad twin out there.'

'Said what?'

Prof brought over the laptop and replayed a YouTube video; the unexpurgated version, blurred and jerky cinéma vérité. By the time the clip started the woman was already alight but still standing, still recognisable. And there he was, coming into the picture like a half-naked wild man, dancing around her, darting in and out (had he really done that, so close, so often?) but always beaten back by the flames until both of them sank to the ground, one still flesh, the other turning to ash.

The man with the mobile had been right; over thirty thousand hits already. Suicide gone viral.

H e had lost his anchor. Or was that too grand an image, to equate himself with a ship? He was more like some rubbish thrown over the side to sink or float according to chance. One of life's rejects. He had been wrong yesterday, to have the arrogance of thinking that two women had chosen him to witness their deaths. No, he was of so little consequence that they simply didn't care if he was there, even at the climax of their lives.

The smell of burning wouldn't leave him, nor the memory of the blue eyes. Such a meaningless death. But who was he to judge meaning, how could he possibly know her motives? Her worries, her miseries, these were all gone. Her eternity had ended. And so had Esther's. It took him half the night to work out that the nagging emotion, the hollowness in his chest, was envy.

THE BIKE WAS BACK. He'd forced himself to leave the flat after turning down Prof's offer of another day of repossessions and there it was, no mistaking those Shimano shifters, padlocked to the railings. It couldn't have been there for long or someone would have taken it. Although people were walking by in tee shirts, he found himself shivering.

So. On the basis that he hadn't become the object of desire for a sentient machine with attachment issues, his stalker had already found him. How long had it been? Five days, six, since the last note? Nothing more than a respite to lull him into a sense of false security.

It must have been the viral video. Start a second life, why don't you, change identity... and then show the world exactly where you are on YouTube. Jennifer had been right. Even the air he breathed could be put to better use by someone else.

Now what? Prof's flat was no longer safe, so he decided to go out and take the bike with him. He leafed through a dog-eared A-Z from a shelf in the kitchen and traced out his steps from yesterday, back to Hyde Park. The shivering hadn't stopped; more of a trembling, he decided, probably coming down with summer flu. That was all he needed.

THE POLICE TAPE had gone from the pavilion, but it would take longer for the breath of ashes to fade from the air. His hands itched as if ants were crawling over them and he wished he was back in the beach hut, watching the waves and coveting the horizon. How many voicemails were waiting for delivery to his crushed mobile, how many emails waiting to tumble onto a screen? He had a vague recollection of a tribunal hearing date; this week, next? It had all seemed so important at the time, but now it was in another life, the problems of another person.

He couldn't help himself, like a criminal drawn back to

the scene of a crime. He wheeled the bike to the bench where he'd sat yesterday, propped it against the armrest and then sat facing the marble portico. If only she would come this way again; he wouldn't let her slip from his grasp this time, he'd change the course of her history. Save her, even if she didn't want to be saved. Save himself.

A man - chinos, pale linen jacket, leather backpack - approached the pavilion from the main entrance to the park. He reached the darkened patch on the ground, sank to his knees, and then curled up on his side like an unborn child. After a while a passing woman with a pushchair stopped, went over to the man and knelt to talk to him, but he turned his head away. The woman stood and walked off, shaking her head, and after a few more moments the man gathered his body together, collected his backpack and walked towards Quincey's bench, staring at the ground.

He looked up as he drew level and stopped as if someone had slapped him.

'You were here, yesterday...' He reached out as if to take Quincey's hands but then took a step back and stared at him.

Why did other people find it so easy to cry? What should he say to this man, shrunken inside his clothes with streaks of grey on the jacket where he had stretched on the ground, and streaks of tears running into the stubble on his cheeks? What should he do?

The man sat beside him, talking to the ground. 'She was my wife, Natalie, we got married five years ago. We'd been trying for a baby - she was desperate - and then four months ago she told me she was pregnant. She was so happy, we both were.' He paused, shaking his head slowly. 'Three days ago, she found some WhatsApps on my phone. I'd been seeing someone; me and Nat went through a tough time when we were trying for the baby. But as soon as she got pregnant I knocked it on the head, I swear. I even bought her a new summer jacket, she'd had her eye on it for a while. Blue, like her eyes. Call it guilt, maybe. When she found the messages I swore it was all over, I promised, but she completely lost it. I didn't know what else to do. Later that evening I thought she'd calmed down but then she said something was wrong, that she had a pain. The next day, she had a miscarriage.'

He found a soft pack of Gauloises in his jacket, slightly crushed, and offered one to Quincey. 'You tried to help her, I watched it on Sky News. It's not your fault you couldn't stop her. I'm the one that killed her.'

Quincey watched as the man walked away without looking back. Now he'd failed yet another person. He might not have killed Natalie, but he sure as hell didn't save her.

FIVE MINUTES LATER, a man in shorts and tee shirt stopped in front of him and lit a rollup; at the second click of the lighter, with no warning, Quincey's stomach spasmed, and he threw up on the ground, spattering the man's flip-flops.

'Jesus mate, if you can't hold your fuckin' drink...'

Before he could apologise, the man strode away, swearing under his breath.

He was glad of the bike now. The muscles in his legs had gone rogue and he wasn't sure he could trust them, so he walked slowly, balanced against the machine, soothed by the rhythm of the wheels and machinery, oiled and self-satisfied. Post-traumatic shock, that's all it was. Why was he surprised? He only wished the woman in blue had chosen someone else as her witness.

He reached the southern edge of the park. There was life

ahead, buses rocking along a main road carrying people with purposes. Kensington? Knightsbridge? Somewhere like that, he should have brought the A-Z. He stopped walking, letting the bike lean against his body. His arms were trembling as if he had been pushing a heavy weight for too long and he stared at the ground, hoping that it would stop ebbing and flowing long enough for him to get his bearings. Deep breaths.

'You realise you look like shit in a microwave.'

He was conscious of someone's shadow nudging his, a horizontal silhouette. The voice was familiar and he recognised the smooth delivery of insult. He forced himself to look up at her hair, haloed by the sun. 'Dr Dust...'

'I'm beginning to wonder if you're stalking me,' she said. 'And have you been sleeping rough? It's a miracle no-one made off with your bike. By the way, I think it best that we forget that conversation at your beach hut the other day.' She reached out to touch the handlebars. 'I had a bike once – borrowed, actually. The landlord left it in the hallway of the flat I was renting when I was studying for my doctorate. I used to ride it along the towpath in summer and stop at a pub for a drink; happy days. And then one day I collapsed and my life changed forever; no more bike rides for me.'

She paused, a change of mood. 'I guess the lawyer gig wasn't working out for you. Can't say I'm surprised. If I'm honest, lawyers need to be less... flaky. Yes, that's the word I'm looking for. No offence, I'd be appalling as a hairdresser. Horses for courses, as they say.'

Some sort of response was called for, but he couldn't think of anything worthwhile to say.

'I was going to find somewhere to sit down,' she said,

'and have something to drink. Join me? You look like you could do with a little something before you fall over.'

THEY FOUND an Italian café with a couple of empty seats on the pavement, and he propped the bike against a lamp post. Was this the same woman who had walked barefoot across the beach, talked with pain of her lost love and acted like a human?

'I can't stay too long,' said Joanna. 'I'm giving a paper at a conference this afternoon, Imperial College, just down the road. A little project I've been working on with a couple of people from Melbourne, looking at the way the identities of people change during the course of their careers.'

He had forgotten the way she fixed him with her eyes, like a mongoose with a snake.

'Please don't yawn, Quincey, people have crossed continents to hear what I have to say. Step changes, proximate causes, psychological polymorphism, the merging and differentiating of identities over time. We see the effects, but what are the causes? Everything has a cause outside ourselves, including our motivations for change. Or do you still believe in free will? Yes, I suppose you do.'

Right now he didn't believe in anything, other than the fact that he had barely understood anything she was saying and that meeting Dr Joanna Dust here, in London, felt like a coincidence too far. He could almost hear the gentle click of pieces falling into place.

She was clever, no doubt about that, especially with that accusation that he was the stalker. Had she thought he wouldn't see the links? Probably, given that she seemed to regard him as somewhere between an amoeba and the missing link on the evolutionary scale. Keep bashing those rocks, Quincey.

All this time he had thought Marcus was responsible for the notes and his disappearing bike, but now he was beginning to doubt. So many suppositions, so little evidence. Esther's body was a fact, so was the arrest of Marcus, so were the notes, so was his errant bike. But all the rest was his own narrative spun from nothing. When he'd withdrawn all his money, the bank manager had said that knowledge was true justified belief. But he didn't know what he believed anymore, or how to justify it, or whether any of it was true.

Perhaps, all along, he'd been looking in the wrong place and at the wrong person. Joanna worked at the same University as Marcus, the same University where Esther had been studying - click - and had she not approached him to act for her not long before Esther died? Click. Perhaps she had secretly been Esther's lover; women were so much more flexible about these things and now he knew that Joanna Dust had form. Or was this a question of unrequited love? Esther disposed of for her rejection of Joanna's advances and Marcus unsuccessfully framed for her death. And now perhaps the spurned academic was stalking him and waiting for the right moment to lunge forward and deliver the fatal bite of death. Why else had she employed him, appeared on the beach and turned up in the park today? And now this psychotic woman was sitting opposite him, smiling.

He tried to ignore the buzzing in his ears, as if he were surrounded by a swarm of bees. 'What happened about your case?' he asked, playing for time. 'I know things didn't work out with me, but...'

'"Didn't work out with me," what an interesting locution. As if you were the pivot on which the entire edifice would swing like a well-oiled door. No Quincey, it didn't work out with you, so I found myself a proper lawyer. She drafted a couple of letters pointing out the paucity of the University's defence, and I sent them to the slime in HR who dignify themselves with ridiculous job titles while they carry out petty battles against their intellectual superiors. It was almost amusing.'

'How did they react?'

'They caved, Quincey, they crumbled like battlements made of sand. One of them has been reassigned as something like Director of Car Park Spaces, and I have been given the accommodations that are my due. A little pressure applied at the right spot can work wonders, especially when it's justified.'

She checked her watch, drained her glass of water and stood. 'It's later than I thought. Sorry we didn't have much chance to talk. Whatever's going on for you, Quincey, I hope you sort it out.

HE SAT up until midnight but there was still no sign of Prof, even though the van was parked outside. The next morning Quincey checked the second bedroom and although the bed was unmade, there was a sense of abandonment about the space, dust in the air. Heaviness.

Quincey circled the laptop on the table as if it were contagious and then made coffee and toast. He ate his supper in front of the TV and checked the news channels for any more items about the woman in blue but she was already forgotten, her molecules dissipating in the air. Then he opened up the laptop but shut it again immediately, and tried to clean a smear of butter from the lid. He had a floating feeling, as if gravity had decided that he wasn't worth the effort.

He turned back to the laptop – no password, thank god – and within a couple of minutes he found the conference that Dr Dust had talked about; so she had been telling the truth. Dr Joanna J Dust; why hadn't he known about the second J, what did it stand for? JJ, he'd like to know someone he could call JJ.

Perhaps the timings of their encounters were coincidences after all and not a conspiracy, but he was finding it increasingly difficult to know what was real and what was a product of his increasingly fragile imagination. This was what happened when you uprooted yourself; now he belonged nowhere, to no-one. But his old life was still out there, even if he'd given it the slip. He could look through the virtual windows and see what was happening. A few more clicks and he was scanning his email, screen after screen of unread messages. His heart raced as the letters in the words rearranged themselves like wanton insects.

And there, at the top of the screen, was the latest message sent this morning. He recognised the sender even through the gavottes of the alphabet; Cath, who would communicate digitally even when they were in the same house. He forced himself to concentrate, but even when he was sure that the letters and words were in the right order the message still made little sense. *Is this your idea of a joke,* she asked, *what have you done to the front garden?*

Soon after they moved into the house, she found a book on Japanese garden design and employed someone who'd won an award at Chelsea for his rocks and gravel. The man allowed one dwarf maple as the sole representative of organic life, and the Duchesses were instructed with diagrams of how to rake patterns in the paths.

He opened the attachment to the message, and for a moment he thought he was looking at a Flanders field where the garden used to be; poppies, hundreds of them, a lake of red where once there was Zen. He stared at the image, but something didn't seem right. Of course, there were barely any stems. The flower heads were almost at ground level. It must have taken ages to plant those hundreds of plastic poppies in the gravel. And Cath thought it was him.

One thing was sure, it couldn't have been Joanna unless her chronic fatigue was a mere stratagem, not with all that kneeling and bending, and she had been here yesterday, in London. But why go to all the trouble of planting plastic flowers at the house when his stalker knew he wasn't living there?

It was a warning, of course - poppies - Poppy. Whoever was torturing him knew about his discarded, hidden little girl. Poppies to Cath; that was the threat, to tell his wife about his daughter.

JENNIFER ANSWERED on the first ring. 'Where the fuck are you, Quincey? Did you know Robyn was going to do this?'

Jennifer swearing was not a good sign. The sweat seeping from his armpits gave off the sweet smell of decomposing hay.

'She came here. I should have known something was wrong, coming into my house dressed like a drug dealer. I always said she was strange, Quincey, but would you listen? She said she wanted to discuss Poppy's future but I said you should be there too, not that you would have been much use.' The words dissolved into sobs that were hard to catch behind the sound of a poorly silenced motorbike outside.

Jennifer collected herself. 'I should have realised when she asked for another cup of tea. I heard the front door close while I was in the kitchen. At first I thought, why is Fenton home so soon, and then I heard the silence. All Poppy's toys are here, Quincey, and her clothes; what will she wear?'

'Couldn't you have stopped her?'

'You think I didn't try? By the time I got to the front gate, the car was halfway down the road.'

'Why didn't you call the police?'

'And said what, that Poppy's mother had taken her? She has every right, although the way she looks you have to wonder. We should have done the proper thing, I said at the time, not gone all hugger mugger just so that you could keep your little secret from your wife. Or if you had stepped up, Quincey, been some sort of father.'

'Did she say where she's living now?'

'From the smell of sheep shit I assume it's the same place, that commune in Wales. What will you do?'

For the first time in weeks, all doubt had evaporated, and he felt a sense of relief. He had a plan at last, a reason to act. It wasn't as if Robyn had hidden herself. Carningli Collective, that was the place she'd come from when her life and his had intersected for a few months.

He went back to the flat and checked their Facebook page. Even from the photos it seemed distant, a windswept mountainside looking out over a sandy bay hundreds of feet below, with dark hollows under grey outcrops of Iron Age rock angled defensively against something unseen. A low-slung farmhouse, wearing a satellite dish the size of a small car, squatted near a couple of patched barns and a giant stack of wood, some of which had been cut into planks. A field with a couple of circular tents and a primaeval tractor the colour of mud. A wind turbine. It looked bleak even though the photos had been shot on a day of unbroken blue skies. Was this where his daughter had been taken, to the edge of the land? Robyn had told him once what Carningli meant; the Mountain of Angels. You'd think they would have chosen somewhere more fitting.

THIRTEEN

He wished he hadn't left his car outside Tansy's. On the other hand, the van was still outside and Prof hadn't been around for a couple of days. The man was a philosopher, he'd appreciate the exigencies of the situation. With luck, assuming that Robyn gave in gracefully, he could be back tomorrow with Poppy.

And then what; return her to Jennifer? That was the obvious choice, and yet now that he'd felt the pain of this enforced loss, he wanted to enfold her. Perhaps, against all the odds, he would be capable of keeping her safe.

But of course not. He couldn't even keep himself safe. He looked at his reflection in the mirror; there were lines on his face that he hadn't noticed before, furrows contouring the stubble like a wheat field in autumn. He'd lost weight. The borrowed jeans hung from the belt around his waist and there was a stain - he suspected vomit - on the hooded top. He sniffed at his armpit; the sweet hay was now a sour, tired smell. He couldn't go to Poppy like this.

He showered and tried a selection of Pashtun's clothes - why couldn't he wear his own? - and settled on a tee shirt in mustard yellow, decorated with a picture of a hamster toting a Kalashnikov. Trousers? A pair of combat pants with only a little sand in the pockets. He thought of shaving but couldn't face it, and running his hand over the roughness of his chin gave him a sense of comfort that he couldn't quite place until he remembered the fragment of sheet, washed until it dissolved, soft and bobbled with wear, that he would hold against his two-year-old cheek as he sucked his thumb and sat under the dining table, entangled in a grove of legs.

THE VAN KEYS were next to the kettle. He scribbled a note to forestall the police being called should Prof come home in the next twenty-four hours. Where was the man? Back with his latest lover, probably.

The engine was running before he realised he had no idea of the address of the collective. Did places like that even have an address? He went back inside and looked them up again on the laptop but all he could find was the name of the nearest town, Port Nyfer. It would have to do, surely someone there could direct him to where his daughter had been taken.

Poppy - poppies. He hadn't replied to Cath's message about the plastic flowers in the front garden and wondered what he could possibly say, other than to deny all knowledge. She wouldn't believe him, of course, but it was either that or do nothing and that was the old Quincey's way. Fresh, new Quincey did things differently; at least, that was the theory. He logged in to his webmail and one glance told him that something was awry. There was nothing more from Cath, but a message from Esther, sent yesterday evening, was impossible for two reasons. Firstly, she didn't know his personal email address, too risky even though Cath wouldn't have bothered to check. Secondly, and more importantly, Esther was dead. He couldn't swear to it but he was pretty certain there were no laptops in heaven.

A video was attached to the message; surely not more suburban poppy fields. He hesitated, the cursor hovering over the Play button. He could ignore it and pretend he had never looked. Denial, the first refuge of the coward. But that would be impossible, even with Poppy waiting for him on some bleak hillside.

The video had no sound, which was probably just as well. He played the clip twice, three times, just to be sure of what he was seeing. All sensation had left his fingers and limbs; it was as if he was nothing but a mind hidden in a body, a brain suspended in a skull. He had the same sense as the day back at home - alien word, had there ever been such a place? - when he had felt as though he were about to float to the ceiling.

He had never seen his own buttocks before; they reminded him unaccountably of an ill-fed and poorly plucked chicken on a trampoline, bouncing up and down to a rather military rhythm. That they were his buttocks didn't seem in doubt. He recognised the belt on the trousers around his ankles, and the brown shoes on which he'd used black polish once by mistake; he'd thought the end result was pleasingly edgy. Cath had simply sighed.

He could even recall when these images had been captured, the same evening that Esther had asked about going away to the Lakes. Her birthday. He was looking at history happening, an aerial view; the webcam must have been on top of the wardrobe, hidden somehow amongst the stacked and ruined masonry of shoe boxes and empty cartons. Had Esther known it was there? Surely not, she'd always been a curtains drawn and lights out girl. Not that he could blame her, now he could see himself objectively. An object. A scrawny, thrusting thing. Esther's face was visible sometimes, her eyes closed. He'd always assumed that her grimaces were passionate responses to his skills as a lover; on the video they looked like spasms of pain.

Whatever was happening to him wasn't in response to her death; this had all been planned long before. An idea was forming; get Poppy back, take her to Jennifer - where she belonged - and then confront Marcus. Just a little longer and he would meet his stalker, the man who had to know more about Esther's death than anyone.

AT LEAST THE van had a rudimentary satnav, even if it took him on a circular tour of Carmarthen and then reset itself after abandoning him in a hospital car park on the outskirts of the town. He found the right road, eventually; right enough, at least, heading west and following the sun. Perhaps that's why migrations always flow that way, he thought, trying to avoid the darkness. Trying to stay alive.

He was driving back in time. The main roads had long since been left behind and he followed the course of a small river lined with woods that seemed ancient, stunted and gnarled as if the growth of every cell had been a grudging decision to carry on for one more day with no guarantee about tomorrow. He imagined the atmosphere outside as a thick gaseous soup through which the branches and twigs forced their way. Would he even be able to breathe?

But when he pulled up by the Post Office in Port Nyfer and unfolded himself, the air was thin and sharp and filled with the complaints of seagulls. This wasn't what he had expected; a short street pointing up the hill to a half-restored castle; a worthy-looking café, a pharmacy, a Spar. No sign of the sea.

The Post Office cum gift shop was unlit, the door locked. He wandered up to the Spar; the cashier glanced over and then continued her conversation - Welsh, Quincey assumed, although it might as well have been Sumerian - with a customer buying a six-pack of cider and two family packs of Cheese and Onion crisps. The man could have been anything from fifty to seventy, with a grey pony tail and a face like a yellow balloon.

When the man, the cider and the carbohydrates had left, Quincey asked the woman behind the counter about the Carningli Collective, hoping that English would be acceptable.

'Such lovely people,' she said, 'even if some of them don't know if they're Arthur or Martha or somewhere in between. But that's the point of a place like this, see, all the flotsam and jetsam washes up and no-one asks questions. We all have our secrets, lovely, nothing wrong with that.'

It all depended on the secret, he thought.

'They're in Pen Deryn Farm, what used to be Dai Parry's place, god rest his soul. Go up to the end by here, turn right, wiggle up past the church and follow your nose for a couple of miles or so. Breezy up on that mountain, mind. Well, we call it a mountain but it's just a big hill really. They say angels used to visit, back in the old days, not that I've ever seen one. Makes you wonder, doesn't it, where all the little buggers have gone.'

THE ROAD CLIMBED out of the town and past a candle shop set back from a ford over a stream. Two thoughts tumbled over each other; that he could stop and buy a present for

Esther, a scented candle for her bedroom, and then came the vision of her body in the bath. So much blood in the world. Where did it all go when it seeped out of bodies? Perhaps that's where the planet's iron core had come from; a coalescence of haemoglobin, a spinning ball of gore.

He left the trees behind and the van rattled across a cattle grid onto the open fell. The landscape shifted; to his right he looked down onto a long sandy bay, with the sea a shimmer of grey. The view seemed almost familiar; the website, of course, he must be near the farm. Without any conscious decision, he pulled into a little passing place by a stunted hawthorn leaning in to the hillside; further up the slope, towards an outcrop of defiant rock, a group of ponies were grazing. One of them, slightly bigger than the others and grey with splashes of white, lifted its head and looked over at him. An appraising gaze, Quincey thought.

To stretch his legs he left the van and cut across the uneven ground, stone and scrub, towards the ponies. Male or female, it was hard to see any telltale signs from here. As he came closer the animals began to back away, all except for the grey and white stallion. The animal tossed its head back, made a strange whinnying call, circled around until it was between him and the road and then charged. Quincey ran towards the rocky outcrop, conscious of the sound of hooves behind him. He was sure he could hear the horse's snorting breath just inches away before he scrambled up and over the rocks until he was out of reach. He turned to look back; the stallion pulled up, tossed its head with contempt and then wandered off as if bored with the unworthy opponent.

He climbed a little higher and looked down the other side of the outcrop onto a small stone circle that had been hidden from the road. In the centre a large flat stone balanced on two others, waist high, for all the world like a prehistoric altar. Not that all altars weren't prehistoric. He'd never got his head around the concept of Mass. What would the poor souls do, in their Sunday bests, if the wafer on their tongues turned to gristle and the wine to salty, sticky blood?

The sun was low on the horizon, silhouetting a headland in the shape of a sleeping lion. Or was it a dog? And why was he stopped here, why wasn't he rushing to the rescue of his daughter? For this moment he could be anyone, anywhere. Or no-one, nowhere. He had been running almost since he found the body in the bath and now he had nowhere further to go.

The ponies had retreated into shapes on the horizon and he couldn't put off the confrontation any longer. He clambered down, made his way back to the van and continued up the single track road, mirroring the contours of the coast and always climbing. After a final bend, visible off a track to the left, were the buildings he'd seen on Prof's laptop. He turned and pulled in by what must have been the farmhouse, next to a muddy Landrover Defender. A small number of sheep were dotted about the stony field, grazing next to the unmoving wind turbine. The sound of a chainsaw stuttered from one of the outbuildings, but he could see no signs of any people. Or yurts.

He swung down from the van and stood shivering in the last horizontal rays of the sun, liquid gold. The salted air caused him to sneeze without warning; please God, not a cold. Or flu. He was halfway to the farmhouse door when a figure came out, a soft little man with cropped hair and thick black spectacles. The face was familiar, and with a kick of recognition he realised that the body had been too, once upon a time.

'I wondered if you'd show up here, said the figure, in a pleasingly light tenor. 'Paternal feelings kicked in at last, have they?'

And then Poppy was there too, holding the hand of Robyn, who was looking at him with a strange, quizzical smile.

'All things must change, Quincey, as they say. To be honest, it was knowing you that clarified what I felt about my identity, if that makes any sense. I'd say I was fulfilling my destiny, but only a wanker would say that and I'm not there yet. Joke. To be honest, lifestyle choice doesn't even come close. For me, the decision was a no brainer.'

'Robyn...?'

'Just Rob. Are you okay? You look like you're about to keel over. You should come in and sit down. I suppose you deserve an explanation.'

Inside the house they sat opposite each other in a room full of unexpectedly beautiful furniture, on hand-carved chairs that wouldn't have looked out of place in a gallery. He had no words. So easy to be liberal in the abstract until reality slapped you in the face. He sat silently, trying not to open and close his mouth like a goldfish.

'I'm getting my life in order, Quincey. Things were hard for me when I met you. I didn't know what I wanted and when I fell pregnant - trust me, *so* not deliberate - I thought, maybe this makes the decision for me. But as soon as Poppy was born, I knew I couldn't keep her. It wouldn't have been fair to her. Letting her go wasn't easy, never think that, but I knew she'd be safe with Jennifer. I knew you'd never cope. I might have been confused, but I wasn't that stupid.'

Rob paused, as if waiting for a reaction; this was obviously his turn to say something so best not disappoint.

'Why didn't you talk to me about it and tell me what you were feeling?' he said.

'Yeah, right. Your brother-in-law thinks people like me should be put down and let's be honest, if I'd turned up looking like this you would have locked Poppy away and I'd never have seen her again. Who do you think the social workers would have sided with, the trans man who used to be her mother, or the reputable solicitor? They're only human, they opt for the safe judgements like everyone else.'

He could have argued the point on 'reputable' but this didn't seem like the time. 'Aren't social workers meant to be woke these days?' he asked.

'I couldn't take the chance.'

'But you went to Jennifer's.'

'People see what they expect to see. I shaved, used a good concealer, and wore a hoodie. People like me get used to hiding our bodies.'

Rob was blushing. Quincey couldn't help looking for the swell of breasts beneath the baggy tee shirt, but there was no sign.

'Yes, they've gone,'said Rob. 'I used to bind them to get a flat chest. Stupid, isn't it? As if a body matters, but it does. You've grown up as a man. You were given a winning lottery ticket at birth so you take it all for granted, but believe me, life as a woman was never easy. Maybe I wasn't the most feminine, but I still felt like a hunted animal. Now I feel more in control.'

He wished he felt the same. He wanted to say, being a man isn't all it's cracked up to be, but why spoil the moment?

Poppy was rolling on the floor, playing with a ginger kitten that had scampered in.

'I'll be honest, Quincey, sometimes I'm not sure

what I am. Not a woman, that's certain, but not a man either. Somewhere in the middle, perhaps. But people like certainty, they like to know how to react. Ambiguity scares them. And I realised gender is just something we make for ourselves. A construction, as my shrink would say. For you, and probably for most people, it's all straightforward. For me it's more complicated, and I had to make a choice that I could live with.'

She sighed and looked away. 'No-one does this lightly. I had a whole medical team involved; the psychiatrist understood. He gave me a year, max, before I opted out for good and left this planet. This way I get to live, which sure as hell is better than the alternative. And once I'd made the choice, I realised that I'd never felt more settled. I wasn't acting anymore.'

Maybe Rob was right. She - he couldn't bring himself to think of her as anything else, not yet - looked complete, that was the word, in a way that she never had before. Grounded, his therapist would have said.

'I'm asking you to let me keep my daughter,' Rob said. 'She's happy here. I can do this and you don't want to.'

'But look at this place in the middle of nowhere,' he said. 'Do you really want to bring her up here, miles from her friends? And you said yourself that you're seeing a shrink. Poppy needs special care, she's...'

'She's a little girl who needs love. I can give her that. As for the 'shrink' - I stopped seeing him ages ago. I can look after my daughter. Don't get me wrong, I'm really grateful to Jennifer. I know she must be hurting. If you try to take Poppy now, I can't stop you. But I'm begging you, try to understand and let her stay.'

'If I do, how confused is she going to be as she grows

up? What will she call you - mum? Dad? How will you support her?'

The front door opened and closed, and a woman came into the room, gave Rob a hug and then sat next to her on the settee. Poppy trotted over, decanted the kitten into the woman's lap, then clambered up to join it. Quincey looked at this person who was so comfortable with his daughter. Mid thirties, at a guess. She reminded him of someone, willowy but with long red-gold hair, a tailored suit and black heels. No doubts here about who was all woman.

She reached out to shake his hand, a formality he found unexpectedly reassuring; her nail polish was midnight blue. 'You must be Quincey, Rob said we should expect you.'

'And you are?'

'Sorry. I'm Caitrin, Rob's partner. Owner and Managing Director of Carningli Security Solutions - *"We See Further"*.' Something about her seemed out of place; an isolated farmhouse on a mountainside clearly wasn't her natural habitat.

'I thought this was some kind of collective,' he said. 'I looked at the website.'

'There used to be a couple of other businesses run from here. An eco-energy outfit - who was that, Rob, the guy with the mole? Aaron, that's right. Nice guy. He decided the world was ending and moved to an ex-nuclear bunker near Wilmslow. And Rhiannon, she tried to set up a little market garden, but there's a reason there are sheep round here instead of vegetables. The only one left now is Davy the Wood. He has a small sawmill and we rent him one of the barns, but I don't think he'll be staying.'

'You said your company was something to do with security?'

'Just a fancy name for private investigators. Security Solutions sounds more upmarket.

'So how did you end up here?'

'I did some work for a security outfit on the other side of the pond, then decided to set up over here.' So that explained the mid-Atlantic accent. 'My family came from the UK. It's a long story.'

She put Poppy and the kitten back on the floor, stood, stretched, and yawned. 'I don't know about you, Rob, but I could murder a cuppa; anyone would think you didn't know how a kettle worked, but that's men for you!'

THEY HAD supper in the kitchen at a table constructed from bleached driftwood and then Rob took him to a cavern under the eaves. Poppy's bed was obvious from the huddle of soft toys; a pink bear, a green giraffe and an elephant with soft, mournful eyes. 'Give us a chance, come back in a couple of months,' said Rob, 'see how she's getting on. Bring Jennifer if you think she could cope with me. If you're really not happy we can talk again, I only want what's best for our daughter.'

He had already surrendered. He slept on the settee under a floral duvet that Caitrin had brought in but at first he had lain awake, listening to the sounds of yet another strange house at night, wondering about Rob. Once he had held her, made love to her, kissed her breasts - although, in retrospect, she had never been keen on that aspect of the whole business. Earlier Rob had talked about change and as he lay there, he envied her. He might still be searching, but she'd found her destination.

HE WOKE to the sound of a window opening. 'It's a beautiful day,' said Caitrin, 'I have a meeting in London, but you should go down and look at the sea, get some fresh air.' He could smell coffee and toast. 'Rob took Poppy to check on the sheep. You should see her with them, you'd think she was in paradise. They're back now, breakfast is served.' She came and sat on the edge of the sofa, her thigh pressing lightly against his feet. 'It must be strange for you, seeing Rob like this. I know it's a lot to get your head around and it wasn't that easy for me either. We met before he transitioned.'

Transition, from the Latin *transire*, to go across. Which implied something in between. Perhaps Rob had been right about ambiguity.

'You're looking at me and asking yourself, so is she a lesbian or what? You're thinking that I don't exactly live up to the image. To be honest, men haven't exactly stepped up to the mark for me. When Rob asked for that special little talk - even I hadn't seen it coming - I had a lot of soul searching to do.'

She patted his knee, stood, turned by the door. 'Time to pay the price, Quincey, and be a man. If Rob can do it, I'm sure you can.'

After breakfast, Rob drove him and Poppy to a car park between a golf course and the sea. The tide was out and the beach stretched into the distance, towards the headland that he'd seen on his way in the day before. Someone was cantering a horse along the edge of the water and kicking up foam, and he tried to remember the last time he had been by the sea. The night of Esther's death, with nightmares in the beach hut? No, he'd been back since, that day he started to wade towards the horizon, and he still wasn't sure what would have happened if the woman and her dog hadn't stopped him.

He walked with Rob and Poppy past a boarded-up café and on to the sand. He knew he should offer money, although quite how he wasn't sure. Now he was in the cash economy, what would he do? Deliver brown envelopes of used ten-pound notes each month? Jennifer had always refused help - '*this isn't the mediaeval church, Quincey, you can't pay for absolution any more,*' - but it felt different, now, as if he were more involved and actually had a choice.

'I won't say no,' said Rob. 'Cait does okay, even though it means she's always away at meetings or investigating someone. Sometimes I don't see her for days. We keep the costs down, but it will be a long time before I earn anything worthwhile. I'll be giving all my time to Poppy.' She picked up a handful of sand and let it trickle through her fingers. 'I thought I saw you online the other day, that YouTube video about the woman who set herself alight in London. Horrible business, did you see it? I would have bet real money it was you trying to save her. I told Cait, but she said you were on my mind because I was stressed over our plans to get Poppy. Don't get me wrong, but you're not exactly hero material.'

'Our plans?'

'Cait talked about us having Poppy even before I'd said that I wanted her back. I'm not sure I would have had the balls to carry it through without her help and support.'

They reached some grass-covered dunes and sat out of the wind, facing the town on the other side of the estuary, watching as Poppy drew patterns in the sand. Rob reached into the bag, and as she pulled out a bottle of juice for the little girl, a red plastic poppy fell out. Rob picked it up and put it back in the bag.

'When we got back from London that was lying on ground near the front door. No idea how it got there, completely the wrong time of year. Someone must have dropped it months ago, then I guess the wind blew it here. I thought it was a sign but it was just coincidence, Cait said, nothing more than the human desire to make patterns and bring order to a chaotic world. She is exceptionally practical.'

Quincey thought of mentioning the field of plastic poppies that had sprouted in his own garden, but decided, on balance, that the situation was weird enough already.

CHAPTER
FOURTEEN

He used Rob's phone to message Jennifer that his daughter was okay, glad that he didn't have to suffer the inevitable outburst, not yet. Perhaps Rob was right and he should bring Jennifer to Pembrokeshire so she could see for herself that a north London Edwardian semi wasn't the sine qua non of the good life, no matter how many distressed Welsh dressers you shoehorned under the sparkling LEDs. And it had been harder than he'd imagined to drive away from the farm, with Poppy waving and smiling - lopsided, heart-stopping - against a backdrop of sheep and rock and sky. In another world he'd turn around, go back and ask to stay. But what role could he carve out for himself now that Poppy had both parents merged into one with Rob; buy one, get one free.

He stopped in town on the way back and bought a Pay As You Go mobile from the Spar; '*they sell everything*', Rob had said when pleading with him to stay in touch. She might have been right; sheep dip next to a boxed laptop, a small library of pre-loved Dick Francis novels, and a selection of polyester pillowcases partially covering a chainsaw.

. . .

THE SUN WAS SINKING below the roofline by the time he got back to the London flat. Everything was where he'd left it with no sign that Prof had been home. He was aware of a sense of vague unease; there was a definite disjunct between what was, and what should be. He went into his room and checked the mirror, just in case he actually was Prof and had merely dreamed Quincey, but the face looking back had enough similarities to memories of himself that his existence was beyond reasonable doubt.

He was drying himself from the shower when he heard a knock at the door. Janine clocked the precarious towel wrapped around his waist as he opened the door. 'Cleared for action, are we? Sorry, I'm flattered, but I'll have to pass if this is an offer. Time and place, you get the picture, and I'm not in the mood. I spent this morning working out how to put parental controls on the laptop at home - mother has developed a taste for gay male porn; it's the bums, she says.'

She made them both coffee while he dressed. 'Is Prof around? I saw the van was back and assumed he'd been on some jaunt. There was a gig last night over in Camden Town but he never turned up, which isn't like him; he might be ethereal at times but he's pretty reliable when it comes to the band.'

Quincey gave her the redacted highlights about the past few days, leaving out the unimportant details about his child kidnapped by a mother who had morphed into a father and his musings on what that made him. Ex-dad, obsolete dad, replaced-with-someone-better dad. Never-wanted-to-be-a-dad-in-the-first-place dad.

'Then twenty-to-one on he's with Melissa,' said Janine. 'Don't tell me you haven't heard him talk about her, the latest squeeze. Pretty, if you like that sort of thing. More like pretty vacant, which probably suits his intentions, and almost young enough to be his daughter, the dirty bastard. She was in the band for a while - thought she could sing, she couldn't - never quite grasped the concept of knicker elastic, as my mother would have said. Actually did say, quite often, usually about me. She had a point; if they give me a choice of parents next time round I'll eschew evangelicals and opt for Catholics.'

She winked. 'Drink up, boyo, Melissa only lives a few streets away. Let's rescue the old bugger.'

THE SIDE DOOR next to a Thai restaurant was peeling purple. Janine rang the topmost of the six bells and a minute or so later the door opened, the smallest crack. The face that looked out was swollen and blotched, the cheeks smudged with mascara.

'What do you want?' The voice was a small frightened child.

'Jesus, Mel, you look a mess. You gonna let us in?' Janine pushed her way past and Quincey followed the two women up the narrow staircase on what had once been carpet but was now compressed to the consistency of cardboard, making small sucking sounds with every step.

Mel led them down a corridor to a closed door and paused. 'It wasn't my fault, we were just having fun. I thought he was joking at first...'

Janine pushed the door open. Displayed in front of them like an art installation, dressed as Wonder Woman complete with boots, bracelets and tiara but with a useful cut-out on the star-spangled pants, and tied to the bed by his wrists and ankles - skeins of red and blue embroidery

silk - was the Prof. His body, at least. The golden Lasso of
Truth lay knotted loosely around his neck and whatever
essence had once animated the skin and bones was long
since departed. Three dead people in little more than two
weeks, four if he counted stuffed Herman and the detach-
able ear; this was becoming a habit.

Janine felt for a pulse; rather unnecessarily, Quincey
thought.

'For God's sake, Mel,' she said, 'how long has he been
like this? You could at least have made him decent.'

'I don't know, a day or so.' Mel was trembling, barely
able to light a cigarette. 'I didn't know what to do. I thought
they'd blame me and say I killed him. There wasn't even
any warning; up till then he'd been so happy, never even
had to use his safe word, not once.'

It must be hard to say anything, Quincey thought, while
being strangled by the truth.

'We have to call an ambulance at least, or go straight for
an undertaker. No, I suppose they need a doctor to confirm
that the poor bugger won't wake up in a chiller cabinet
while they're waiting to do an autopsy on him.' Janine
moved one of his legs out of the way, sat on the bed and
sighed. 'I don't suppose you play the ukulele, Quincey?
There's another gig tomorrow - cash in hand and free beer -
and we're a man down. No? Well, worth an ask.'

Mel was still standing in the doorway. 'But what will
happen to me?'

'I wouldn't worry,' said Janine, 'this must happen all the
time. Mind you, I'd lose the lasso before anyone else gets
here, might just give the wrong impression.' She looked
more closely at the neck. 'How did he die, exactly?'

'I'd tightened the noose, just enough and not too much,
but he was looking a little peaky and I told him maybe we

should have a rest. The cough reminded me of grandpa after his sixtieth Marlboro of the day, but the Viagra had kicked in and he didn't want to waste a hard-on. When he started to have the spasms I thought it was Geronimo time, then he just stopped. Moving, breathing, everything. Except the erection, that stayed.' She began to cry. 'I was being fucked by a corpse!'

THEY LEFT before the ambulance arrived, after briefing Mel to forget that they had ever been there, and went back to Prof's flat. The home of a dead person; the sense of abandonment he'd felt earlier was even stronger. They went into Prof's bedroom; a tumble of clothes on a chair, a framed photo of a young woman against a backdrop of the Doge's Palace in Venice – his ex-wife, perhaps, or a young lover who hadn't managed to kill him. A ukulele propped against the wall, next to its open case. A drowned moth spreadeagled on the surface of a half-drunk glass of water on the bedside table, next to a packet of pills. A single sock over the radiator. And a wilting spider plant; after a nuclear winter it wouldn't just be cockroaches that inherited the earth, there would still be spider plants clinging on to life because they didn't know any better.

'He never mentioned any family,' said Janine, 'except for the ex. Poor bugger - still, what a way to go.' She emptied the water and its moth into the plant pot. 'What about you - planning to stay on? As long as Marek gets his rent, he probably won't care who lives here. Not a bundle of fun, that man. I met him a couple of times, he came to one of our gigs. Looks a bit like the Incredible Hulk in a borrowed suit. Apart from not being green, of course, that would be weird. Before he moved here he was in the Polish equivalent of the

SAS - I think he said that to impress me. I never have understood how men think.'

HE PACKED a few things in Herman's rucksack - the cash was
still safely stashed at the bottom in its Waitrose bag - then
hesitated over the laptop. He should never have used it at
all, and now it would have to come with him; at least Prof
wouldn't be missing it. Such a shame that one couldn't
enjoy the freedom of death.

The ambulance would have been at Mel's place long
since, the police as well. With a suspicious death to investi-
gate, they'd find this flat before too long and there was no
more time to waste. He stashed the bike in the back of the
van; at least it had stayed put this time.

Tansy had promised that she'd keep his room free. It
was as good a choice as any and now that he was going on
the hunt for his nemesis, what was there to fear? Just one
task to accomplish first, for which fear was an utterly
appropriate emotion. He headed north, back to Crouch End.
Jennifer deserved that, at least.

HE HAD FORGOTTEN it was a weekend and Fenton would be
there.

'Q, dear boy, it simply won't do. Jennifer told me all
about it, Robyn proving once again just how unsuitable she
is to be a mother.'

'I don't think it's a mother that she wants to be.'

'Don't be so obtuse. We all know what we mean. If you
won't do it I shall simply have to motor to Wales myself -
does one need a passport? - and collect your daughter. *Your*
daughter, Q. Or have you abdicated all responsibility?

Heaven help any of your poor clients, not that I should think you have many, looking like that. What on earth has happened to you? Jennifer said she thought you might be having a breakdown; was she right? Come on, man, speak up.'

How had Jennifer landed herself with this creature? Perhaps there was something in the Oedipus complex idea - or was it Elektra for women? Greek literature had never been a strong point; perhaps that was what one got for going to a minor public school on the outskirts of Avonport rather than Harrow, like Fenton. He'd probably read Sophocles in Greek. Prick.

Perhaps it was his height. How could his sister bear to be with a man who liked her to walk in the gutter so that he could look her in the eye? How did he ever imagine that Poppy could grow up here?

'Where's Jennifer?' he asked. 'I wanted to explain and put her mind at rest.'

Fenton snorted, looking slightly more like a Gloucester Old Spot than usual. 'That woman's mind is a law unto itself; I gave up trying to fathom its depths years ago. I'll be honest with you, Q, I never wanted the girl here in the first place. Can't pretend I did. But family is family and some of us are prepared to step up to the plate, do our bit. And Jennifer wouldn't take no for an answer, so there's an end to it.'

'So is she around?'

'Wasn't expecting you, wanted some distraction. Gone off to one of her good causes to bludgeon the undeserving into gratitude. If people want to top themselves, let 'em, that's what I say, no point in talking about it. Always was a rescuer, that woman.' He patted Quincey's arm as if it were an uncertain puppy. 'I know you want what's best for the girl but letting her be brought up by some kind of pervert really isn't on. She's already damaged goods, let's call a spade a spade, and Jennifer has her heart in the right place. I know you think I'm a pompous ass, and perhaps I am, but we both know you haven't got much to write home about either. Why Cath ever married you when she could have had someone normal - don't get me wrong, Q, but I didn't get where I am today by saying black was white.'

QUINCEY LEFT after extracting a promise from Fenton that there would be no rescue missions to the Welsh coast, bought with the concession of a 'family meeting' with Jennifer at some unspecified point in the near future. 'And don't think I'll just forget,' said Fenton, 'we wouldn't want Cath to find out about your little secret, would we?'

Given everything else that was happening, Quincey thought, he was almost past caring.

TANSY WAS STANDING by the front gate as he drew up outside her house and seemed unsurprised to see him. 'You're just in time,' she said, 'the others will be there already and I sense a questing aura around you today; nice.'

As he decanted from the van into her camper - it was already evening, what else would he do? - Tansy handed him some moulting, turquoise earmuffs and signalled him to put them on. 'Trust me, hon, Lili Marlene is a tad frisky at the moment and a little non-discriminating when it comes to the difference between rodents and human body parts. I'm beginning to wonder if she's losing her sight. Or her mind, which would, I guess, be hard to judge.' The camper's engine juddered into life and they swung out into the road.

'It started after Herman's ear fell off,' said Tansy, 'that day you went into my room. Took me days to find it again, and the lobe was chewed ragged. Lili has her own secret stores, she moves them around so I don't get to find them, or so she thinks - hah! I ain't been beat yet by a damn parrot, not gonna start now.'

He heard a flapping of wings from behind him in the van, and then a squawk of disagreement before the weight of the bird settled on his shoulder.

'Does Lili always come with you?'

'She has a thing for vans, don't ask me why. Doesn't matter how careful I am, she always manages to hide away until I'm on the road.'

'Where are we going?'

'Not far. Gonna be the first time for Horatio, he thought if we used his house she'd be more likely to turn up. I said to him, hon, I said, I don't think the spirits do geography, but makes no odds to me and if it keeps the man happy... and he's a judge, they like to get their own way, bit of a habit.'

'The turning up... are we talking macaw here?'

'No honey, his wife.'

They drove along the coast road, heading south and past the crumbling pier, past his beach hut, past the drooping sign to the Samaritans. Up to his right, a couple of streets away, was his old house. Would Cath be there now? What would she say if he asked Tansy to divert and turned up at his own front door? The prodigal husband, hold the fatted calf.

They left the street lights behind, drove for another ten minutes and then swung into the driveway of a brick-built Victorian pile, incongruous and isolated on the main road. The building seemed to be reaching into the sky with its turrets and dwarf spires, as if aspiring to be a church. They parked between a white Range Rover that could have come straight from the showroom and a Ford estate with non-existent suspension that looked as though it had spent its life wallowing in the Glastonbury mire. A pizza delivery moped was propped a few metres away and the smell in the air was a melange of petrol and toasted cheese.

The man who answered the door looked wearyingly familiar. A judge, Tansy had said, so he was probably on the tribunal circuit. They walked down the hallway to join two people already sitting at the circular table in the dining room, a monochrome teenage girl with white, pastry skin and hair like black straw hidden under a scarlet beret, and Romola, the woman whose shag pile still haunted his dreams. 'It's Ouija tonight,' Tansy explained. 'I channel the spirits sometimes, but they can be downright feisty; last time - well, best not talk about last time.'

Quincey sat next to the girl, it seemed safer that way, with Tansy on the other side. 'We're going to reach out to Horatio's wife tonight,' she said, 'see if she has any messages from the other side. How long has it been, hon, since she passed?'

'Thirty-seven days,' said the judge, checking his watch. 'Would a photo help?'

'No need, she knows what she looks like. Not that the spirits have bodies, just a kind of morphic memory.' Tansy took a set of cards from her bag and laid them out around the edge of the table, each one a letter of the alphabet and another two saying 'YES' and 'NO'. 'We need a wine glass. Crystal works best; the spirits, they kinda shy away from impurities.'

If that were the case, then they were going to have a very unsuccessful session, Quincey thought. Each time he caught Romola's accusing glare he felt the rug wrapped around his naked body, tight and constraining, leaving him helpless.

'Okay,' said Tansy, turning one of Horatio's cut crystal whisky tumblers upside down in the middle of the table. 'One finger on the glass, everyone, no pressure. Empty your mind, don't crowd out the spirits. They tend to get skittish when there are new people around.'

Quincey reached out, wondering why he was here. '*You're a sheep*,' his mother used to say. '*Always a follower, never a leader. It was the same when you were born, I should have known then, God help me.*' He'd never been able to understand quite what she meant by that, but then his mother, like all women, used language in a way that sounded normal but where the words had subtly different meanings.

Tansy was speaking again. 'Is there anybody there? Don't be shy, no-one here gonna hurt you.'

Nothing.

'Come on now, just a little sign, don't take much effort.'

The glass seemed not to move but to hum slightly under his finger, a tingling, a vibration on the edge of feeling. And then the hum turned to a tremble, and the tremble to a spurt of movement, almost leaving his finger behind as the glass skittered across the table to the 'YES' card. The judge let out a muted yelp.

'Cool,' said Tansy, 'now we need to know who you are.'

'Suzy, is it you babe? Please, say it's you.' The girl broke in with the hint of a sob in her voice.

The glass moved back to the centre of the table, circled slowly, and then went back to the 'YES'.

'I miss you babe but I'll be with you soon. I tried, but that bridge is so fuckin' high. Soon, don't be angry.'

The glass moved away, then back again, and again, and again. YES, YES, YES.

He hadn't noticed before just how cold it was in the room.

Tansy again. 'Is there anyone else out there, any messages for someone in this room?' She turned to the judge. 'Your wife, hon, what was her name? Elizabeth? Are you there, Elizabeth? You got anything to say to Horatio here, the man's grieving.'

The glass was still vibrating but immobile, ticking over.

'Don't be shy, all friends here, give us a sign.'

The glass moved again in a lazy figure-of-eight, then the circling stopped and the glass moved slowly, stutter-ingly, across to the E.

Quincey looked across at the judge, whose eyes were bulging.

'Lizzy, darling, is that you?'

The glass was off again.

S

T

H

E

R

'Esther,' said Tansy, 'anyone here know an Esther?'

He'd read about Ouija boards. All nonsense, of course. The glass was moved by the people taking part; subcon-sciously, perhaps, but still by human intervention, not some non-existent spirit. He'd spelt out her name himself, axons and dendrites firing in his brain without consulting him, sniggering as they made his wish become act. There were no ghosts.

He thought of taking his finger away, but it would have

been an admission of sorts and he wasn't ready yet for any form of disclosure.

U
B
R
A
S
T
R
A
D

Tansy said the letters out loud. 'Beats me, anyone know what that means?'

'Obvious, innit,' said the girl, 'you bastard. Not you, the letters. Looks like we conjured ourselves a dyslexic spook.'

LIZZY NEVER DID APPEAR, to the obvious annoyance of the grieving Horatio, and Quincey didn't even feel surprise when he got outside, after the session had finished, to find his bike leaning casually against the VW with Lili Marlene preening herself on the shit-covered saddle.

TANSY CALLED IT MAN-FLU, but it felt like the plague. Not that he knew how that was supposed to feel but surely it couldn't be worse than this; his chest and arms were covered with a burning rash as if the surface of the skin had been sanded away prior to a light dusting with cayenne, and the sneezing had brought on a nose bleed. 'A day in bed,' Tansy said as he appeared in the kitchen next morning, mopping his upper lip with a wad of toilet tissue, 'one egg or two?' The breakfast tray that arrived in his room a few minutes later was accompanied by Lili Marlene, who hunched on a curtain rod and muttered verses of romantic poetry to herself in passable German while he dipped Marmite soldiers into perfectly soft yolks.

He lay back on the plumped up pillows, eight years old and excused school, trying and failing to make sense of what was happening to him. Perhaps this was what paranoia felt like, suspecting everyone. And then he slept, dreamlessly, until Lili woke him with a nip to the earlobe as the daylight faded and the windows became indigo.

TAKE CONTROL, that's what his therapist had said all those years ago. But Poppy was safe for now, whatever that meant, and Jennifer and Fenton wouldn't go rogue for the time being. And whether he was haunted by spirits, a consortium of stalkers, or by himself, he needed to do something to take back control. After twenty-four hours the rash had gone, ditto sneezing and the threat of nasal exsanguination, and if he wanted a prime suspect then Marcus was back at the top of the list. He was human and alive, and not living in Quincey's head; where else to start the fight back?

IN THE AFTERNOON he drove to the Uskmouth Law School car park, Prof's van acting as a comforting cloak of invisibility. The last time he'd been here was when Esther's car had been in for a service and he'd picked her up after a lecture, not wanting to give Marcus an excuse to take her home. She'd called her professor a victim of presenteeism, which seemed to mean that the man went to work every day. Soon, Quincey thought, he'd have to go back to his own work. Or perhaps not. The mere thought of clambering to his feet in EJ Minchin's court was sending his bowels into a spasm.

At just past five-thirty, as Quincey wished he'd brought a sandwich for a snack, a man loped out of the building, dressed in running shorts, singlet and rucksack. For a moment he paused as if making a decision, with the crescent moon profile of his face against the sky giving him away.

Quincey had assumed that Marcus would drive in to work like normal people, but now that he was on foot would it be too obvious to follow him in the van? On the other hand, no-one ever noticed white vans crawling around the roads although it was harder than he'd imagined, a stuttering journey of inching up close and then waiting while Marcus jogged on, the bright red rucksack melding with his body and deforming him into a resurrected Plantagenet.

They edged down into the bay where the masts in the marina were jiggling about as if eager to be out of the harbour and fulfilling their destinies. Anthropomorphising had always been a weakness. He parked the van on a verge outside the barrier and watched Marcus slow down - the man had jogged non-stop - and then turn up one of the duck-boarded alleys between the boats. Was this where he lived? Surely not; a professor at one of the better Unis would earn enough for a decent place somewhere out of the city. Perhaps he was visiting a friend or a lover. A wife, even; a complication. Or maybe sailing was a hobby - that would work. But whatever the real situation, it was time at last to meet his rival.

The back of the boat Marcus had boarded was painted dandelion yellow as if destined for somewhere warmer.

Maybe he was about to make a run for it and sail across to Somerset or down to Spain.

Quincey clambered out of the van and then saw Marcus coming back between the boats, this time with a small white dog on a lead. Poodle? No, too small. Bichon Frise; one of his clients used to bring hers to every meeting and sat with it on her lap, a lump of white froth with a ridiculously happy face. Perhaps a dog would make him happier, love unadulterated by the expectations of sex. It was definitely worth a thought.

Marcus turned in the opposite direction, towards the path that ran around the bay. Time for action. Quincey locked the van and scuttled furtively to the boat, the *Princess Dorothy*. There were no signs of anyone else around and the neighbouring yachts seemed deserted too. A prickle of sweat threatened under his arms; he wasn't sure if he had a comfort zone and if he did, it wasn't here. But it was too late to back out now, especially if he wanted to reach some kind of resolution, and he had no idea how long Marcus would be away.

Getting on board was more difficult than he'd imagined, but he succeeded in scrambling over the side with an inelegant clatter of legs, and then barely managed to stay upright; he hadn't expected the deck to move so much.

He opened the door to the cabin and clambered down to a distinct smell of damp dog, overlaid with pine disinfectant. He should search the place, that's what people always did in circumstances like this, but he had no idea what to look for.

The small galley reminded him of the beach hut; happy days. A hollowness spread in his chest; to go back in time and say different words, make different decisions - he would do that in an instant, accept anything Esther wanted if it would keep him off the road to this little hell.

He moved towards a small sitting area further down, a foldaway table with the rucksack tossed on top. He was just unzipping the main section when he heard a sound from the doorway, the dog was yapping at his ankles and Marcus stood at the top of the steps, blocking out the light.

'I don't know who you are, my friend,' he said, 'but you'd better have a fucking good explanation for being on my boat.'

CHAPTER
FIFTEEN

The dog's teeth caught in his jeans, a little below the right knee, and the small creature hung there heavily, gradually pulling them down. The belt was holding, just, but that fried egg buckle had never felt too secure.

Marcus was in the cabin; now that he was no longer back-lit he seemed smaller and pale, his corrugated hair shot with grey. On TV, after they released him from custody, he had looked more thickset and threatening. And now he was holding up a mobile in his hand as if it were a weapon.

'I'll call the police unless you leave,' he said. 'Now.'

The man's voice held a quaver of fear; not an emotion, thought Quincey, that he usually evoked in people. And how was he meant to leave? With Marcus between him and the doorway there was no other way out, no escape. Trapped on a yellow boat by a potentially psychotic murderer and his dwarf attack dog.

Marcus leaned forward and stared, his mouth working like an old man's. 'I've seen you before. The woman in the park, the one who burned...'

The dog pulled its teeth free with only a small rip to the denim and sat back by its master's side, looking smug.

'What do you want with me?' said Marcus. 'Are you with the police? I had an alibi, you let me go. Esther's death was nothing to do with me. This is harassment!'

The man was making no sense.

'I should be asking the questions,' said Quincey. It felt like the right thing to say. 'You want to talk about harassment? What do you think you're doing to me; following me around, leaving notes, moving my bike.' With luck, the tremor in his own voice wasn't noticeable.

'What on God's earth are you talking about?' said Marcus. 'I don't know anything about a bike, I can't even ride one.' He sounded close to tears. 'As for following you, what do you think I am, some kind of stalker? Are you sure you're with the police?'

'You were there last night,' said Quincey, not feeling quite as certain about Marcus' involvement as he had been. 'You followed us to the seance.'

Marcus and the dog edged back towards the doorway. 'I don't know what you want,' he said, 'but if this is a joke you have a twisted sense of humour.'

'No joke, I promise you.'

'Well, if this isn't a joke and you're not the police, who are you?'

Quincey looked over at a framed certificate on the wall, which hadn't registered until now. A decorated border and two names; Marcus Haremountain and Patrick O'Brien, celebration of Civil Registration, 4th of April two years ago.

'He passed away if you must know,' said Marcus, noticing his glance. 'Three months ago, a massive stroke. I found him when I got home, didn't even have a chance to say goodbye.'

The dog had done more than rip the fabric of his jeans; Quincey became conscious of a burning pain and he looked down to see blood seeping through.

'I have plasters,' said Marcus, 'in the drawer. No? Suit yourself, just don't drip on the carpet tiles, they're a bastard to keep clean.'

IT WAS a while since he'd drunk neat gin from a teacup in the afternoon. The dog hopped up next to him on the vinyl-covered bench seat and licked his hand. Not quite worship, but better than outright hostility.

Marcus faced him across the cabin, on an identical benchette. In the fluorescent light his yellow skin was a moonscape of acne scars, and a depression in the centre of his forehead spoke to him having been dropped on his head as a baby. He was already on his second cup and the gin filled the small space with the scent of juniper.

'Esther never mentioned your name,' said Marcus, 'but then she didn't talk much about her life. She had her struggles like we all do, perhaps that's why we got on. I was her personal tutor and I confess, the boundaries got a little blurred and we became friends.' He stopped talking to the floor and looked up at Quincey. 'You'll have gathered it was nothing sexual; a lovely girl, but women aren't my style. I could see she was attractive, that was part of her problem. Insecurity and beauty can be a toxic combination. She found it hard to turn people down, and I know she was having a relationship with a man. Was that you? A woman was on the scene too; poor Esther really didn't know what she wanted other than love, and I'm not sure she found that with anyone. Some people are users, others are used. She was the latter. And social acceptance also came high on her list, which doesn't help when you find your feelings don't run down the usual channels; I should know.

The dog gathered itself and leapt across the divide to sit beside its master.

'I don't know why I came out to Esther. Perhaps I was modelling appropriate disclosure, as Pat would have said. She'd guessed anyway, and said I should just be honest about who I am. Who cares, she said, and I realised I did. Perhaps it's different when you're young.'

He was absent-mindedly playing with one of the dog's ears while he talked. 'The break-in was what really affected Esther, I didn't know what to say to help her.'

'Break in?' said Quincey, but Marcus wasn't listening.

'When Pat died she was the only person I could talk to. His family had always hated me; he had two sons from when he was married and they blamed me for "turning" him. As if. Whenever he visited them I had to stay behind because they refused to meet me. When he died, they sold the house from under me; it had always been in Pat's name and we never got around to putting me on the deeds. Who thinks about the future when the present is perfect? They left me with this boat and nothing else - we never thought in terms of "mine" or "his", everything was "ours". Except that it wasn't.'

How hard to watch a grown man trying not to cry.

'They didn't even tell me about the funeral. I crept in at the back after the service had started; I didn't want a fuss but I couldn't let him go without a last goodbye. They had a priest conduct the service even though Pat was a humanist. Such a gentle soul, he hated conflict.'

Cup three.

'I never realised how much I relied on him. Nothing works any more; I can't focus on teaching or research, barely anyone turns up to my lectures, the seminars are torture and as for the marking... the IT system was hacked and now I have 450 printed essays in my car that should have been done weeks ago.'

Bottle emptied, the last few drops.

'We used to walk in Gwenstow woods, me and Pat - do you know them? There's a tree near the centre, a little off the main path. Small-leaved lime, over four hundred years old. There's a split in the trunk you can walk through, it was a seedling when Elizabeth the First was on the throne. I can still hear Pat telling me about it - he loved the serendipity of knowledge. We called it the Answer Tree, we'd go there with a problem and somehow it never seemed quite so bad when we left.'

Marcus had given up any attempt at self-control and the tears on his cheeks looked as if they belonged there while he cried with the quiet familiarity of despair.

'We used to sit under the branches, summer and winter, eat ham sandwiches and have a snifter or two; a half-bottle of Bombay Sapphire, tonic if we were feeling virtuous, lemon slices - Pat used to say that a G&T without lemon was like sex without love. I wouldn't know.'

He found some kitchen roll, blew his nose and wiped his face dry. 'Sorry. You came here looking for answers and all I've done is talk about myself. I wish I could help, but I don't know why Esther took her own life. I told the police about the break-in; she hadn't reported it, I never worked out why, but they didn't seem interested especially as nothing seemed to have been taken.'

He had to ask. 'So why did they arrest you?'

'They suspected someone had been on the scene with her body after she died and they found my fingerprints in her flat, and some hair on the sofa. Well, they would. I told them I used to visit her. It isn't a crime, having a friend.'

Had they found anything else, that was the question.

'A neighbour thought she'd seen a man there earlier, but she didn't pick me out in a line-up even though I thought my heart was going to burst. How could she? I wasn't there the day Esther died. I wish she'd called and talked to me for all the good it would have done.' His voice had dropped. 'Perhaps she was the one with the answers after all.'

He went to the tiny fridge, took out an opened tin of dog food capped with clingfilm and spooned some into a yellow plastic bowl on the floor. The dog jumped down, sniffed the food and then started to eat, its little body quivering with excitement.

'There was one strange thing,' said Marcus. 'The neighbour said the man was carrying a bunch of flowers and they found roses at the flat, but Esther was allergic to pollen. I guess it couldn't have been you; whoever brought them didn't know her very well.'

THE DISCUSSION about Poppy couldn't be put off much longer and when he told Jennifer he was back in Kilvercombe, she suggested meeting him there. Either she was being conciliatory or she and Fenton fancied a day out, not that it mattered. He told them to come to the beach hut, thinking it best to keep Tansy to himself for now as someone he could trust. When he'd returned from seeing Marcus she'd taken one look at him and prescribed a chicken liver omelette. 'Get some iron into your blood,' she'd said, which had seemed safe enough until she continued, as he was into his third mouthful, 'I always knew Sarkozy would come in useful one day, God knows he did enough to piss off the hens.'

As for Marcus; the man had seemed genuine enough and had even thanked him as he left the boat for being a friend to Esther. But the world was full of impostors; he used to see them every week or so in the tribunals, telling lies, wearing masks. Look who's talking.

THEY WERE ALREADY WAITING the next day when he arrived at the beach, just before lunchtime. Fenton's low-slung Audi barely fitted into the parking bay and they were sitting inside, prematurely old, watching the sea through the windscreen.

The hut usually smelled musty if he hadn't been there for a while and today there was that sweeter smell, not unpleasant but hard to place. Jennifer had brought a selection of M&S delicacies and Fenton produced a bottle of Gevry Chambertin from his briefcase. 'What d'you say, Q, no need to be uncivilised about these things, oil the wheels as it were.'

They sat on the terrace, balancing mismatched plates of sweet potato falafels and quinoa salad; the wine tasted of rust. He should have prepared for this, but how? What compromise could there be?

Fenton was the advocate today, the only person to whom Jennifer had ever deferred. 'It won't do, y'know, using us like this. We dug you out of a hole when the girl's mother dumped your little mistake on you, we kept the secret from Cath - don't think that was easy, woman has a glance like an emerald laser beam - and it changed our lives.'

Quincey couldn't let this go unchallenged. 'Jennifer wanted children but couldn't have any. Poppy was a gift.'

'A gift you want to take back. You can't just move the child from pillar to post, it's bad form, Q, very bad form.'

He had to think about how to word this. 'Robyn gave birth to her. She's been through a hard time and come out the other side.'

'You're forgetting something,' said Jennifer. 'Robyn isn't exactly stable, is she, and I don't see you accepting any responsibility. You just take from everyone and never give back. It's always been the same. You're a parasite, that's what Ma called you and she was right.' She was crying now, tears of anger. 'She always said the wrong one was taken!'

Jennifer looked across at Fenton, who shook his head. 'None of that now, old thing, you promised.'

'Who was taken?' Quincey asked. 'What was Ma talking about?'

'A long time ago, Q, much water under bridges.' Fenton the conciliator. 'Jennifer's just upset, aren't you, old girl? No point in going over the past. Your Ma was a bitter woman, said lots of things she didn't mean.'

'And you don't think she had a right to be bitter, married to that silver-tongued old goat?' Jennifer poured herself the last glass of wine, sank it in one, and turned to her husband. 'We both know Quincey is a fool but he has a right to be told. God knows how Ma kept it quiet all that time.'

She looked older today. Fifteen years between them, a generation. How could he have ever thought she could bring up his daughter?

'It was a shock to us all when you came along,' Jennifer said. 'I was a teenager and it was so embarrassing to have a pregnant mother. Parents having sex was disgusting, you have no idea what I went through. I was on my way home from school one day and a group of girls, a couple of years older than me, wouldn't leave me alone. They kept asking if I listened to Ma and Pa when they were at it and then they threw me over a garden wall onto a rose bush. When I got home Ma belted me for ruining my uniform.'

She shook the empty wine bottle, more out of hope than expectation, and scowled. 'She wasn't happy about another baby, not in her forties, and she was always in a mood. Pa spent more and more time at the office. At least, that was his story. I don't know whether they'd told her she was having twins, I suppose they did, but she said nothing to me and I didn't want to talk about it.

'And then you were born, two of you. One boy, one girl. She came out first, but you were heavier. And you were so ugly, Quincey, like a misshapen frog. Ma cried when she saw you, yet your sister was so pretty. Her eyes never seemed to blink, just stared as if you were the entire world.'

A twin, he had another sister. 'What happened to her?' he asked, not sure if he wanted to know the answer.

'She died,' said Jennifer, looking out at the sea, 'and you lived.'

Fenton reached out to touch Jennifer's arm.

'No,' she sighed, 'I've said this much now. He might as well know the rest.'

Quincey felt, unaccountably, as if he were in the dock.

'Ma was so tired all the time,' said Jennifer. 'She went to bed one afternoon and took the two of you with her. I can't remember exactly how old you were, not more than a few weeks. She was bottle feeding; couldn't face all that other nonsense, as she called it.'

He focussed on the new scaffolding around the pier, grey and orange. When had that happened?

'When she woke up, you were cuddling your sister. She almost liked you for a moment, and then she realised that something was wrong. You were warm, but your baby sister was already turning cold. It was as if you'd sucked the life out of her.'

Jennifer had never been able to hold her wine. But why couldn't she have let him carry on in ignorance of the fact that he'd been a murderer almost since birth?

The conversation about Poppy had been hijacked; he asked them to leave and even Fenton didn't demur. 'Not your fault, old chap,' he murmured, 'I think Jennifer was thrashing about a bit, wanted to get her own back for losing Poppy. Perhaps it is for the best after all, letting the girl stay with her mother, or whatever we're supposed to call Robyn these days.' He sighed. 'Things used to be so much simpler.'

Quincey folded the chairs, stacked them in the beach hut and made himself a mug of coffee. A woman could handle this, multitasking and keeping all the threads in order. But he was floundering, sinking into an oncoming tide that he couldn't outrun.

What had Marcus talked about yesterday, the answer tree? A ridiculous notion, of course, but he had nothing to lose. He locked the hut - the smell seemed to have dissipated, he should come here more often - and set off towards Gwenstow. When he was small Ma and Pa used to take him to the woods there, a Sunday afternoon trip down the motorway from Kilvercombe, and then a winding, meandering set of lanes to the small car park with its picnic tables and litter bins. He felt a surge of familiarity as the old landmarks appeared; the ruined marble folly on a small hill, the farmyard that straddled the lane, littering its surface with mud and straw, the avenue of trees that met overhead creating a dappled green tunnel. And as he used to feel all those years ago, the sense of entering a magical world.

One other car was parked inside the entrance, dandelion yellow, a marque he didn't recognise. He had hoped to be alone here but no matter, there were enough trails through the beeches and oaks and limes, dotted with patches of viridian spurge in the undergrowth that glowed almost metallic against the ferns. Four paths led into the trees, but he knew from memory that they would bifurcate again and again, branching and crossing, demanding choices. The nearest main roads were miles away and the only sounds were a soft rustling above him even though there was no sense of a breeze below the leaves, the muffled sound of his footsteps and the occasional snap of a twig under his feet.

Where was the birdsong?

The mid-afternoon sunlight stood in slender columns like the ghosts of vanished trees, almost reachable, and dust glimmered in the air. He passed the crumbled foundations of a small building, never more than a room or two even in its pomp, the pocked stones barely visible through an overgrowth of brambles. Empty for centuries, perhaps, Sleeping Beauty long since discovered, woken and taken. He had played there once, called it a palace and himself a king. You couldn't make it up.

The path was curving ahead; he was close to the middle of the woods now. A thin, canine keening reached him before, after a few more steps, the perspective changed and a sudden sense of space unfurled around him as he entered the clearing. No doubt this was the right place, open to the sky with an ancient lime isolated in the centre. No doubt this was the right tree; small bright leaves, thin branches sprouting from grey, pollarded stubs and a trunk riven to the height of two men and wide enough to walk through without twisting. No doubt either that this was where the answers lived.

The white dog was sitting by the tree and staring up at its master, who was hanging from one of the lower branches like a cat strung up by a boy. Marcus's body seemed framed as if posed in front of the crack, twisting slowly in the barely perceptible breeze with his feet pointing to the empty bottle of gin on the ground a metre below. No lemons for Marcus, not today.

And the little dog, bereft in a world emptied of joy, threw its head back and howled again to the sky.

THERE WERE STILL JUST the two vehicles in the parking area, the van and the car that must have belonged to Marcus; it was, after all, his colour. Quincey peered in; the back seat was a slither of papers, hundreds of word-processed essays waiting to be marked.

What would it feel like to put the weights down, to turn away and never have to look back, to feel no guilt? What would it feel like at that penultimate moment with the noose around the neck, the harshness of rope against skin? He imagined it, rasping and uncomfortable, the unaccountable worry about the mark it would leave. A last, indelible love bite.

He wondered why Marcus had decided to go through that final, one-way door. The loss of love, or perhaps it had been pressure at work. Perhaps he had nothing more to give; no ideas for new research, nothing to say to his students. Living a lie; Quincey knew how that could feel, the familiar shiver at the fear of discovery. And had he been responsible, after all, for what happened to Esther?

Whatever the truth about Marcus, he was gone now. Quincey wondered if he'd feel some sort of relief, but all he felt was another weight pulling him down. 154 pounds at a rough guess, the lead weight of another dead body. Marcus may have slipped the surly bonds, but he, Quincey, was still shackled to life.

HE STARTED DRIVING, not sure where to go. Deracinated like a weed on summer tarmac, desiccating. His thoughts went back to Saturday night, driving in a daze with Tansy through the streets of Kilvercombe on the way to the seance. They had been two streets from his home and he'd had a sudden, unfamiliar urge to see Cath and catch her scent. Home calling Quincey.

As he slipped up onto the motorway at Gwenstow, he wondered if he should have called the police or an ambulance and told them about the body in the woods, if only for the sake of decency. There would be flies. But Marcus was beyond caring, nothing more now than a bag of chemicals embracing entropy, and this was no time to put his head above the parapet. Someone else would drawn there by the sound of the little dog's cries and raise the alarm.

A fine drizzle started and the windscreen wiper on his side shuddered with each pass, leaving smears of damp grime. He should probably stop driving the van soon, they might be on the lookout for it now that Prof was gone.

The road in front of him was moving in the wrong directions and he felt as though he were swaying on the edge of a precipice. The klaxon of a lorry jolted him back as it undertook him; he was doing forty in the fast lane, not a good idea. He weaved back to the left-hand side, ignoring the hooters of the cars he barely missed, and came off at the next services.

He hunched in the toilet cubicle, studying his legs; there was a bruise on his thigh the size of a saucer that he hadn't noticed before. It was already turning yellow; body consciousness wasn't really a man thing. A prick-height hole in the side wall was stuffed with tissue that looked as though it had been in and out a number of times. And on the back of the door was a green and white poster with the photo of a man who looked like a failing plumber, stubble and haunted eyes: *A Samaritan,* he proclaimed, *Helped Me Take Control Of My Life.*

Well done you.

As he paid for a coffee and danish, eat in, he realised that his hand was trembling so much that the woman behind the counter had to chase the note he was holding.

CATH'S CAR was outside the house, but that signified nothing. *Taxis are chargeable*, she always said, *what's not to like?* He parked the van a little further down and sat for a while, looking out at the familiar street. The cat woman's house, three doors down; Beth and Joe's place with their matching Porsches, changed each year; the home with 'those' children. A mother had been spotted from time to time, rara avis, but the father had left a year ago after murmurs of a Lithuanian au paire, and the six children had gone feral. He had never been sure where the neighbourhood stood in the tectonic shifts of gentrification, or in which direction it was drifting.

At least he still had a front door key. Should he knock, or ring the bell? No, that would be an admission of defeat. As he shut the door quietly behind him, he heard a radio playing classical music. That didn't sound like Cath. In her view music was an unwanted distraction, neither necessary nor sufficient for a civilised existence. Perhaps it was a Duchess day, not that they had ever shown an interest in Mozart or Mussorgsky.

A maroon briefcase sat at the bottom of the stairs, unfamiliar and expensive.

We are not alone.

He walked slowly up the hallway towards the kitchen of granite and chrome, almost certainly unused since he left. The radio was here and so was a man, sitting at the table, sipping tea and reading the Telegraph. Probably not a good sign that he was wearing the moccasins that Cath had given Quincey for his last birthday; who said romance was dead?

So this was how it happened, the changing of the guard.

The man looked up, vaguely familiar. Salt and pepper hair curling over the white collar of his pink chalk-striped shirt, gold and emerald cufflinks, signet ring, signature smile. Why was their local MP sitting in his house, wearing his slippers?

'Hello Radlett, we wondered when you'd turn up. Cath was doubtful, but I said, a dog always goes back to its mess because they don't know any better. And here you are.'

It wasn't quite the greeting he'd expected.

'Tea? I made a pot, always think it tastes better that way. Single estate Darjeeling, you'd be surprised the difference it makes, although by the look of you I suppose you're a PG Tips man. Dash of milk? That's a boy - might as well be civilised, what?'

The man handed over a cup, folded the newspaper and

leaned back. He'd probably gone to the same school as Fenton.

'How long...' Quincey asked. He didn't know what else to say. He wasn't even sure what he felt. Numb? Yes, that seemed to work.

'It's not as if you two were exactly Romeo and Juliet, were you? Cath and I have no secrets. She's a feisty bitch, Radlett, needs a strong handler. Stronger than you. Did she tell you that the Party had approached her? All bullshit but there are mutterings about not enough women in the House, especially on the front bench, and our dear Leader has decided that we need to be seen to be "doing something." Cath's a moderately well-known silk, photogenic, and I was asked to co-ordinate the approach. Between you and me I didn't expect it to go this far, but my wife upped and left and moved in with her best friend the same week that our youngest went up to Brasenose.' He shook his head in wonder. 'There must be something in the water these days. As for Cath, she's surprisingly passionate under all that psychological armour, not that you'd have found out. What was a chap to do?'

Should he hit the man? Probably the honourable thing; Cath would not appreciate the idea that she needed 'handling', but her honour wasn't his responsibility and never had been if he was honest. And he'd never liked those slippers.

The tea was pale and tasted of straw.

'It all happened rather quickly once you went walkabout; "Do It Now", that's my motto. I didn't get where I am by prevaricating, especially in the lists of love, what? In the circumstances, probably best if you collect your things - we put them in the third spare room. 'Fraid I needed your study - poky little room, always smells of coal - but we've talked about a bit of remodelling once I sell mine, always assuming my darling wife doesn't take me to the cleaners. I should be all right, courts don't look kindly on weirdos.'

Classic FM, not Radio 3.

'Quite a few letters stacked up for you, I'm afraid. Cath tells me that's she's heard on the grapevine about questions from one of your Toytown employment judges - the name Minchin ring a bell? - rumours that you'd gone rogue, and I gather it isn't the first time, eh? She's put it about that you're seriously ill and hors de combat, which is probably pretty close to the truth. Must say, you look frightful.' He sniffed the air. 'Bit ripe too. I'd invite you to have a shower before you go but I have an appointment and we don't take too kindly to leaving strangers in the place.'

THERE WASN'T much to collect. The CDs that had moved in with him, three screwdrivers and the hammer with a handle that gave him splinters. And a framed photo of Ma - shrunken and frightened - in the residential home, the week before she died unexpectedly in the night with the secret she had kept all those years. Had his dead twin ever haunted her dreams?

The letters were in a plastic bag; he tied the handles together and dumped them in the dustbin on his way out. Ring out the old. The van's engine was churning out its usual particulate-rich effluvia before he went back, reached in and retrieved the bag. One never knows.

CHAPTER
SIXTEEN

Tansy left him a note the next morning. '*Out most of day, hens need feeding, say hi to William. Mind your ankles.*' He scouted the house in case Tansy had picked up another waif, but there were no signs of life other than his.

He went out into the garden; the hens seemed not to be missing Sarkozy although how could one tell? They were still scratching in the dirt and Sarkozy had been transformed into feathers, bones and the remains of a chicken curry in Tansy's fridge. The lot of all males, he was realising. You think you're doing the fucking, but in reality you're the one being fucked.

Another little enclosure had been created near the shed, with a low shelter in one corner. He wandered over and a small, mottled pig trotted out to view him.

'William?'

The pig smiled briefly, grunted in a manner that signified a desire for friendship, and continued its examination. There was an air of expectancy about it although the note had mentioned hen food only. He wasn't even sure what pigs ate; everything, he seemed to remember, or was that goats?

William was shuffling now, dancing decorously from side to side in the muck. Quincey leaned over and ran his fingertips along the little creature's back; he'd expected the softness of fur, but this was like stroking strands of wire. He stood back, but William butted the fence post and squealed for more.

'Sorry sunshine.'

The pig seemed to understand and wandered, a little disconsolately, back into its shelter.

Quincey walked slowly back towards the house, wondering whether pigs ever felt that they had a choice about anything. Free will; someone had talked to him about that recently. Joanna Dust, sitting outside the Italian café in London. She'd implied that there was no such thing; how could anyone believe we had choices, she'd said? Everything was mapped out from birth and the universe was peopled with puppets.

But how much better to believe in freedom and the ability to take control of one's own life. Someone else had said that, the plumber on the poster at Gwenstow services. Clearly the Samaritans were on the other side of the argument from Dr Dust, so perhaps a chat wouldn't hurt.

HE MUST HAVE DRIVEN past the end of this road a thousand times, a cul-de-sac half way between his old home and the beach hut. A small Victorian terrace on one side, fenced-off wasteland on the other. Not many cars. He didn't know what he had expected; a converted chapel, perhaps, or a local authority style office. Not this slightly seedy domesticity. Reassuringly, the woman who answered the door met all his expectations. Seventies, county, and a smile that hinted at condescension. She showed him into a small room off the hallway and asked him to wait while she got them both a nice cup of tea.

While she was out, he looked around. A sash window, locked. A coffee table with a half-empty box of man-size tissues, a faded Constable print of Salisbury cathedral, three Ikea easy chairs, not too stained. CCTV in the corner of the ceiling, blinking at him, and a rather obvious alarm button.

It was a different woman who came back with the tea. At least fifty years younger, a gold stud in one eyebrow and pale green hair. 'Deirdre was coming to the end of her shift so she asked me to see you.' Her voice made him think of the salt air at Carningli; perhaps synaesthesia was catching.

'Is there a name I can call you?' she asked. Such a strange question. 'I'm Kassia,' she said.

Somehow that seemed improbable, but it would be rude to say so. 'Bob,' he said, 'you can call me Bob.'

'OK, Bob.'

Just OK? She was smiling at him, with the security camera high above her shoulder. He couldn't help looking up at it, then back at her.

'Everything you say here is in complete confidence. We don't record anything, the camera's just for... for...' She hadn't needed to explain this before.

'...training purposes,' he volunteered, 'my safety and convenience?'

He wondered why he was here.

'Health and Safety,' she said, 'will that do?'

As good as any. If he were her, he'd want someone keeping an eye on anonymous visitors. Anyone could come through the front door, probably did.

'Was there something you wanted to talk about, Bob?'

Scarcely imaginative as an opening, but he wasn't help-ing. Perhaps this was normal, people phoning or calling in and then being struck dumb. Why would that be? Perhaps they simply realised the enormity of their problems, or just how small and insignificant they were. Or perhaps they simply didn't know where to start. And what could someone like Kassia possibly know of life? What insights could she offer?

'Have you been in touch with us before?' she asked. 'No? Perhaps something happened recently that you're worried about.'

'I seem to be killing people.' That hadn't come out the way he meant. Was it his imagination or was the camera flashing faster? And Kassia was no longer leaning back, but sitting upright on the edge of the chair.

He waved his hands as if to shoo the words away. 'Not literally, it's just that I keep meeting people who end up dead. I think I'm up to five, and the timescale between meeting and dying seems to be getting shorter. I'm not sure that Sarkozy fits the pattern but we ate him, and we'll prob-ably do the same to William when he gets a bit bigger. No, don't look so worried, William's a pig. I only met him today but I think he's safe for now.'

This definitely wasn't going to plan.

Kassia sipped at her tea as if playing for time. 'So how do you feel about these people dying?'

'Three of them killed themselves, one I murdered; I was a few weeks old and I don't think it was deliberate, so it probably doesn't count - and the other was an accident. Well, I think it was an accident, bit hard to tell as I wasn't there at the time. I don't think the lasso had anything to do with it, not tight enough.' Unlike the rest of the costume;

that Wonder Woman bustier had been reinforced with some sort of boning which, on reflection, was probably not optimal for catching one's breath at moments of passion.

So many images crowding in all the time, unfiled memories. They were all there in the room with him, clustered in the corner, watching silently. How much had it been his fault; where had he taken the wrong fork in the road, time after time?

'These people that died, did you know them well?' Kassia asked.

He wondered if he really knew anyone, least of all himself. But here, if anywhere, he could try out honesty.

'One was my lover, she slit her wrists in a bath. I think that's what she did, but I'm being stalked by someone and I wondered if he had killed her. At least, the person I thought was stalking me hanged himself, but he'd fallen behind with the marking and his boyfriend died and I don't think it was him after all. The woman who burned herself alive, I'd never seen her before. Wrong place, wrong time. The last one, the man who let me share his flat, I thought he died happy but now I'm beginning to wonder. And I seem to have cuddled the breath out of my twin sister, but I didn't know that until today.'

'It sounds like you've been through a lot, Bob,' said Kassia. 'How many of these events are recent?' She would have used the same calm tone of voice if he'd said he was an emissary from the Andromeda galaxy, come to enslave mankind.

He counted the days. 'Apart from my sister it's three weeks from the first death until now. I keep wondering who will be next; I thought it might be my daughter after she disappeared, but I found her safe with her mother - well, she was her mother but now she isn't. I know it sounds a little complicated but I really don't think I'm to blame, not this time.'

'Do you feel guilty about the other deaths? That's a lot to encompass in such a short space of time?'

'If you thought someone had committed a crime,' he asked, 'would you call the police?'

'Are you saying that's what you've done, Bob?'

It all depended on how you defined crime.

'And what about you, Bob? Have things ever been so bad that you've thought you couldn't go on?'

Aye, there's the rub. Who hadn't contemplated the bare bodkin, and who hadn't held back for fear of the dreams that might come in the everlasting sleep of death?

There was a knock on the door that had been left ajar, and a man leaned in with the same practised, apologetic smile. 'Kassia, could I have a word?'

As soon as she left the room he peered into the hallway, but there was no sign of either of them. A mid-term report, no doubt, time for them to discuss the loony and time for him to leave. As he drove out of the dead-end street he wondered why he had gone there in the first place. He felt no different, the fardels were no less heavy. And he still had no answers to his questions.

HE WAS BEGINNING to wonder if he should, perhaps, see a doctor. Get something to slow down the flow of time and give him a chance to find solid ground for a while. Could doctors do that? And while he trusted the Samaritans to treat him as a deluded mad man and ignore his mutterings, he wasn't sure that his GP would be quite so accommodating. As if it mattered; Cath was lost to him. Perhaps she'd known about Esther all along, Poppy too.

Yesterday he had felt like an uprooted weed. As he pulled up behind Tansy's camper van he realised that there was nothing keeping him here in Kilvercombe, not any more. His clients would have written him off by now and he regretted salvaging the bag of mail. There would be reprimands, there would be threats. Some would be from HM Courts and Tribunals Service. Perhaps he could write 'return to sender' or 'not known at this address'. It might buy him some time and get the monkeys off his back for a while.

LILI MARLENE WAS PERCHED on the newel post at the bottom of the stairs. There was a sly look about her sideways glance, as if she were debating whether to share a secret. As he climbed to his room she hopped heavily onto his shoulder, nipped his ear with what he took to be affection and, in an approximation of a parrot whisper, said 'fuck me big boy'.

'Sorry Lili, not really my type.'

'Naughty mummy. Fuck me big boy.'

'I'm not your mummy and trust me, neither of us would benefit if I fucked you.'

There was another sound in the house, coming from Tansy's private room off the hallway. A muted shriek, a crash, then someone groaning. Perhaps she'd fallen, which would be easy enough in that place of shadows peopled by a host of stuffed dead. Please God she wasn't about to join them; he wasn't sure he could cope with yet another corpse.

He went back down, knocked and listened. Was that a voice? Was she murmuring to herself in pain? He opened the door and peered in; this time the heavy curtains were fully drawn over the bay windows, casting a dull red light into the room, and the air was sweet with the smell of dope.

There had been a rearrangement. Herman, Fay Wray, the stoat and mouse in the domed glass case, as well as a stuffed badger that looked rather fresh, were all positioned around the taxidermy table like students at a nineteenth century physiology lesson.

And bent over the table was Tansy, completely naked except for a paisley headband, trying to stifle a giggle as the judge from the seance struggled to extricate himself from her body.

'Hey honey,' she called over to Quincey, 'don't mind us. Feels just like the old days, you learn to lose the shame. Whatever happened to free love, huh?'

She twisted round to look at the judge, who was muttering imprecations under his breath.

'You give in yet, sweetheart? Guess this is the last time you take a bet on muscle control; I *invented* pelvic floor exercises. And I told you, Horatio, not so many of the little blue pills - not that I'm complaining, but I hope for your sake you brought a long coat.'

Lili flapped over to the judge, landed heavily on his comb-over, threw her head back and squawked in triumph: 'SEND ME DOWN BIG BOY!'

HE CLOSED THE DOOR, leaving the three of them in a tableau of flesh and feather; that was the second time in a week that he'd seen a man's buttocks in the process of having sex and he wasn't sure his own came out well from the comparison. At least he had a better appreciation of the term 'hairy-arsed'.

He wandered through the garden towards the chickens

and the pig, conscious of the smells of thyme and rosemary from the herb border. As he reached the end of the garden he saw William in his pen, snuffling around at what looked like a scattering of papers on the ground. Was Tansy feeding him on old birthday cards? Pigs might not be choosy, but still. He reached over and pulled one out of danger before William could grab it. Definitely not a greetings card, but a photo - 4x6, matte, shallow depth of field, so probably a telephoto lens. Excellent light quality. Film club at school had a lot to answer for.

Thinking about the past couldn't stop him from focusing on what he was holding. Had Marcus really been that far from the ground? Had the little dog looked so bereft? And why hadn't he seen the photographer who had captured him so perfectly, looking up at the hanging body as if he were a pilgrim hoping for the first relic?

William was gradually consuming the other images; were they all the same? He bent down again, just missing the pig's questing snout, and hooked another card.

Different. Very different.

The marina, the masts, the dandelion yellow boat, and him looking out piratically from the cabin door; a suspicious cove if ever there was. He considered leaving the images there for William to dispose of but decided against, too risky, so he jumped over the low wall and collected the photos. He'd have to find somewhere to dump them where they couldn't be found and used in evidence.

BACK IN HIS room he sat on the edge of the bed, listening to the judge's remonstrations, Tansy's laughter and the front door closing. Unless Marcus had returned from the dead, which he couldn't exclude as a possibility given everything else that was happening, his stalker was still out there and playing mind games. If someone would just tell him what he'd done wrong, he could apologise and try to make amends. But perhaps it was already too late; he could almost feel the breath of Nemesis on his neck as she closed in on him.

THE NEXT DAY he was on the road by nine, heading north towards the bridge and the border. In the silence of the night he had decided on a respite day; he had been tracked everywhere he'd gone since Esther died, so perhaps the emptiness of the Black Mountains would prove a more formidable barrier to covert surveillance.

He remembered a ridge walk from years before, when he was pursuing an athletic girl at Uni. A year older and six inches taller than him, Lisa was all legs and shoulders and her daddy worked for the TUC. Even her memory made him feel exhausted; knowing her had taught him never to date a woman whose biceps were bigger than his.

The start of the walk was easy enough to find, a lay-by next to a small church half an hour the other side of Abertrothy, who needs a map? He laced up the walking boots Tansy had lent him, still caked with mud from Herman's last expedition, then walked up past the church-yard and the wych gate, the sunken lane, the farmyard, and started to climb.

Surely the slope had been less steep the last time he was here, the ridge nearer. It was too early to stop and eat the cheese and pickle sandwich from the petrol station en route, but maybe a sip of water was allowed. He tightened the straps on Herman's rucksack - don't think about the finite quantity of cash stashed in the plastic bag at the bottom - and moved on, across a final cattle grid and onto the open hillside. If anyone tried to follow him here they would be visible from miles away, and for the first time in weeks he felt safe.

At last he was on the ridge - more of an edge, if he was honest - heading north. On his left the ground dipped slightly and then rose again towards the flattened summits. On his right it dropped steeply away, scree slopes like skirts flaring out from the cliffs. The path rose and fell, well-worn, always tracking the edge until he reached a crossroads at the head of the valley below. Left, he remembered, that had to be the way.

The land had become almost featureless, a plateau of grass and peat with patches of charred heather, but the path still curved towards the highest ground. What had been a clear sky was now veiled with a light gauze of cloud attenuating the light, and the breeze had swung round to the north, thin and sharp. He looked for somewhere to shelter while he ate the sandwich; a dip over there might suit, out of the wind. As he reached the depression he stopped, shocked. It was deeper than he'd thought and revealed, now that he was almost upon it, the wreck of a light aircraft. One wing had been bent back from its struts like a broken limb and the single propeller at the nose had churned itself into the peat.

Yellow spindles of grass had grown over the wheels and the glass around the cockpit was cracked and stained. The whole depression was a sheep magnet with piles of half-rotted droppings covering the ground. The crash wasn't recent, then, so no need for heroics. But would there be bodies?

He slithered down, picking his way through the dung, and put his hand on the fuselage; it was still warm from the recent sun, making it feel almost alive. The door was ajar, just reachable, but it fell from its hinges as he pulled on the handle with one ragged edge catching him on the cheek as he tried to dodge out of the way. Blood trickled down towards the corner of his mouth; he wiped it away, wincing as he felt for the damage.

The cockpit was empty. The pilot had either walked away or been carried. Or perhaps he'd parachuted to safety, leaving the plane to fend for itself.

His weight caused the plane to rock, but he'd seen a photograph taped to the dash. Sunlight and damp had faded it to a pale brown wash, but the picture was clear enough. A woman wearing a headband, leopard skin leotard and legwarmers. She reminded him of one of his teachers, Miss Everett; she hadn't lasted long. He had been in love, as much as you could be at seven. A memory intruded, long since boxed away; one afternoon, he was in Popinjay class - they'd call it remedial these days, he supposed, at that age he was stupid, not dyslexic - and an older child came in to show them how to make a paper flapping bird. He tried so hard to make it as a present for Ma, but the paper just crumpled in his sweaty little hands and the folds never lined up. The older boy came over, made a couple of adjustments and suddenly there it was, slightly grubby and with a wonky beak, but if you pulled the tail - not too hard! - the wings flapped up and down. He couldn't wait to get home and presented it to Ma when the woman from next door dropped him off - Ma had a trick of getting neighbours to work for her - and watched as she pulled the tail clean off, ripping the paper, before throwing it in the bin.

The plane lurched again and he lowered himself back onto the ground, slipping on the damp grass and falling face down inches from one of the piles of sheep pellets, narrowly missing their progenitor who had come to check out the excitement. Strands of bramble, caught in its dirty yellow wool, were trailing on the ground.

He clambered out of the dip and looked onto a changed world. The earlier veil of gauze had thickened and become an opaque mist, damp and penetrating. The last features of the landscape disappeared as he stood there, leaving him alone on the few feet that he could make out of the path. Alone except for the sheep which had clambered up beside him.

'I guess you're used to this.'

The sheep gave him a sideways glance, then bent down and started to browse on his left bootlace.

HE FOUND an overhanging rock after trying to retrace his steps. It hadn't been there before, but at least it felt like some shelter while he ate the sandwich. A flask of tea would have gone down well; planning had never been a strong point, Ma had been right about that. The sheep stood a couple of feet away and together they watched the mist thicken like soup. If he wasn't careful the daylight would go altogether, and night on Sheep Mountain was not an enticing thought.

His only option was to follow the path, it had to lead somewhere. He struck out again and the sheep kept pace for a few minutes, but the next time he looked back, it had disappeared. He slowed down, hoping it might reappear, but at last he had to admit defeat. Deserted, as ever.

A shape ahead slowly resolved into a solitary tree leaning at an improbable angle, and as he got closer he saw the path was running only feet away from a sheer drop and the rowan tree was clinging to the edge of the cliff. He didn't remember that either. Damned path; there had been no fork that he could remember, no choice to be made. It had twisted in the mist out of sheer malevolence.

He looked over the edge into nothingness. The drop could be five hundred metres down or fifty; no matter, either would be enough to put an end to everything. Not that there was much left to end. He balanced on the edge, holding onto the tree for balance. Should he let go? It would buy him a few moments of freedom, and then would come the darkness. That would be welcome enough if it were the end, but knowing his luck someone would find him alive and then it would be 'does he take sugar' for the rest of his existence.

He stepped back onto the path. Life had come down to two choices: either retrace his steps or carry on. If he went back, he knew that the overhang would have disappeared and the plane sunk out of sight. He would end up walking in spirals and getting nowhere on this grey mountain. Being stalked in a city was feeling more comfortable by the second.

This mist had coated his skin and clothes with a film of water, worse than rain, insidious and inescapable. After another hour, the path led to an outcrop of tumbled rocks and petered out. There was no way round, so he scrambled and slipped across the cold, wet obstacle course. He could almost see the ghost of the path starting again on the other side when his foot caught in a crack and no matter how he twisted and pulled, it seemed stuck fast. He made another attempt and felt something in his ankle reach breaking point, so he sank back, bracing himself against the slimy surface of the stone. His left leg was still twisted and if he stayed like this for too long he'd find it hard to walk at all.

With a few more contortions, he managed to reach down, unlace the trapped boot, and pull his foot free.

He wondered if he could hop all the way down the mountainside but it seemed unlikely, and the walking was hard enough even through Herman's Vibram soles. Never leave a boot behind, probably an SAS saying. Prying, tugging, pulling, twisting - nothing worked. The pockets of the rucksack were empty of anything he could use to free the boot; funny, he would have had Herman down as a bushcraft knife kind of guy. His fingers were bruised, bleeding and one fingernail lighter.

And his foot was cold. Wet and cold. The sheep was back, looking a little more goat-like as it perched on the rock next to him.

'I don't suppose you have any ideas?'

The sheep looked bored, as if standing on a rock in the mist was so yesterday, and ejected a spray of pellets.

'Shit. That just about sums it up - thanks.'

The sheep picked its way across, nuzzled the boot which tumbled free, and then ambled off into the mist, trailing its strands of brambles back the way it had come.

THE PATH HAD BEGUN to drop which, on balance, seemed like a good thing. After another hour a dry-stone wall came to join him, running parallel for a while before veering off again. He was walking through a field now, rather than the scrub of the fell. More trees appeared ahead, proper ones this time, bordering a stream crossed by a short wooden bridge. And after the bridge, mirabile dictu, a surfaced lane. He hadn't even noticed the mist fade away.

The house was hidden behind a bend in the lane, all stone and slate, with a couple of outbuildings and a stable block. A large chestnut horse and a small donkey were grazing together in a white fenced paddock, an old Land Rover sat parked opposite the house and the elderly border collie dozing by the front door showed no interest when he knocked. If nothing else, he needed to know where he was.

'Can I help you?' The woman who answered his knock wasn't what he'd expected; a walnut-faced farmer, perhaps, or a dumpling-armed wife. But the person smiling at him from the doorway was slim as a whip, with café latte skin and glistening black hair pinned up in a bun. And the scar on her face was a crescent moon, pale and enticing.

'Are you okay?' she said. 'You seem a little... dishevelled.' Her voice was low, with the unexpected hint of a soft Scottish accent. 'And that cut on your cheek looks rather nasty. Come in, I'll clean it up and get you a plaster.'

On the outside an ancient farmhouse, on the inside a Docklands apartment; glass and chrome and open spaces.

'Your boots - would you mind? One hates to ask, but the dog is bad enough, bless him.'

He left them by the front door, along with the rucksack, and followed her through to a kitchen that had probably cost more than Tansy's entire house. She sat him on a stool, wiped away the blood from his cheek with a piece of kitchen towel and found an Elastoplast in one of the concealed drawers. She smelled of cinnamon.

'You might want to clean up your hands - use the sink there. And some coffee? You look like you could do with it.'

She moved a laptop to one side on the glass-topped table. 'I find it easier to work down here - something about the kitchen being the heart of a home, I suppose. And I guess we should introduce ourselves. I'm Parvati McNeil, most people call me Pav. And you are...?'

'Quincey Radlett. I'm so sorry to bother you. There was

mist on the mountain and the path didn't live up to expectations. I don't think I'm where I should be.' Best not mention the sheep.

'It can be treacherous up there if you don't know the terrain. No problem. I just got to the end of a chapter, so I deserve a break. I'll make us something hot to drink and then I'll give you a lift to where you need to be.'

THEY TOOK the coffee through to the living area. The dog had let itself in and was occupying one of the armchairs.

'Worse than children,' she said.

He looked around for clues but the paintings on the walls were suitably abstract and there was just one framed photograph on the side table next to the sofa, Pav and a friend, arms round each other against a backdrop of gondolas on a canal lined with Gothic palaces.

'Your house,' he said, 'it's lovely.'

'The last couple of books did rather better than I'd hoped. When I left the day job everyone said that writing was a mug's game, but I guess I got lucky.'

'Day job?'

'I started off in the police, ended up on secondment to the Civil Service. Technical stuff mostly, very boring.'

'So that's why you don't mind inviting strange men into your home,' he said. 'The police, I mean.'

Her smile curved into the crescent scar. 'Don't turn down experiences, that's my motto. And although Tommy there looks docile, all it takes is one word of command and he goes straight for the jugular.'

The dog opened one eye and then closed it again.

. . .

AFTER HE FINISHED the coffee he said that a cab would be fine, but Pav insisted, 'Have you tried to get a taxi out here on a wet evening? Not going to happen,' and drove him back to the van in the next valley.

'Try not to get lost next time, Quincey, and keep an eye out for my next book. You never know who might make an appearance.'

———

TANSY WAS out and an envelope sat in the centre of his unmade bed, his name typed on the front. The same paper as last time, almost the same message, and a copy of one of the photos William had been munching on. '*Marcus send off. Tomorrow, 2 pm, same place as Esther. Don't be late, none of us can hang around forever.*'

CHAPTER
SEVENTEEN

There were no crowds at the crematorium this time. He arrived after the undertakers and sat at the back, wondering who the others were in the small clump at the front, five black crows. Family? Marcus hadn't mentioned any. Colleagues, perhaps, from the University.

The coffin looked so small on its dais, with one ring of white flowers lying on the top. The sounds of Handel faded from the tinny speakers and a stooped man in grey stationed himself behind the lectern and began. 'We are gathered here today to celebrate the life of Marcus Rothko Haremountain.' He paused, checked his notes, scratched his nose, looked around the audience as if for confirmation, and continued.

It was all too late. Quincey filtered out the cut'n'paste words and wondered who would do the marking now. He wondered what had happened to the dog. He wondered who was watching him.

The sounds of Bruce Springsteen pulled him back into the room: '*I'll wait for you, and if I should fall behind, wait for me'*. And a sax solo, while he realised that no-one would ever wait for him.

When the homilies were done, something jauntily classical faded back in while the congregation filed outside. In the perfectly timed drizzle, one of them detached itself from the rest and came over to him. 'Which of us is the bad penny, I wonder.' Joanna seemed more stork-like than usual, disguised in heels, black skirt and a hat. 'And how did you know Marcus?' she asked. 'Were you and he...?'

'God, no, I'm not, you know...'

'Who am I to judge, Quincey? I had wondered about you, but if you were gay you'd be more normal.'

'You don't think I'm normal?'

'Bad choice of word; what is normal, after all? Would "healthy" work better, or "sane"? Sorry, I should be charitable on a day like this. Marcus had his own demons, but he could never be honest with himself, let alone with anyone else.'

Joanna unpinned the fragment of hat and shook her hair free. 'It's a mercy any of us came at all. The University like to hush up this sort of thing. Happens with students more often that you'd think, now it's the staff. They have an image to maintain, everything rosy on the campus. And of course, we don't have students anymore, just customers. I remember reading about the Falklands victory parade, Thatcher refusing to let people in wheelchairs take part. It's the same attitude; if it's broken, keep it out of sight or throw it away, don't spoil the party. What sort of person acts like that?'

They walked together towards the car park. 'You still haven't told me how you knew Marcus,' she said.

'He was the friend of a friend.' So much for honesty.

'He sent an email,' Joanna said, 'to everyone on his

contacts list. Just one word, "Sorry". When you realise what he was going through, it puts your own problems into context.'

The next cortege had arrived already, another stream of sadness funnelling into the building behind them.

He walked with Joanna to her car and knocked on her window as she was about to pull away. 'Was it you who sent me the note about today?'

'Note? You are a strange man, Mr Radlett, I have no idea what you're talking about. And I really must go now, a lecture theatre full of first years to frighten. Good luck.'

IT TOOK a while before he found the source of the sound as he pulled up outside Tansy's; the mobile that Rob had persuaded him to buy, stuffed in a side pocket of Herman's rucksack.

He called back, thinking it could be a problem with Poppy; had Jennifer and Fenton reneged on the deal and executed a reverse kidnap?

The tenor tones had gone and on the phone Rob's voice sounded like a teenage boy going through puberty. 'Are you around tomorrow?'

Where else would he be?

'Cait has a meeting in Avonport in the morning and she wondered if you could meet her afterwards for a chat. She likes you, Quincey, I think she has a proposition.'

'She wants to marry me?'

'Don't be obtuse. She thought you could help her out with a project and it's not as if you're exactly over-committed at the moment. Do you know the Portofino Arts Centre? She'll be in the café, around one. Don't forget, Quincey, she doesn't like to be stood up.'

. . .

HE'D WALKED past the entrance many times, stashed on the gentrified Avonport dockside between an upmarket Tex-Mex restaurant and a bar with swollen men in suits guarding the door after six in the evenings, but the Portofino had never felt like something he was entitled to with its subtitled films and poetry slams and feminist speakers at events where they debated such excitements as 'The Relevance of Men in the Twenty-First Century'. If he remembered rightly, Cath had been invited to speak at that one; he hadn't enquired further.

Cait was already in the café when he arrived, talking on her mobile while alternately tapping at an iPad and sipping a latte. What was it about powerful women? She was wearing her hair up and that green jacket hadn't been stitched by children in a south Asian slum.

Esther would have liked it here; wholefood and worthy but definitely on trend, the sort of place that served mung bean sprouts on vodka jelly.

'What a morning.' Cait ended the call as he got to the table. He felt strange seeing her here, not knowing why he'd come. One day he'd grow up and stop doing what women asked without question. Some women.

'You must be wondering why I wanted to meet,' she said.

'To talk about Rob?'

'God, no! I wouldn't gossip about Rob behind his back. No, I wanted to ask you a favour. Are you doing anything next week? Clients to see? Hearings to go to?'

'I'm taking a break for a while.'

'How do you fancy a trip to Vancouver?' asked Cait, 'all expenses paid, naturally. I have some loose ends to tie up and I could do with a bit of professional support... what do you say?'

This was ridiculous. Sitting in a café with the lover of the mother of his child, a woman he'd met once, asking him to travel halfway round the world with her. He sipped the latte, stalling for time. Sitting in a café with an attractive woman who was smiling at him.

'I practice employment law, not commercial.'

'I don't need an expert, just someone to be a pretty face - well, you know what I mean. To be honest, I need to put on a bit of a show; don't worry, I'll make all the decisions.'

This was familiar territory at last. 'You want a bag carrier.' Donkey Quincey. 'There must be people working for you who know what they're doing. Why not take one of them?'

Ma would have called it a knowing laugh. 'You haven't met my staff because there aren't any. I run a lean operation, very selective projects. And I thought that maybe you and I ought to spend some time together and get up to speed, as it were. So I want to kill two birds with one stone; would that be so bad? Come on, we'll have fun, I think we have a lot in common. I'm going to help bring up your daughter, after all.'

Not exactly diplomatic, but probably true. 'When are you leaving?' he asked.

'Monday, from Heathrow. Business class, obviously. I'm guessing you've had a hard time recently, so maybe you could do with a change of scenery. I'll show you the haunts where I grew up and share some of my life with you.'

'Vancouver? You're going to love it, hon.' Tansy had prepared a chicken and nettle pie - Sarkozy was the gift that kept on giving. At least it wasn't roast pork. 'I had a lover came from Calgary, other side of the mountains; I was on a break from Herman and she reminded me somehow of Lori - same kindness, same gentle spirit inside. We used to drive into the Rockies and go hiking; the rivers in Alberta - man, you gotta see them. Like the world is new and that turquoise water ain't never been anywhere else.'

'Why didn't you stay?'

'Herman turned up again like the proverbial bad penny.' She shrugged. 'Things were different in those days.'

She cleared the plates away and poured them both another glass of red from a carafe. 'You wanna share a smoke? I ran out of home-grown but my man got me some new stuff, way more mellow - just like the old days. Kids these days with their skunk and coke and ketamine - sometimes gentle and slow is best.' She winked. 'You sure?' She took a pre-rolled joint from the kitchen drawer and sent a blue smoke ring towards Lili, perched on the back of the chair next to him.

'You gonna tell me more about this Cait?,' said Tansy. 'Not heard her name before, all seems a bit sudden. Not that I'm judging, honey. Lord knows I'm far too well acquainted with the short path betwixt frying pan and fire.'

'She's a friend... of a friend.'

'Have it your own way. But be careful, secrets are like boulders in a backpack. They weigh you down; try to carry too many and one day you'll find you just can't take another step. Leastways, not till you let some of them go.' She drained her glass. 'But while you're here and hale, what say we go tease William.'

They wandered down the path towards his pen; there was no sight of any incriminating documents today, which had to count as some sort of blessing. Tansy had brought a plate of scraps from their supper and threw them over the fence. 'When I was a kid, if ever I felt life was unfair I'd go look at the pigs. And you know what I realised? Just how lucky I was that I would never end up on someone's dinner table next to a jug of apple sauce.'

As THE FLIGHT ATTENDANT PASSED, Quincey changed his mind and asked for a glass of champagne along with the orange juice. Just the one, to relax him. At least the seats in business class were comfortable enough; more like individual pods herringboned along the cabin. As the Airbus left the British coast, he tried to read the thriller he'd picked up in Departures, but this was one of his bad days and the words were dancing a mad tarantella on the paper.

'Book not cutting it?' said a voice. 'Don't blame you, it's not one of her best. Me, I like character as well as plot. But they have some good in-flight movies; trust me, I've seen them all. Give yourself a break and relax, the boss can't see you here.' The woman settled herself into the seat across the other side of the aisle. Sixty, maybe a little less, with brittle, blonde hair framing her face like a spun helmet. She strapped herself back in and then smiled across. 'Or maybe you are the boss? Not that you have that sort of look. No offence.'

'None taken.'

'Who can tell these days? My daughter, now she'll be the boss one day - she's in advertising in London. The clients love her, she has a flair with words. A sentence or two from her and you'd buy anything. But that's not your business, I can tell. PR? No, I don't think so. The movies maybe? Or television; you're going out to pitch an idea for the new Breaking Bad. They do a lot of filming in BC – we got the space and the forests, maybe not the weather, but who wants to be in California these days?' She drained her half empty glass of wine and signalled for another.

He closed the book. 'None of the above. I'm a sort of lawyer, or used to be. Not quite Hollywood.'

'Lawyer - there's a word to conjure with. "The first thing we do, let's kill all the lawyers." Henry Six, Part Two. Whenever my Sasha gets too full of himself, I quote that at him. You have offices in Vancouver?'

'No, I'm helping a friend, just a short trip and then home.' At the end of the cabin, the food trolley had started its progress and the air was tinted with the scent of gravy.

'So what were you doing in the UK?' he asked.

'It was my daughter's wedding. In my day it was family and a few friends, now they invite the man who sells them skinny latte in the morning.' She leaned across the aisle and dropped her voice. 'And the stuff that goes on before! I spent my hen night in a friend's apartment, smoking joints and discussing The Female Eunuch. They were trying to persuade me not to go ahead; maybe I should have listened harder. But my daughter – a week in the Caribbean with her entourage, I don't want to know what she got up to.'

'So what about your husband, did he come too?'

'My Sasha?' She shook her head. 'That man... You know, he told me that if I went to London, I'd find the locks changed when I got back. My daughter and him, they don't speak, don't ask why. Five years I have to put up with this shit, being their go-between, and now he thinks he can tell me what to do. I'll show him "change the locks".'

'You don't look worried.'

The woman laughed, and her gold earrings fluttered. 'He gives me the backchat, I call his mother in Florida. Ten seconds on the phone to her and he's like a five-year-old who never got potty trained. I get no trouble after that until the next time.'

'Sounds like you know what you're doing.'

'You wonder why I stay with him. I wonder the same. When you're young, you make these compromises and you call it love, maybe you even believe it. He wanted free sex and someone to tidy up after him, never mind the food, and I wanted kids. We both got what we wanted, so what's to complain about? It's like a dance you do around each other, all those years, until one day you realise the music stopped a long time ago. And then you look around and think, where else would I go? I have a good home and a good car, I play golf when I want, and the bed's big enough that we don't embarrass each other by touching in the night. And you should see my tennis pro!'

After the meal the woman put on headphones to watch a film, but when he looked across she was asleep, her mouth slackly open and her glasses on their chain rising and falling on her chest, along with her breaths.

HE HAD EXPECTED A HOTEL, but the taxi dumped them in the rain by a tree outside an anonymous 1980s building. In the middle of a confluence of streets stood a stunted, nineteenth century clock tower that wouldn't have looked out of place in a mill town in England. 'I keep a base here,' Cait said, 'never burn all your boats.'

If the weather stayed like this, they were going to need them. He was too tired to take in the apartment; after the ordered-in pizza he crashed in his room. 'Day off tomorrow,' Cait said, 'get your bearings before we settle down to business.' At least she took a civilised approach to life.

. . .

ALTHOUGH THE OVERNIGHT rain had long since stopped, the streets of Gastown were still steaming the next morning as he wandered slowly without a plan, other than to find somewhere for coffee. He had slept poorly, propping himself up in bed, uncomfortable and damp in the humid air and listening to the storm. As the large windows of the apartment had turned from dark blue to pale grey, he wondered if he would ever again wake up next to a woman who might love him. He wondered if he ever had.

A couple ambled out from a café onto the street in front of him, holding hands and lost in a shared joke. They look so incongruous, the boy way more than six-foot tall with shaggy blonde hair, the dark-haired girl barely up to his chest; Japanese, he guessed, or maybe Korean. Look at it the right way and the ocean here faced east. Behind them trailed the smell of coffee and pastries and he felt the need for a shot of caffeine and some sugar, to kick-start his body. He took an empty seat by one of the large windows and ordered a double espresso with a glass of water, hoping it might dispel the spacey, disconnected feeling.

Cait had been gone when he woke, leaving him a set of keys, fifty dollars, and a note saying she had chores and would be back later. Such an early abandonment. It usually took them much longer; at least this time he'd been given keys rather than asked to relinquish them.

He signalled to the waiter wearing his 'I'm a Smart Mouth' T-shirt and ordered another coffee, the best he'd had since that tempestuous weekend in Lucca with... Who was it with? It took him a second to remember the name, even though he could picture the freckles on her face, the swell of her small breasts, he could hear the tenement in her Sauchiehall voice. Lynn, of course, playing away from home in more ways than one while her husband served the final months of a two stretch for burglary. Benny, that was her man, a 5'5" package of shaved head and strut. They'd gone for a meal, the three of them, a couple of days after Benny got out; '*He's a puppy dog, babe, but he don't bite.*' Somewhere on Upper Street in Islington; they'd sat in a conservatory at the back of the restaurant and Benny had paid. Best not ask where the money had come from. '*Thank you,*' Benny had said, '*for looking after my girl while I was away.*' The 'now you can fuck off' was there in his off-centre smile.

On the pavement outside, the summer night over-used and warm while a bus rumbled down to the City, Lynn had kissed him on the cheek while Benny watched; a slow, Silk Cut valedictory. '*Thanks babe,*' she'd whispered, and that was it. Chapter end, move on.

He pushed the cup away and signalled for the bill, wondering why every memory had to be such an irretrievable death.

CAIT WAS WAITING for him back at the apartment. 'We have a car,' she said, 'fancy a ride?'

They drove out of the city towards the mountains, the highway soon surrounded by tracts of forest for which the term 'virgin' could have been invented. 'I thought I'd show you where I grew up,' she said. 'I always think knowing more about someone's background gives a context to their actions.' Her accent was stronger here, as if she'd stopped trying.

They turned off the main highway, passed a green sign to 'Fraserwood Lookout, Elevation 415 m' and after another mile or so, he saw a barely readable notice as the car slowed; 'Fraserwood Trailer Park.' Someone had sprayed a fluorescent yellow tag across the faded letters, the only colour left. 'We'll park here, by the entrance,' said Cait, 'easier to get away quickly if we need to.'

Which didn't sound auspicious.

There was no order that he could divine, no purpose in the placing of the trailers; why couldn't they call them caravans like normal people? They were dotted about the couple of acres of scrubby grass and gravel, most of them resting on concrete blocks, washing lines de rigeur. The puddles, he felt, might be bottomless.

Cait led him along what passed for a path. 'Don't mind the stares. People dressed like us, they'll assume we're social workers. No-one else would want to come out here.' She stopped by a trailer that looked no different from any of the others - rusted white, an aerial on the roof, a jerry-built set of wooden steps leading up to the open door, and a couple of opaque windows.

'Can't show you the actual shit heap where I lived; there was a fire and it burned down. My mom died along with the man who was fucking her, which was a mercy for us all. But this is the plot.' She looked around. 'Last time I was here it was covered in snow – and don't go having any fancy notions about White Christmases. It's crap now, and it was crap then.'

She didn't seem to expect any expressions of solicitude, which was just as well; at least he wasn't the only angel of death in the vicinity.

'I guess it's a little different from the Radlett residence where you grew up,' she said.

'It's not what I expected.'

'I don't think my mom ever expected to be here, either. Me, I didn't know any better.'

'So what happened?'

'You really want to know?' She scuffed her foot in the dirt. 'I never knew my dad. He cut himself out of our life because he had another family, so much better than us. I used to wonder; did he send us away because we were trailer trash, or is that what we became because of his cruelty? An interesting conundrum, huh? Chickens and eggs and all that shit.'

She sniffed the air, looked around the park and then up to the distant peaks. 'I was much older when I found out how mom was paying for the rent and the weekly groceries. There were always guys around. At first she used to see them during the day when I was at school, but when they started to turn up in the evenings, I'd go stay with Maria in the next unit.'

A man appeared at the open door of the trailer; the black dog at his feet, a barrel on legs, was wearing a Vancouver Canucks tee shirt. Neither seemed pleased to see them.

'You guys need any help? See you staring at my place here like I'm some kinda sideshow.'

'We were looking for Earl,' said Cait, taking off her sunglasses and propping them on her head. 'Earl Lekker – you seen him?'

'Ain't no Earl here. If I was you, I'd move on.'

As they made their way back to the car, Quincey asked, 'who's Earl.'

'Unlucky shit, Earl, wrong place at the wrong time. He paid his dues, though. I saw to that.'

An indeterminate child cycled past on a bike held together with duct tape, missing Cait by an inch.

'You have no idea how much I wanted a bike when I was a kid,' she said, watching the child wobble away. 'No way mom could have paid for one, food was hard enough.

I said to her, doesn't have to be new, but I wasn't top priority.' She turned back to Quincey. 'When you were young, I bet you had some great wheels; no way Quincey Radlett would go without, huh? You probably think, why's she so worked up about a fucking bike, but it was as much about what it signified as what it was. When you're a poor kid with nothing you don't reason like that, you just know you drew the short straw. Life isn't fair, never could be fair.'

'So your father didn't help out?'

'He was the one paid for us to come out here from England, to get us far out of the way so we didn't intrude on his real life. At first he looked after the rent on an apartment in Eastside, so mom said, which was crap but better than this shithole. When I was eight the money stopped. My mom didn't know why at first, but then she found out; my father had died, not that I knew who he was.'

The clouds opened again, a rainforest downpour through the humid air, and the puddles were joining into lakes.

'I don't know how she managed, but mom found the money to take us back to England. More "uncles" visiting, I guess. *"He won't have forgotten us,"* she said, *"at heart he was a good man, he'll have left something."* I didn't know who she was talking about, not then. But she was wrong and her "good man" left us nothing. In death, as in life, we were the fucking dregs.'

She stood by the car, her hair straight and dark in the rain.

'We went to the funeral and sat apart from everyone else. I remember insisting on wearing my baseball cap, it wasn't as if I knew what was going on. We were at the back while the real family was at the front. But if it hadn't been for them, I would have had a life.' She shrugged. 'And I guess that was the first time I saw you.'

Water trickled down the back of his neck and under his shirt and his shoes were patterned with mud.

'I don't understand...'

'That's your trouble, Quincey, you never understand. You know why I brought you here? So that you could see what you missed because our father chose you instead of me. All of this; would you have swapped?'

He tried to think of something to say, but she didn't give him the chance.

'I had plans,' she said. 'All the work I put in to change my life and get what I was owed. I played a long game; you have no idea what I had to do to get by, to succeed and not end up like my mother. When I got to the UK and found you I took your possessions, your lovers; I even took your child. And all of that was going to come to a climax right here. This would be where I delivered my coup de grâce. But now we're together in this shitty little place, it feels like dust in my mouth. It's not enough. Perhaps nothing could ever be enough.' She spat on the ground. 'To think I used to envy you.'

Dust in her mouth, stones instead of words in his. The rain was running down his back and his chest, his feet had sunk into the mud, and all he could do was watch silently as Cait drove out of the trailer park, down the track, and out of his sight.

CHAPTER EIGHTEEN

H is leg felt suddenly warm; the dog in the tee-shirt had arrived, along with its owner, and pissed on him.

'You still here? Lady friend dumped you? Too fuckin' bad. I'd get my ass outta here if I was you, fuckin' loser. Go on, fuck off back where you came from. We don't need your sort round here.'

Weren't Canadians meant to be nice? Still, it sounded like a plan. He shouldered the rucksack and started down the road in the general direction of the city, trying to make sense of what Cait had said. His father's funeral, the child at the back - that had been her, another sister. Lose one, gain one. And she blamed him for her crappy life.

He massaged the back of his neck and tried to ignore the headache. What he wouldn't give now for the beach hut, a mug of coffee, and only the sea for company.

Twenty minutes later, he was by the turnoff to the lookout that they'd passed on the way in. Two cars had driven by, neither of them the right one, but at least the rain had stopped. He got out the mobile phone but there was no signal to call for a taxi even if he knew a number, even if any would come out this far.

He wished he still smoked. For some reason he wanted to be off the road, at least for a while; it was a week since he'd walked alone in the Welsh mountains, but the cut on his cheek had refused to heal and his jaw ached as if he had been chewing leather for days. He turned into a small parking area and took a path from the sign that led through the woods, the trees so different from the homely beeches and oaks of Gwenstow. He'd felt it from the moment he came out of the terminal building on Monday, as if everything here was scaled up. The trees were no different; ridged red bark, their tops lost in the mist. Not so easy to hang yourself from one of these.

The path, though, could have been transplanted from a municipal park, including the occasional used condoms like tapeworms in the grass. He was about to turn back when the ground ahead fell away behind a wooden railing and he looked out across a sea of dark green trees towards the towers of the city in the distance; it would be a long walk home.

A bench faced the vista and he sat on the edge, not trusting his legs. For sure, he had been evil in a previous life if this was his karma now. Or perhaps there was no plan, nothing but blind chance and his luck had run out. And yet; other people starved, lived through wars or were eaten up by disease. Other people hated life so much they left it of their own volition. As for him, he was simply going to wear out a bit of shoe leather unless he got a lift back, or his new sister reappeared from wherever she had taken herself.

Try as he might, he couldn't wrap his thoughts around what Cait had told him. Images chased themselves in his mind; a child in a baseball cap at his father's funeral,

Jennifer at the beach hut, calling Pa an old goat. Lying in bed, listening to Ma and Pa arguing downstairs, knowing that in the morning there would be one less glass or plate in the cupboard.

He turned suddenly at a noise behind him as a man appeared, a walking advert for the benefits of steroids and gym membership. 'Hi, mind if I join you?' he said. A statement rather than a question. The man sat a little nearer than felt comfortable; perhaps personal space here was in inverse proportion to the size of the country.

'You want one?' The man held out a pack of cigarettes. 'Having a smoke together always feels more sociable somehow, breaks the ice.'

Why not? Perhaps his luck was about to change, his wishes about to be answered. The smoke hit the back of his throat, burrowing down into his lungs. His heart started to race, and he felt the faintest hint of nausea.

'You been here before?' the man asked. 'Not seen you around, not that it matters. Nice to have new blood on the scene.' The man shifted a little closer. 'You okay? Not your first time, goddamn! Man, I love me a virgin.'

No, his luck hadn't changed. Same old.

'I'm so sorry,' he said. 'I think there's been a misunderstanding.'

'A Brit? Even better, Ain't never had a Brit before. They say you guys are tight-arsed, guess we'll find out.'

A hand was on his groin now, palpating. He pushed it away and stood, grabbing the rucksack and backing away from the bench. 'There really has been a mistake. I was just sitting here, I'm not looking for anything else.'

'Come on, look at you. Bet you're not a virgin after all, bet you were a real chicken when you were younger. Bet all the guys wanted a go. And you let them, didn't you, fuckin' prick tease. You want it, don't you, you're gagging to feel me inside your tight little arse, you fucking little faggot.'

The man got to his feet and, from nowhere, a knife was in his hand. He shrugged, almost apologetically. 'I'm going to fuck you,' he said,' alive or dead. Don't matter to me. Maybe then you'll learn not to sit in the wrong place and talk crap. Someone less thoughtful than me, he'd think this was all part of the chase, bit of a game. Is that what it is, my friend? Because I'm not playing, I'm here to teach faggots like you a lesson you won't forget.'

A long time ago, when the world was different, there had been the karate classes to make him feel more like a man - hadn't worked - a dojo in the back streets of Avonport. Wado Ryu, the Way of Peace. But here, it didn't seem so easy.

'You're wondering, aren't you? What are my chances?' The man painted a circle in the air with the knife point. 'I can tell you now – zero. Don't worry, I don't really want to kill you; makes such a mess. Unless I have to, of course. Hurting, that's a different matter.' Against the backdrop of trees, his face was lit by the afterglow of sunset. 'Think about it, that would be like a farmer killing his milk cows. Cut and come again, that's what I say.' He was playing with the knife now, tossing it in the air and catching it by the handle. 'Do you see what I did there, cut and come again?' His voice had become a little softer, a little quieter. 'Just because I hate faggots don't make me a mindless animal, you know.'

Quincey realised that while he'd been talking the man was slowly moving towards him, forcing him backwards along the narrow trail between the trees. In the cleared space between the path and the undergrowth were fallen branches, detritus from the recent storm.

'Faggots like you, you think you can pick and choose. Not good enough, am I? Have you looked at yourself? You drip privilege like pus.'

He stopped moving, his head a little to one side like a bird. 'On the other hand, you're very quiet. Very controlled. I like that in a man – nothing extraneous, just get down to business. Not like women, always shrieking and leaking. Tell you the truth, I wish there were more like you, life would be a lot less messy. Take your licks, learn your lesson. So what d'you say, shall we stop playing and get down to business? From the moment you sat on that bench, there was only going to be one outcome.'

Maybe the man was telling the truth. Maybe all that would happen if he gave in was a rough fuck in the bushes, and then he would be left alone with twigs in his hair and scratches on his legs, ashamed and bruised and bleeding. But he'd seen the look on the man's face, he'd heard the craziness in his voice. No way he was going to go free, no matter what happened next. So he had no choice; it was either run or fight and he wouldn't put money on either. The only other alternative was to negotiate, wasn't that what you were meant to do? Show that you were a person, not an object, and build some empathy.

'We don't have to do this,' he said. 'You haven't told me your name. I'm Quincey, I...'

'Jesus, you even got a fag name. You see, we're past all that, *Quincey*, a situation like this moves things on a bit. You and me, we're like old friends now; we've walked our poodles in the park together, had coffees afterwards, a couple of cosy meals in that cute restaurant we both like in Kitsilano, that lingering first kiss. Isn't that what perverts like you dream about? Don't matter, it all leads to the same place, where we are right now. I just like taking shortcuts to cut out the uncertainties.'

It wasn't the sex, he realised, although it shouldn't have been a revelation. It was the power and the control, that's what this bastard was getting off on. This must be how women felt, powerless in situations they couldn't control. Scared to death. And how many times had he allowed himself to hear a 'no' as 'yes'?

The knife was quite steady now, held low. Even through the shadows, Quincey could sense the man's muscles tensing as he prepared to make his move, adrenaline kicking in. The man was a grizzly in jeans and sweatshirt but, with luck, he wasn't that fast. Steroids could make a man strong, for sure, but clumsy. And they messed with the brain.

Quincey was a realist. Negotiation had failed, and fighting would only have one outcome, but he was pretty good at running away. All he had to do was stay out of his attacker's clutches, and at least the waiting was over.

The knife was in the man's left hand, and as he made his move forward, Quincey feinted to the right, ducked past and ran into the woods.

He swerved through the undergrowth as he heard crashing behind him and the man swearing, then jumped a small pile of logs and resisted the temptation to turn and look backwards. The main road was just ahead now; he swung around one of the ancient red cedars, feeling the bark rough under his hand, and then caught his foot on something - a branch, a root. He stumbled for a couple more steps, flailing his arms to find some balance, but the gyroscope in his head was spinning out of control and he fell too heavily, catching his side on a tree stump, feeling something inside him tear and break. He tried not to cry out with the pain, but a noise escaped anyway, an animal's whimper. He managed to push himself upright; a few more metres and he'd be out of the trees and by the road. As he staggered into the parking area, a car pulled in. He allowed himself a backwards glance for the first time and saw, through the branches, his pursuer disappearing now that there were witnesses.

A couple of men climbed out of the newly arrived car, on their way for a little fun after a day in the office.

'Are you okay? You look like shit, my friend.'

If anyone else said that, he'd have to start believing it. 'I fell in the woods. I'll be fine.'

'If you say so, cupcake, you take care now.'

He could barely put any weight on his right leg and the stabbing pain in his side was probably a cracked rib, but he had no option. The clouds had almost gone and the moon lit the road ahead of him. Time to go home, wherever that was.

IN THE DREAM he was standing on a high cliff, dangling a line in the river hundreds of feet below. The water was silver with fish, twisting and leaping in the moonlight. He begged them not to take the hook as he couldn't bear the thought of dragging one into the poisonous soup of oxygen, to watch it dull before his eyes. But they weren't listening and he swung the line like a pendulum, backwards and forwards until one fish - as large as a pony - landed on the ground beside him. 'You can't sleep here,' it said in a voice like honey, 'storm's coming back, need to get you inside.'

The fish took his arm in its mouth and shook him gently. He opened his eyes and looked into the face of a woman crouched beside him, framed with black hair that was highlighted by the moon. 'You took some waking, thought I was gonna to have to call 911. Let's get you in the truck 'fore the next storm hits, gonna be showtime tonight.'

She was stronger than she looked which was just as well, given a leg which was proving completely recalcitrant and the sharp pain in his side. 'Wondered if I'd found me some road kill when I saw you lying there,' she said. 'That's it, lean your weight, I ain't gonna snap.' She opened the door of an ancient red pickup while he steadied himself against the bonnet, enjoying the warmth of the engine.

'Now we just got to get you up - there you go, sorry there ain't no more elegant way to do this.'

She climbed up beside him and pulled away. 'I'm guessing if you had someone to call you woulda done it already. No matter, my place is 'bout five klicks away. I'm proposing we go there, get you dry and put some coffee into you, then make a plan. You okay with that?'

THE COFFEE CAME FIRST, then a plate of salmon. She watched him while he ate, cleared the plate away and felt his forehead. 'You got yourself a temperature. Anything I should know? Apart from that leg, you got any other pains?'

'I think I cracked a rib.'

She made him pull up his shirt and felt his side, making him wince. 'Can't be sure unless you have an X-Ray but wouldn't change nothin'. Painkillers and don't lift nothin' heavy. What else? That cut's a coupla days old at least but don't look too good - how'd it happen?'

'A plane door fell off when I was looking for bodies, caught me in the face. Then I slipped in some shit, not that I'm complaining about the sheep. She freed my boot from the rock, which was more than I could do.' He really would have to stop these streams of consciousness or people would think he was weird.

'You on something or do all Brits act like this?'

'I wish,' he said. 'Sorry, it's been a bad few weeks.'

'All the same, you should have a shot. My husband - long gone and good riddance - he cut himself when he was clearing a patch of land we used to own, down by the river. Got tetanus, shook like an aspen for weeks.'

'What happened - did he die?'

'No, he moved to Seattle with the woman from the grocery store. Man, she was ugly.'

'What about you?'

She waved at the paintings covering every square foot of the walls, except where there were weavings and arrangements of feathers. 'I paint, I make, I teach. Sometimes do a bit of healing, unless antibiotics are called for. On which point, we should get you seen to. One benefit of having a very discreet friend and neighbour who's also my personal medic, we don't have to drive into the city. Trust me, you don't wanna wait all night in one of the Emergency Rooms. No arguments. You can tell me your story after Freddy's gone.

HIS ARM WAS sore from the injection. 'We should really get you in a hospital for observation,' the doctor said, 'but for now I've given you a shot of TIG to kill off any tetanus bacteria that might be careering around your bloodstream. We could be lucky but Alice, you see any symptoms, don't take no for an answer, get him down to St John's.'

Alice showed him into a bedroom covered in posters of a band he'd never heard of. 'My son's. He crashes here from time to time when he gets back from a tour. That's him...'

she pointed to a figure on one of the posters. 'Plays bass, pretty damn good. You can catch them on YouTube, got their own channel. He says no-one wants a recording contract these days; you give more'n half the money away, so why not do it all themselves? I say, if that's the way to go why do you end up here with your dirty laundry, looking half-starved, but that's kids for you.'

When she'd gone, he lay on top of the bed, staring at a ceiling painted turquoise. The same rucksack, another room. One day, maybe, he'd be able to start another life. And then he thought; maybe I already have. The only trouble was, it didn't seem any better than the first.

Breakfast came in piles: bacon, pancakes, hash browns, fried eggs. 'Figured you needed sustenance,' said the woman, 'you're looking kinda skinny. Didn't have you down for a yogurt and blueberry guy but maybe I'm wrong. You started shaking yet? Good, looks like Freddy's jab worked - more coffee?'

After he'd finished, she took him through into a back room with canvases stacked against the walls and cupboards. 'The gallery in town offered a one-woman show and I have to decide what to take in. And I'm working on something new.'

The canvas on the easel was half sketch, half painting in vivid reds and yellows. He walked over to look more closely. 'Do you mind?'

'Knock yourself out. I stopped being precious 'bout my work a long time ago. I usually create from imagination but this is based on something real. Nothin' wrong with a bit of change every so often.'

'I'm sorry, I'm not sure...'

'It's a totem pole, or will be. Freddy's son, he decided to get back to his roots, trained with a carver over on Vancouver Island. This is from one he finished recently, made from a piece of four hundred year old cedar. I took photos, made a sketch, now the imagination comes in. The original isn't decorated, I'm adding the colour in the painting.'

'What is it?'

'That top face, that's a wolf - see the teeth? And he's holding an owl, keeping it safe. It represents strength guarding wisdom - can't argue with that.'

She cleared a chair of rags and half-used paint tubes. 'You mind if I work? No matter what else is happening I do a little every day, helps keep the soul toned.'

He sat to one side, next to the large glass doors looking out onto a garden with a small stream running through, watching as she painted over the sketch touch by touch.

'Don't want to put any pressure on you, cowboy. We all got stories we wanna keep private. But the spirit, some-times it needs confession, stops the tubes from getting clogged. You and me, we're strangers. What you tell me stays here, ain't gonna share it with no-one. Got no-one to share it with.'

Her long, black hair was tied back in a scarf and the pale blue smock was dotted with paint. She was so... complete, that was the word. Most people had blurred edges where they leaked into the world, but hers were firm. Was this what contentment looked like?

'I guess there's a woman in there somehow, usually is for a man. Am I right?'

Perhaps she was, perhaps he needed to purge what passed for his soul.

'Her name was Esther,' he said, and after that the words wouldn't stop.

IN ALL THE time he was talking she didn't turn around once, didn't interrupt, never needed to prompt. When he stopped nearly an hour later, drained, she put down her brush and looked around.

'You were lucky. Been a series of attacks by that lookout, one boy died coupla months ago. Was always a favourite place for guys to hook up with each other, most of them found some place else I guess.'

She stood back from the easel. 'So, what do you think? It's meant to be seen from the ancestors' side, that's why the colours are different. Otherwise why bother? Might as well get your phone out and upload a photo to Instagram.'

'It's very impressive.'

'Don't worry, can't like everything you see.' She went over to the sink in the corner and washed her hands and arms like a surgeon after a procedure. 'This Cait, you say she's your sister and you never even knew?'

'Half sister, if it's true.'

'You don't believe her?'

'I'm not sure what I believe anymore.'

'So all this time, all this crap been happening to you, it was this woman stalking you 'cause you had a Pappy and she didn't. I know there's crazy folks in this world but she sounds like a real doozy. I guess there's one way to start finding out more; you know the address of the apartment you were staying in?'

'No, but I could find it if I was in the right part of town. There was a sort of clock tower, and I know it was near the sea.'

'Gastown.' She checked her watch. 'We leave now, we'll be there by lunchtime. Get that bag of yours, cowboy. If you feel up to it, let's go see what's occurring.'

Was it only yesterday he had walked down these streets? They passed the coffee bar, found the building, and Alice insisted on taking the stairs up. 'Don't hold with elevators, not natural.' He thought it best not to ask why she didn't walk everywhere instead of perching in the cockpit of the battered pickup.

His key still worked, which was a bonus, and there was movement inside, the sound of a vacuum cleaner which stopped as they shut the door behind them. He half expected to see a duchess, but it was a young woman in cut-off jeans with a basket of dusters and cleaning sprays.

'Sorry,' she said, 'I didn't think anyone else coming in till later. The agency...' Eyes to heaven. 'They give till two pm to get done, new tenants come at three, that's the rule.' She looked at them both more carefully. 'You guys sure travel light.'

He looked at the key as if it had betrayed him. 'This is the right place...'

'All depends which place you mean. This apartment 403, only me and agency got master key so I guess you where you should be.'

Alice was prowling through the rooms - a bit like a wolf, he imagined, sniffing for the scent of clues. 'That Cait sure ain't around. This place is stripped; hope you weren't expecting to pick up any of your gear 'cause it ain't here now.'

She turned to the cleaner. 'You said tenants; my friend here, he says this belongs to a colleague of his from the UK.'

'No way, this whole block vacation apartments. Company own it has places all over town.' She had her mobile out now. 'Maybe I call agency, ask what you guys doing here. Sound like fuckin' big time balls up, no way they blame me. I got kids, you know.'

Quincey handed her the key. 'You're right, it was a mistake. Sorry to have bothered you.' And then, slo-mo and strangely peacefully, he felt himself fold to the floor.

ALICE HAD SWALLOWED her distaste for the elevator and they were sitting in the café. 'Should have let me call an ambulance.'

'I'm okay, caught that cut on my cheek when I tripped just now.'

'That weren't no trip, you collapsed like a stunned steer. Not surprising, the shocks you had.'

One way to put it.

It felt as if blood was trickling down his face. 'Even this apartment was a lie. She said it was hers, but it was just a holiday rental.'

Alice balled a paper napkin and reached over to dab at the cut. 'When you arrived, was there any personal stuff around? Photos, clothes?'

It was only two days ago, but it felt like a year. 'I don't know, I was whacked. We ate pizza and then I went to sleep.'

'That's guys for you, never look at what's around them. My husband, he'd say "where's the scissors," and I'd say "in the drawer" and he'd open it and say "no they ain't" and I'd go over and move a bitty piece of paper and there they'd be. If it ain't in front of your eyes, you don't see it - am I right?'

Alice ordered mushroom soup and a croissant, he chose

a maple bacon scone. None of this made sense, but then nothing had in the last month. One change, that's all it would have taken. After going through those documents from Joanna he should have gone home, or stayed at the beach hut, anywhere but to see Esther. A high price to pay for such fleeting pleasure. But on balance, she'd paid more.

The bill came, and he realised that he was almost out of dollars.

'My treat,' said Alice, 'looks like it's about time someone took care of you.'

HE SAT IN THE STUDIO, watching Alice as she painted. The glass doors were open and the stream in the garden glinted in the afternoon sunlight, reminding him of the sea at Kilvercombe. A world away; would it matter if he never saw it again?

'Could you pass me that rag, the one by the sink?'

He took it over to her, aware of the scent of walnut from her hair. He had never known anyone so un-needing of him, of anything. He handed over the cloth and let his hand touch hers. Time was he would have reached for more, perhaps he should now.

She hadn't moved away. Her head was no higher than his shoulder, and the warmth from her body was almost palpable.

'Not so easy to paint with a body standin' by your elbow.'

There was the hint of a shadow on her upper lip, fine black down that cried out to be kissed. She reached to take the hand that he'd stretched to stroke her cheek: 'No-one asks first, not where you come from?'

She was standing so close but still looking up at him; an

animal would stare like that. He pulled away until there was clear air between them. This, he thought, is where I've been going wrong.

Alice wiped at a spot of paint on her arm, making a comet's tail of gold. 'Did I tell you 'bout the land we're on here? Where we are now, this is First Nation land. It was ours long before you people came over the plains and the mountains and stole it, herding us into reserves like we were animals. We didn't just live on the land, we lived *with* it. We never took more than we needed. Then you came with your guns and your germs and your steel and we had no chance. Like we learned at college, you changed the paradigm and we were the losers.

'And what you did to us is what men always do to women. You take whatever you want without asking because you think it's your right. You take more than you need simply because you can, and you never think you have to pay.'

'You can always say no,' he said, already realising how weak that sounded.

'You know how many men hear that word? Honestly? I seen the red mist come into a man's eyes - and you know the first time? Was my father, his true love was Jim Beam whisky. Which meant he spent pretty much all of his life drunk. When my mother walked out on him - I was twelve, I didn't have that choice - I had to take her place every which way. And I learned never, ever, to say no. So remember, just 'cause you got the strength don't give you rights. Not over a thousand bodies, nor just one.'

She was standing at such a strange angle, but then so was the rest of the room. Everything tilting, a slow progression from the vertical to the horizontal just like watching a forest from the perspective of a falling tree.

'Aw shit,' he heard Alice say, 'here we go again.'

HE WASN'T sure how they got up the stairs. There had been halts along the way, he seemed to remember, while Alice alternately swore and cajoled; at one point she had her shoulder under his arse. Shame would be an appropriate emotion, but he hadn't enough energy. He wasn't even sure what shame felt like.

He was shivering again, about five on the Richter scale. Hard to undo buttons and zips when the hands are enjoying a spell of palsy. He gave up the fight and let Alice undress him, then felt her lying beside him, earthing the tremors as she held him close.

When he woke, the curtains were open and a blade of moonlight lay across Alice's face on the pillow next to his. Under the covers, her arm was light on his chest and her breasts moved gently against him with her breathing. The shivering had stopped.

Alice opened her eyes. 'I guess you're awake, feeling better too.' She reached over and felt his forehead. 'Temperature's okay. Maybe it was just a reaction to the shot Freddy gave you. He always has a heavy hand with the meds; him and germs, it's personal.'

THE PILE of breakfast pancakes next morning was no less high and the bacon no less crisp. Alice brought a fresh jug of coffee. 'How you feelin' this morning? Freddy reckons you're exhausted, but I still think he overdid the meds. Sleep should have helped.' The sheen in her hair was like oiled steel. 'What I said yesterday, I meant it all. Still do. But

I see you had it hard too, in your way. All I ask is, don't put yourself first all the time.'

She asked for his phone. 'Gonna give you my number, case you end up staying around for a while, gettin' yourself well. Damn... don't you even turn this thing on?' She punched in her number and handed it back. 'You don't read your messages neither, new one there for you by the looks of it.'

Eight thirty in the morning here. That made it four thirty in the afternoon in the UK, on the hillside overlooking the sea. Rob answered on the first ring. 'Where are you, Quincey? Cait said you got delayed. Did you screw up again?'

On a crappy phone call from over four thousand miles away was probably not the best time to explain what had happened. Joy deferred.

'The police came round, and the social,' said Rob. 'Someone said I'd abducted Poppy, that she wasn't mine. I thought it was Jennifer, but when I called she said not. The woman from social services, real bitch, she obviously didn't believe me. I could see the look on her face as she sat here, looking at me as if I were dog shit.'

'So what happened - is Poppy ok?'

'She's still here, for now. But Quincey, what if they take her away? I know I screwed up when she was born, but it's different now.'

This was the day he should have flown home, bag carrier to Cait, job done. How could he have forgotten? Denial, of course, that old friend.

'I'll be back in the UK tomorrow morning,' he said, 'your time. I'll get to you as soon as I can, we'll talk to them. Try not to worry.'

Alice poured more coffee as he ended the call, not looking at him. 'Leaving today? You never said.'

'I'd forgotten.' How could he admit that, right now, all he wanted to do was eat more pancakes, watch Alice painting in her studio filled with the scent of turpentine and listen to the stream.

'Sorry,' he said.

'Don't be. Let's look up that flight and get you to the airport.'

'I wanted to stay, for a while.'

'The world is full of wants and might-have-beens. People you meet a few years too late, in the wrong place, the wrong time. People who can't see their way clear to changing direction and taking a different road with you. When that happens, you have to learn to walk away else you'll get eaten up from inside. And Quincey...'

'Yes?'

'Just remember that sometimes you get more when it's given, not taken.'

ANGEL MOUNTAIN

Fraserwood had solved nothing. Confrontations might work in books or on film, but in life they leave a lot to be desired. It had been the same with Ches and Buck, satisfaction at first and then a feeling of anti-climax, as if nothing had been solved. No sense of completion or resolution.

Cerys negotiates her way out of the airport car park and onto the road back to what, for now, she calls home. Quincey's bound to have spoken to Rob but his credibility has always been in doubt, and after her mind games of the past few weeks he barely knows what's real anymore. That's one result at least.

The search for vengeance has filled her life and given her a meaning, been her friend and her lover. Since that day in the trailer park, twenty-one years ago, the path has always been clear. Apart from vengeance she hasn't needed anything or anyone, but now that the final confrontation has played out - so unsatisfactory - what is the point?

The traffic heading west is light and she stays in the fast lane, overtaking everything. Her mind works double time, thoughts tumbling over each other. Vengeance, retribution, nothing but words. Abstract concepts that mean nothing until they're translated into actions. And what was she going to do if she ever tracked down the person responsible for her life? Her father died a long time ago and whatever biblical injunctions might have sustained her, the son could never really take his place. Killing Quincey, whatever fantasies she'd entertained in the dark reaches of the night, was never going to happen. He was nothing but a small child when she was born, so he carries only the echo of blame. And from what she's seen, happiness has evaded him too, despite the house and the family and the education and the job. Fucking with his mind had been fun, a lot of fun, for a while. But in the end it was too easy and all froth, no substance. Their father was the one responsible for both their miseries, and he's beyond her reach now. He always has been.

She stops briefly at Reading services for a coffee and sandwich, then gets back on the road. What are her choices now? She could disappear again, down that well-trodden road. Pick another name and another identity, become someone new. Even the thought makes her weary, though; what would it solve?

As she drives across Wales a storm blows in from the west, rocking the high-sided lorries she passes on the motorway. By the time she gets to Pont Abraham services at the end of the M4, her windscreen wipers are working overtime to clear the rain falling in sheets of water.

Ninety minutes later she parks outside the farmhouse at Carningli, turns off the engine and headlights, and sits in the darkness, listening to the comforting howl of the wind. They call this the Mountain of Angels, but she has both an angel and a demon, one on each shoulder. Is this what it's like for normal people, she thinks, having to choose the right thing to do without knowing what 'right' means? And right for whom?

There are three actors left in this play, apart from herself. Quincey, Rob and Poppy. She's not been squeamish in the past; people are expendable if they get in the way. She's never believed in such thing as sin, there's no last judgement day to fear. Just what is, in the moment.

On the journey from the airport, one elegant possibility had presented itself. All her life, since the death of her mother, she'd been alone. The occasional lover never even scratched the surface, which on reflection comes as no surprise. But there is someone now, family of a sort, someone who could fill the space left by the depleted quest for revenge. She can take Poppy to be her new reason for living, someone to fill the void. Someone to love, whatever that means. Quincey's loss - if he feels any - will be a bonus. Rob will just be collateral damage, not even worth thinking about.

The rain eases off a little and the seesaw in her mind tilts the other way as reality bites. She doesn't really want to burden herself with a three-year-old. Love is just another abstract concept, and she has no idea what it means. Poppy would be a ball and chain, not freedom, and Cerys knows what a loveless parent feels like. Taking the child would be a mistake.

But what to do with Poppy, that's the question. She's become the fulcrum, the nexus. So much responsibility for such a small creature to carry, and that doesn't seem fair. Life is shit, no matter how you want to spin it. On balance, would it be better, perhaps, not to put the child through all the pain and misery that living inevitably brings? Saving anyone from that would be a kindness. Wouldn't it?

Cerys feels the car rock gently in the wind, considers all the options and comes to a decision. The angel and the demon shake hands on it, the seesaw is level and the way ahead is clear once again.

The farmhouse door opens with Rob silhouetted against the light from inside. A strange, queer little figure; he'll survive, given time. He might even be grateful; loss just leads to new opportunities. Cerys opens the car door, forcing it against the wind. It's almost time to go onstage for the final act, and she's going to make it a show no-one will forget.

CHAPTER
NINETEEN

He asked Alice to come into the terminal with him but she dropped him off on the concourse, leaving the engine running. 'Don't do goodbyes, cowboy, don't believe in endings. Anyways, this is all just shadows in the sun.'

'Shadows?'

'You think this is real life? If you got a god who listens, better pray not.'

THE WOMAN at check-in shook her head sadly as she looked between the screen and his passport. 'I'm sorry sir, this reservation was cancelled.'

'But I didn't cancel it.'

He saw himself through her eyes as she let herself take in the totality of the creature who was Quincey Radlett. A suit two sizes too big, festering cut on one cheek, stubble both too short and too long to be fashionable, only luggage a battered and bulging rucksack which, he realised, he was holding as if it were a precious child. And an unfortunate tendency to shake.

'Perhaps your assistant?' she said out of habit rather than with any conviction.

He made the walk of shame to the nearby customer service desk, only to encounter another sad shake of a head. 'There are seats left if you'd like to purchase a ticket,' said the woman behind the desk.

'I already have a ticket!'

'Not according to our system. You're welcome to write to our customer championship department.'

'I don't want a customer champion, I want to go home!'

The woman flashed her best smile. 'I can do that for you. All I need is your credit card and passport and we can pop you on that flight in a jiffy.'

Such a simple thing to hand over a little plastic card. There was no money in his bank account, but he could worry about the bill later. Except that there was no card in his wallet. He'd been part of the cash economy since the day he moved into Tansy's so the card could have gone at any time in the past three weeks or more, not that the answer was too hard to work out. There was only one other option; he reached into the bottom of the rucksack and pulled out the plastic bag of cash.

The plastic bag of newspaper, carefully cut to the same size as banknotes.

'Sir, are you okay? Do you want to sit down? Hey, someone get a doctor, stat!'

'I TOLD you I didn't like endings.' Alice sat next to him in the small, windowless room just off the departure hall. 'You're lucky I got stuck in traffic, hadn't gone far when you called.'

She handed him a few bills. 'Five hundred dollars, best I could do at short notice. And I've paid for your ticket, could only run to coach. Best you go now and get yourself to the gate, they'll be boarding any minute.'

'You didn't have to do this.'

'So why did you call? You'll pay me back, or you won't. Don't matter either way. Just do one thing for me, cowboy, stop drifting. Anyone can see, ain't what you were made for.'

HE CHANGED the dollars into sterling, rather less than he'd hoped for, then called Jennifer from the Arrivals hall at Heathrow and asked her to meet him at Hornsey station. Neutral territory, he'd decided, for hard conversations, but he let her drive him to a café not far from her home.

He waited until the scrambled eggs and bacon arrived before explaining to her about Cait.

'You told me about my twin,' he said, 'why didn't you mention my other sister?'

'You think life was hard for you, said Jennifer, 'but it wasn't a bed of roses for me either. Ma was a hard woman to like, let alone love, and as for Pa...' She paused, sipped her flat white and looked out of the window onto the decaying street. 'Believe it or not, I always wanted to protect you. Such a strange creature you were, so hard to love, but I did my best.'

'And that meant hiding the truth from me about my own family?'

'I always wondered when you'd find out about her. I suppose I hoped you never would.' Jennifer had aged a decade since the day he had come here for Poppy's birthday.

The grey around the hairline was advancing, another little defeat that she would never have allowed before.

'You don't know what it was like,' she said, 'you were too young. Her mother was Gwen Morgan, we were at school together. Not that we were friends; the wrong sort, Ma used to say. She said a lot more later. Then there was all the gossip when Gwen fell pregnant. She'd just turned seventeen, a bottle blonde with attitude, when she turns up at the house with a bump that looks like it's about to burst and says that Pa is the father, what's he going to do about it. It couldn't have happened at a worse time; you had whooping cough, it was three years to the day since your twin sister died and so Ma was already in a state. Pa was out somewhere, as usual, probably with some other poor cow.

'When he got home later, Ma had bolted the doors and wouldn't let him in the house. I never heard her swear before then, but it taught me a few new words.

'Times were different then and it was hard on Ma. Gwen was never someone to keep her mouth shut so everyone knew that Hugh Radlett had a bastard daughter. And that was just the one we knew about, God knows how many more the old sod littered around the neighbourhood. By the time you were old enough to understand, they'd left the area. There were all sorts of rumours, but I found out later that Ma had given an ultimatum. She said that either they had to disappear, or Pa could get on his bike. So he did what he always did, paid money to make the problem go away.'

'Cait blames me for what happened. She says I had her life.'

'Is that what she's calling herself these days? She was Cerys as a baby, Cerys Morgan. And she's kidding herself, there's no way Pa would have left us for her and her mother.

His taste in women wasn't socially acceptable; he liked them young, blonde and dressed for a night's work around King's Cross. Good enough for fun, but he needed someone like Ma for the client dinners and the golf days.'

She pushed her food away, untouched. 'We were happy, Quincey, until your daughter's mother – no, don't purse your lips, she has a womb and that's good enough for me – had to assert her "rights". Provenance isn't everything, it's love that counts.'

SHE DROVE him back to Paddington. 'I don't know what's happening to you, Quincey. You're my little brother and I love you, but sometimes I look at your face and all I see is this alien creature. I can't tell you how to live your life, but don't screw up your daughter's any more than you already have. And call me when you know what's happening.'

HE'D PLANNED to use his own car for a change now there was no-one to hide from, but all the tyres had been slashed and one of the wing mirrors was missing, so he picked up the van from outside Tansy's and found himself driving towards the beach. It had been the same when Ma was dying. The nursing home had called, warned him that there were only hours to go, and yet he had stopped on the way for a coffee which he didn't need and a pack of mints which he never used.

Too much had happened, too quickly. He felt viscerally tired, as if exhaustion had seeped into the very marrow of his bones. A short respite was all he asked; to walk on the sand, smell the sea and steal a few hours' sleep on the little truckle bed in the beach hut.

At least now he knew who his stalker was and why. He just didn't know how far she was prepared to go.

LATE AFTERNOON and the beach was empty, the tide on its way in. He decided to walk first; took off his shoes, rolled up his trousers and let the cold wavelets roll over his feet, turning his blood to syrup. As he moved away from the water's edge, the Kilvercombe amalgam of sand and mud oozed through his toes, feeling almost erotic.

The clouds were ragged today in a pale sky that had strayed from winter, and the pier, rising from the sea on its elegant arches of wrought iron, had a defiant look now that the scaffolding had gone. But where were all the people? The breeze was blowing more strongly, green with the scent of seaweed, and he climbed the slope, up the beach, towards the rocks that led to the toll-house at the pier entrance.

Cath was a trustee of the Kilvercombe Kinema and Pier Heritage Trust; he'd offered his own services but been turned down - 'we're looking for someone with a higher profile,' they'd said, 'someone with the right kind of face to raise funds. No offence.'

The entrance turnstile was unmanned and he eschewed the honesty box, £1.85 worth of revenge. A peeling poster advertised some boy band that had appeared a few weeks ago. Even he recognised their name; Cath had connections, so this was probably down to her. He would have had closer horizons; a forgotten TV chat show host, perhaps, or a retired soap barmaid. So that's what the right kind of face could do.

He walked towards the pier-end buildings with their faux-Chinese roofs and curlicues. The view would be better without them, he thought. An infinity pier, a sense of being able to walk away from life and into eternity. Cath had always said he was too romantic; it had taken a few years before he realised it wasn't a compliment.

He knelt for a moment on one of the wooden benches that lined the edges of the walkway and leaned out over the sea. The breeze had stiffened and the incoming tide was rolling faster across the flat beach, with sticky outriders of spray reaching up to his face and stinging as if he had been over-enthusiastic with a shave.

A sudden wave of tiredness washed over him and he felt the threat of the tremors, waiting to shake him until he came to pieces. Entropy, there was no escape. He was cold, that was part of the problem, and thirsty. I'll continue to the end of the pier, he decided, and then go back to the beach hut. Strong black coffee would be like wine, and the desire for sleep in his own little cot was almost irresistible.

As he stepped away from the bench, a colourful, centaur-like shape appeared from the main structure in the distance. As they approached each other, the shape resolved into a sad-faced clown with a yellow jacket, cerulean trousers, and scarlet shoes, riding a donkey. The creature's hat - green felt with a feather, rather Tyrolean - had a perky air at odds with the overall demeanour of the duo. Quincey stood aside to let them pass; the clown was engaged in a mournful conversation on his mobile phone and seemed oblivious to his surroundings. When they reached him, the donkey paused and turned its head.

He reached out to give the beast a stroke, but as he did it lunged forward and sank a mouthful of teeth into his hand. He shrieked with pain, dropped the shoes he'd been carrying and with one flowing movement, and an elegance that could have graced the stage at Sadler's Wells, the donkey bent down, picked up one of the shoes in its mouth - sock included - and flung it over the side. The shoe flew into the air with a graceful arc, the laces trailing like tail feathers, and then it was gone into the tide below.

The clown had missed the sideshow and was pleading now on the phone, begging his unseen interlocutor for some intercession as the satisfied donkey turned back to its path and carried its rider away.

Quincey sat on the bench and examined the tops of his feet, salted with fine sand; one of his toenails was looking rather precarious. The remaining shoe was a reproach; he stood, faced the sea and threw it as far out as he could. Not quite up to the donkey's performance, but good enough.

A FINE DRIZZLE had set in by the time he reached the beach hut and no five-star hotel could have looked more welcoming. How long had it been since he sat here on the wooden terrace, surrounded by the files of Joanna Dust's case? The day he went to see Esther and his world began to crumble.

He went inside and shut the door behind him against the rain. The sweet smell was still in the air. Perhaps something really had crawled under the hut to die; a rat, a dog. Or a seagull; where did they go when the sea lost its sheen? When had he last seen a dead gull, or any dead bird? Another one of life's unanswered questions.

He filled the kettle from the plastic water canister and scouted in the little drawer for some matches. The light through the small, plastic windows was soft but sufficient as he fumbled with the tap on the gas bottle, turned on the ring, struck a match, and realised as it sputtered to life that he recognised the smell after all. Gas, gently leaking.

The explosion happened, as all good explosions do, to a

slower timescale. The door blew outwards, and the roof lifted itself and tumbled through the air, ridge over rafter, followed by the gas canister itself which just missed him on its launch trajectory.

Thank the Lord for shoddy workmanship. The force had gone upwards and outwards, leaving him relatively unscathed apart from the smell of scorched hair. He put his hand to his head in case he was becoming a Roman candle, but all seemed in order.

The terrace and steps had shifted a few feet away from the hut as if in self-defence before the explosion, some sixth sense embedded in the bleached wood. Quincey lowered himself down onto the sand; the roof and canister had landed a few metres away, and the door was planks of driftwood. At least there were no flames.

As the ringing in his ears subsided, the only sounds were gulls screeching overhead and the susurration of the sea. He picked his way across to something sticking out from under one of the pieces of wood - a blue, plastic flip-flop, plus its mate.

No-one seemed to have noticed what had happened, the beach was still deserted. This, he thought, would be a good time to leave, so he slipped on the flip-flops and walked towards the road. He succeeded, with a little difficulty, in not looking back.

CHAPTER
TWENTY

He spent the night at Tansy's, foregoing the roast pork even though Tansy assured him that William was safe in his little shelter. The next morning, he took Prof's van and drove to Port Nyfer. The last time he had made this journey it was to bring his daughter back. This time it was to make sure that she could stay. And then there was Cait, or Cerys. How much had she said to Rob, what spin had she put on her story? And how was he going to tell Rob that the person she loved was a stalker at best, maybe even a murderer?

He pulled in, just as before, to the lay-by looking out over the bay. Throughout the drive he'd imagined a soft scuffling from the back of the van. Perhaps the squirrel from another life was following him around, or perhaps he was imagining it.

The hillside was empty today with no ponies to watch him, but a layer of cloud had settled like a shroud over the highest ground. He climbed out of the van and pissed against the rear wheel - no better than a dog - then looked out across the water as a ship nosed its way around the headland, the Abergwm ferry skirting the bay on its way to Ireland.

He shouldn't have stopped; Rob would be waiting and worrying. He tightened the lace on one of Herman's boots that he'd requisitioned again and carried on to the farm.

The only car was Rob's old Landrover and he realised how tense he'd been, worrying that Cait would be there. Surely she and Rob wouldn't stay together, not now, which begged the question; what would happen to Poppy? Would Jennifer have her back, or would it be his turn at last?

Something was missing, and it took a few moments for him to realise; sound, the place was silent. The wind turbine was immobile, the sawmill wasn't sawing, even the sheep seemed disconsolate and mute. The main door was ajar and he called out a greeting, but there was no answer. He tried the kitchen, then the living room, but still nothing. This felt wrong. Rob knew he was coming today and would have been here, unless she had taken fright and disappeared, taking Poppy with her. They could have been on the ferry he had seen earlier, on its way across the Irish Sea, taking them to safety. He went back to the kitchen and made himself a coffee; how would it be if that were true? It was hard, but honest, to admit that it would be a reprieve.

It was, however, just a hypothesis. If they had left, then he was off the hook for now, with just Cait to handle - and maybe even she would leave him alone now that he knew about her games. There was nothing more he could do here other than wait for someone to arrive, just in case they were out for a walk somewhere instead of heading into exile. Catastrophising had always been a weakness.

After a few minutes he realised that he really wasn't

thinking straight, too long off the grid, so he called Rob's mobile, hoping for a signal. It began to ring and then he realised the sound was in stereo; her phone was somewhere in the house. Not a fugitive, then. The call cut off and went to voicemail, so he tapped out the number again and tracked the sound up the stairs to one of the bedrooms.

He knocked, just in case, then pushed the door open. Rob was lying on the bed, eyes shut, garden twine tight around her wrists and ankles. No sign of breathing.

He said her name, and her eyes flickered open, breaking the spell.

'Quincey? Oh shit...'

He freed her from the restraints and helped her to sit up, propped against pillows. 'What happened?' he asked. 'Where's Poppy?'

'We were talking, me and Cait.' The words were thick and sticky, hard to make out. 'No, not talking, arguing. She said that you'd attacked her on your trip. She said you were planning to get Poppy for yourself and stop me seeing her because I was unfit.'

'You really believe that?'

'She said you were stalking us, that she'd had you tracked by one of her people.'

'Please... she has no people!'

Rob looked at him for the first time as if he were a stranger. 'What are you saying?'

'You can't believe anything she tells you,' he said. 'Cait's not right. Trust me, the woman is seriously deranged.'

'She was so angry,' said Rob. 'She was shouting about how awful you were, then she calmed down a bit and I think she got us both a beer. I remember us talking, and next thing you were here.'

'She must have drugged you somehow.' He'd been deluding himself, thinking that Cait would leave them alone.

'How do I know it wasn't you?' said Rob. 'I wouldn't remember, and Cait said you were a psycho. Perhaps you drugged us both... oh Jesus.'

He took her hand. 'It wasn't me. I only just got here. Call Tansy; I stayed there last night, and she was around when I left Kilvercombe this morning. Call her if you don't believe me. Cait is doing this because she hates me.'

'Why would she make up lies about you?'

'There's something I need to tell you about Cait,' he said.

'Please Quincey. If something went on between you both in Canada, I don't want to hear it. I just want Poppy back.'

She swung her legs onto the floor, tried to stand, failed, and sat back on the bed.

As if his life wasn't bad enough, as if he hadn't spread enough mayhem, now he was about to puncture another dream. There was no point in trying to dissemble; Rob needed to know the truth.

'Cait is my half-sister,' he said. 'Caitlin isn't even her name - she was born Cerys Morgan. I didn't know we were related until we were away in Canada. That's why she wanted to make the trip, to rub my face in her crappy life and tell me it was all my fault. Jennifer told me more when I got back.'

'I don't understand.'

'Cait hooked up with you to get at me; sorry. It's complicated. I'll explain later; right now we need to find her and Poppy. Any ideas?'

And then he remembered the ferry.

Rob asked him to slow down as he gunned the van's engine on the track leading back to the main road to Abergwm. 'If they're on their way to Ireland, we can't stop them now.' Her voice cracked. 'I thought Cait loved me. She was the one person who seemed to understand.'

'Just because she wanted to hurt me doesn't mean she didn't like you. Love you.'

'I might be different, Quincey, but I'm not deluded.'

'At least we can find out if they bought tickets or not.'

'I'm not sure. It's not like they would have needed passports.'

'Someone might remember seeing them. If you have a better idea, now's the time to say.'

The earlier cloud had lifted, and the hillside was clear of its mantle again. The ponies were back, clumped together near the outcrop he'd climbed on his first trip to the farm. They seemed strangely intent on something other than grass and as he slowed down they pulled back to reveal a car, driven across from the road and leaning at an angle by the edge of the rocks.

Rob turned to see what was happening and then grabbed the wheel, sending them skidding across the tarmac. 'Stop! It's Cait's car.'

The van's wheels caught the edge of the road and as Quincey fought the steering for control, they seemed to drift sideways towards the steep slope down towards the bay, hundreds of feet below.

He pumped the brakes, wrestled the wheel, and they eventually came to a halt straddling the white line.

'Shit. Never do that again.'

But Rob was already out of the van and heading for the car, scattering the ponies like a starburst. Quincey backed the hundred metres to the lay-by and then followed her across the uneven ground. The car was a silver Merc, convertible. He'd thought of getting one for himself, a couple of years ago, until Cath saw the brochure on the kitchen table and choked with laughter on her G&T.

The car was empty and one of the back tyres was flat, but the doors were unlocked and he opened the boot slowly, too many TV images in his mind. Would Poppy be in there, bound and gagged, scared almost to death? Would it be her lifeless body? But it was empty.

Rob sank to the ground. 'I should never have taken her from Jennifer. It was Cait who said we should become a "proper family" and I bought into the fucking stupid fantasy, daddy and mummy and little Poppy.'

He looked out across the hillside, searching for clues, and realised that this local mountain was just a bump in the landscape, one of the foothills of a bleak expanse that stretched for miles, always rising.

'They can't have gone far,' he said. 'Poppy would slow her down.'

'If Cait hasn't done something to her already.'

'Stay here. I'm going to climb these rocks and get a better view.'

The surfaces were slippery from the earlier mist and he scrambled up on all fours. A good thing Tansy had gifted him the boots; the flip-flops would have been a tragic mistake.

He reached the top and straightened up. He'd forgotten the stone circle, but he never would again.

'You took your fuckin' time!' Funny how some people's

voices carried. Cait was in the centre of the circle, next to
Poppy lying on the altar, unbound but unmoving, her eyes
shut. 'I'd stay there if I were you. Any closer and you'll lose
your precious daughter.' She held up a knife. 'Not that she
ever was that precious. You gave her away, Quincey, like a
puppy that outstayed its welcome at Christmas. People like
you don't deserve anything.'

Rob had scrambled up beside him; he took her arm and
held her back as she tried to run towards the tableau in the
dip. If he knew one thing about Cait, it was that she was
capable of anything.

His sister took off her sunglasses and propped them on
her head. 'Do you have any idea what the two of you look
like up there? The clown and the pervert, you were made for
each other. That's right, "Rob". Even the sight of you
disgusts me. You're a neuter, a nothing, just a creature; you
and Quincey deserve each other. But don't expect too much,
he'll throw you away like he does everything else. Oh, I
forgot, he already did that.'

With a sudden jerk he felt Rob pull herself free, and she
slithered down the slope.

'Shit.' He tried to follow but tripped after a couple of
steps, twisting his ankle, and started to tumble. Rocks and
stones cut into his hands as he tried to protect his face and
head and something hit his damaged rib, making him grunt
with pain.

At last the slope flattened, and he came to a stop near
the edge of the circle. Twenty feet away, Cait was holding
the knife to Poppy's throat while Rob circled around them
both like a prowling lioness.

'Why do you want to hurt her?' said Rob. 'She's just a
child.'

'Stupid as well as a freak,' said Cait. 'Hasn't he

explained yet? That man behind you stole my life. He had everything he wanted - a home, a father, a career, a marriage, lovers. But when they got tiresome, he got rid of them, if they hadn't come to their senses and dumped him first. God's love, one of them even killed herself to get away.' She was throwing the knife hypnotically from hand to hand. 'And did he ever start young; he began culling the competition when he was still in diapers. That was a surprise even for me; I wish I could have seen your face, Quincey, when Jennifer told you. Don't look so shocked, listening in to conversations is easy these days. And I had to grow up with nothing, just the dregs. But for a time we coped, while the money kept coming from my father. Our father. But then he died, and who caused that? Take a bow, Quincey, you couldn't even leave us that small mercy.'

Rob stopped moving and twisted to look back at him. 'What's she talking about?'

Poppy's eyelids were flickering as if she were dreaming, or about to wake.

'No good asking him,' said Cerys. 'Years of therapy, and it got him nowhere. An expert on denial, my half-brother. But there are no secrets in this world; it's amazing what you can find out with enough money and a persuasive personality.'

He felt the old emptiness inside, as if something had sucked away everything under his skin.

Cerys was still talking. 'Always had a fascination with water, haven't you? My mother found out the truth, someone told her at the funeral. The boy who didn't listen to his parents and swam out too far. The father who tried to rescue him but was pulled under by a current and drowned. The wrong one died that day, Quincey, I wish to God it had been you. It wasn't enough that you had his love, you wanted his life.'

Poppy half-opened her eyes and tried to move, but Cerys pushed her back. 'It was always going to be hard depriving you of something you loved because, let's be honest, you never really loved anyone except yourself.'

'That's not true,' he said.

'Perhaps not, even you must realise what a useless fuckwit you are.'

The light seemed hazy and he realised that a mist was coming in from the sea, tendrils reaching into the stone circle; he was already watching the scene at the altar through a film of gauze. Rob stopped her prowling, and he realised what she had seen; behind Cerys the mist was solidifying into shapes. The wild ponies, the grey stallion at their head, were silently moving forward.

'Well, can't stick around here,' said Cerys. 'Places to go, things to do. It's time for a little sacrifice to even things up. But I'm not cruel; they say that slitting a throat is a humane way to kill animals so it can't be different for people, huh? We can only hope.' She stroked Poppy's hair as if she cared for her and lifted the knife, but then turned suddenly as she heard something. The stallion was charging straight towards her with his head down like a battering ram, his harem spread behind him in support like an equine arrow-head. Cerys backed up against the altar with nowhere to go as the galloping ponies reached the perimeter of the circle, flooded through - and past - and blended back into the mist.

She turned back to face them across the altar, looking almost disappointed. 'You see Quincey, even the horse gods refuse to take sides. No matter, as ever it's left up to me and I think, finally, it's my turn. A life for a life.'

He started to move but Rob was ahead of him, darting forward as Cerys lifted the knife like a priest.

'You took everything from me, brother. You might as well have my life too; I have no use for it any more.'

She gave a nod of complicity, the shadow of a bow, and with a sudden, balletic, double slash across her throat, Cerys swayed for a second, looking surprised, and then collapsed behind the altar.

The bones were back in his legs. Quincey ran forward, but Rob was already holding Poppy, crying and stroking her hair.

'Get the knife before Cait recovers,' she said. 'Quickly!'

There was no need for that. He looked at the body on the ground; blood was pumping from the deep wounds in her neck and he tried to staunch it with his hands, knowing it was useless. His sister's eyes were still open, and he murmured meaningless words of comfort as the blood flow slackened and her eyes, at last, lost their focus. He felt, for the first time in his life, as if part of him had died.

HE DIDN'T REALLY WANT Cerys's Welsh malt whisky, but Rob insisted after Poppy was asleep.

'Are you okay, Quincey? You've barely said anything since we got back.'

What was there to say? In the past couple of weeks, he'd discovered two sisters he didn't know existed and lost them both again.

'We shouldn't have left Cait there,' Rob said. 'The police will come here and ask questions and you know Poppy, she's not grasped the concept of lying.'

'We didn't kill Cerys,' he said, 'she did that to herself. I just don't understand why.'

What is it about me, he thinks, that causes women to take their own lives? First Esther, now Cerys. A lover and a sister. Even Robyn had died, in a way, to become Rob. Something inside him must be twisted and broken, even though he'd always thought of himself, vaguely, as a good person. Not perfect, but then who is? Perhaps, though, there could be a life ahead for his daughter and her mother.

'You should leave here,' he said. 'Both of you. Go away, today.'

'Go where? Who would want me? Perhaps Cait was right; I am a freak.'

The neat whisky burned his throat. 'What do you want, Rob, really?'

'To live in peace with my daughter. Not to be ashamed.'

'And you should. But you're right about the police,' he said. 'They'll want to know what Cerys was doing by that altar with the knife. I touched it so they'll get my fingerprints.'

'You could go back and find it before they do.'

'And leave more evidence? What if someone sees me, or the van?'

Rob paused. 'We could all go away together.'

For a moment, he let the images play in his mind and saw them as they would appear to others. A strange household; two mismatched creatures and a little girl. He imagined the comments, the barely concealed laughter. This wasn't the life he had dreamt for himself, but neither was the one he was living.

'It wouldn't work, not with me. Sorry.' And he was.

'So what will you do?'

'I have a few loose ends to clear up.'

'And then back to being a lawyer?'

'There's a woman I know,' he said, 'Alice. I met her

when Cerys abandoned me in Canada and she was kind to me. I'm sure she'd let you stay with her for a while, at least until it all blows over here.'

'I never got round to changing my passport after the transition.'

'Perhaps that's a good thing. If the police look for anyone, it would be for a man, not a woman. And travelling with Poppy - I'm just saying.'

HE WATCHED the Landrover's lights moving away down the track; the hazards flashed twice, and it disappeared around the bend. Poppy had barely woken as they strapped her into the child seat; a small hug, a kiss on the forehead, and his daughter was gone. With Rob he hadn't known whether to offer a handshake or a hug; in the end it was neither, just a shared smile of goodbye.

The clouds and mist had cleared, and the moonlight was bright enough to read by. He could go back to the stone circle; no-one would be there now. He needed to find the knife and check that Cerys really was dead; knowing his luck, she'd come back as a zombie to feast on his brains. And the way he felt right now, he'd probably let her.

HE LEFT the van in the lay-by and picked his way carefully towards the rocks, crossing the hillside which had become a dreamscape in the pale light, drained of colour. On the edge of the bay, far below, the lights of Port Nyfer seemed almost tawdry.

The sound of an engine rose and fell in the distance, leaving him with the small sounds of a different world. He climbed the outcrop but hesitated just before the crest, wondering if he really wanted to revisit the aftermath of the afternoon. Lose lose; either her body would be there, which would make the whole nightmare real, or the stone circle would be empty, in which case the zombie scenario would come into play.

There was always option three; turn back without looking. The Quincey way. Never know. But on balance, that strategy hadn't worked too well in the past. He clambered up the final few feet and looked down; Cerys's body was where it had fallen, but the head appeared to be moving slightly. Surely she hadn't survived; there hadn't been a pulse when he checked unless he'd felt in the wrong place, which was always possible.

His legs wanted to take him back to the van, but the knife was still waiting to be retrieved. He slithered down, fearful of turning an ankle again or breaking a leg that could trap him at the scene, and made it safely to the bottom.

From this viewpoint her body was hidden behind the altar, all but her long hair which seemed to be moving slightly in the still night air. What if she were still alive and in pain? He could hear Pa's voice, the day they came across a blackbird in the garden with a broken wing. '*Put it out of its misery, like so,*' as he brought his heel down on its head. Even Cerys didn't deserve to suffer.

He wondered why he was trying to move so quietly. He took the final few steps around the altar; the knife was under her out-flung arm, but what he'd seen as her moving was nothing more than moon shadows from drifting night clouds.

.   .   .

HE WIPED the knife clean on damp grass, took it back to the farm and stashed it under the passenger seat of the van, then worked through the rooms in the farmhouse like a repo man, loading the van with anything personal. Cerys's laptop, her clothes and shoes; not as many as he would have guessed. This had always been a temporary stop. Then on to what he guessed were Rob's things. At the back of a drawer of men's underpants and socks, he came across a blue make-up bag. Why had she kept that? A reminder, an anchor? A lifeline back in case it all went wrong? He unzipped it and smelled the faint perfume of the cosmetics, reminding him of home.

He made one last sweep through the building and then left. And when he reached the main road he realised that he had no idea where he was going, or why. He turned in the direction of the bay and the town, but a mile later swung right on a whim when he saw a sign to the Gwm Valley. Serendipity, he thought, let that be the watchword of the night.

The road switchbacked down, away from the coast, until he was driving alongside a small stream. After a couple of miles, the valley opened out and he reached a crossroads sans signpost. The toss of a mental coin, and he turned left this time. The road quickly narrowed, became a track through the trees, and then faded away by the shore of a lake, its water still and dark under the moonlight.

He shut off the engine, climbed down, and walked to the water's edge. The cries of owls echoed, hidden and mournful, and the lake felt full of secrets.

He looked back at the white van. Where was Prof now? Where were the people who had dropped by the wayside? Ash, all turned to ash; perhaps it was time the van joined the others. He felt in the side pocket of the driver's door and found Prof's pouch of tobacco, a wrap of dope, and a lighter. Serendipity indeed. It had been a long time since he'd attempted to roll a joint and the first couple of attempts wilted like dying shoots, but at last he achieved sufficient rigidity and sat on the gravel of the lake shore, coughing gently as he half-inhaled and gazed over at the shadows of the trees.

When the last puff burnt the joint down to scorch his fingers, he flicked the butt away and retrieved the rucksack; time to say goodbye. There was just one problem; he had no idea how to set light to a van. People did this all the time, destroying evidence, so how difficult could it be?

One of Rob's shirts did the trick, fed down into the tank until it had soaked up enough fuel. He opened the back doors of the van, stuffed the shirt under a pile of clothes, and flicked the lighter. Another mistake. The soft crump of flame singed his face and he stumbled backwards, surprised at how quickly the fire took hold and wondering what had brushed past his head as he turned away.

The van was too close to the trees. What if the flames leapt upwards and over, setting off a forest fire? Would that be his legacy, the deaths of hundreds or thousands of creatures in the woodland?

The flames were still confined to the body of the van, but the cab was untouched as yet. He circled round to the driver's door, pulled it open and reached in to release the hand brake. The van shook itself slightly, as if flexing its muscles, and then rolled slowly down the sloping shore. All he had wanted was to move it away from the trees, but it picked up speed before it reached the water's edge and continued its progress until it was half submerged, floating slowly away from the shore. A shower of sparks arced upwards with a muffled explosion, and the van slowly sank out of sight.

He watched until the ripples had subsided and the haze of smoke dissipated and listened for any sounds of discovery, but there was nothing except a call and response of hooting; the owls were back.

CHAPTER
TWENTY-ONE

A break in the trees shows where a stream flows out of the lake. He takes the narrow footpath alongside, sometimes veering away from the water, sometimes back again, once crossing on a wooden bridge. At last the trees start to back away and he comes out by the headland at one side of the bay.

There's a change in the sky, the stars beginning to fade. Nearly dawn, and nowhere else to go. This is the end of the world. He slings the rucksack off his shoulder and fills it with stones, surprised at how many it's able to contain until it's almost too heavy to lift. When it can hold no more he fastens the straps, walks to the edge of the sea and stops. The boots are wrong, he wants to feel the sand beneath his feet. He bends to unlace them and tosses them up the beach.

'Thanks, Herman.'

In the light of the full moon the waves are like dark mercury, heavy and slow as they roll across the damp sand. The opposite headland slumps like the silhouette of a sleeping dragon at the entrance to the bay, and just above the horizon the moon sits low in the sky, where the sun sets in autumn.

A breeze has started, light but chill, and there are no colours; the sand oozes grey through his toes, damp and clinging but not as cold as the sea which has covered his feet as he stands at that border between land and water, between being and nothingness.

He turns and looks over to the shadows of the rocks where they sat once, he and Rob and Poppy, one of his many No Through Roads.

He walks through the waves and the water is all around him now, climbing past his ankles. The tides are quick to advance and retreat here, where the sands are flat. How far would the water come if he stood without moving?

The loose strap from the backpack flaps against his calf with the movement of the water, and he hefts the sodden bag up into position, feeling the weight of the stones pull him down into the sand. He tightens the straps around his waist, across his chest.

He wishes now that he'd thought of a way of tying his hands together to stop them betraying him, but it's too late. In the pockets of his jeans, then, a casual way to leave. He would whistle if he knew how.

The water is past his knees and his feet feel heavy and numb, but he can't stop now. He wades further out until the water is above his waist and then, without warning, the rucksack splits and the stones fall out. The sudden shift of weight unbalances him and he falls backwards into the water, but the rucksack acts like a buoyancy jacket and he floats, looking up at the lightening sky. The current twists him to face the shore and he watches as a flash of blue and yellow resolves into a bird taking off from its perch on one of Herman's boots. It glides towards him and lands so softly on his chest that he barely sinks any deeper. The current turns him like a compass needle, spinning slowly as dawn spreads from the east, and he realises that he doesn't know if the tide is coming in or going out.

THE END